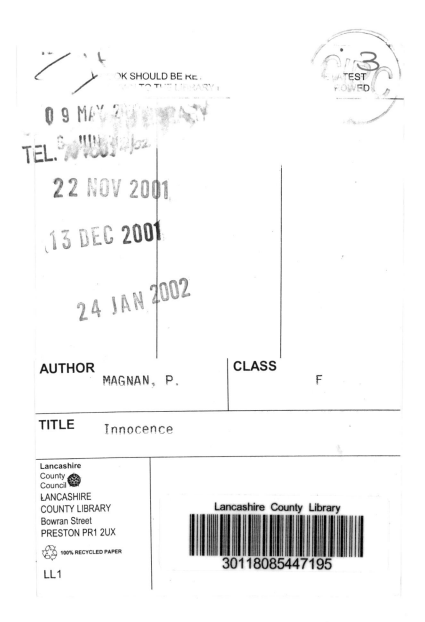

AUTHOR   MAGNAN, P.

CLASS   F

TITLE   Innocence

INNOCENCE

Also by Pierre Magnan and published by The Harvill Press

THE MURDERED HOUSE

Pierre Magnan

INNOCENCE

Translated from the French by
Patricia Clancy

THE HARVILL PRESS
LONDON

First published as *Un grison d'Arcadie*
by Éditions Denoël in 1999

First published in Great Britain in 2001 by
The Harvill Press
2 Aztec Row, Berners Road
London N1 0PW

www.harvill.com

1 3 5 7 9 8 6 4 2

© Éditions Denoël, 1999
English translation © Patricia Clancy, 2001

Pierre Magnan asserts the moral right
to be identified as the author of this work

A CIP catalogue record is available
from the British Library

This book is supported by the French
Ministry for Foreign Affairs, as part of the
Burgess programme headed for the French Embassy
in London by the Institut Français du Royaume-Uni

li institut français

ISBN 1 86046 879 9 (hardback)
ISBN 1 86046 880 2 (paperback)

Designed and typeset in Minion by
Libanus Press, Marlborough, Wiltshire

Printed and bound in Great Britain by Butler and Tanner Ltd
at Selwood Printing, Burgess Hill

"Ferrante: I wrote, 'much better and much worse…' For I have been much better and much worse than the world will ever know."

Montherlant, *La Reine morte*

To my dear friend Maurice Brun, in memory of all those times when we both put the world to rights.

The author has given a lot of thought as to whether the erotic scenes that appear towards the end of the novel are justified. He knows they may alienate a section of his readers, but given the particular nature of the characters in this story, it was impossible to bring the episode to a conclusion by any other means than eroticism.

Otherwise, why would the heroine weep while she was making love, and what explanations could be given if she didn't?

I

I WAS 15, WE WERE POOR AND THE WINDS OF WAR WERE still blowing around us. I'd got up at half past three in the morning. It was the end of June and in the hills the line of the horizon was already separating the land from the sky. Down in the Asse valley, a shaft of light made the summits of the Estrop and the Cheval Blanc rise up out of their night and their stars. The castle tower stood out like a receding black rectangle against the early dawn.

I'd taken my father's *biasse*, an unbleached linen shoulder bag which flapped at my side. I was rigged out in a long coat of jute flour bags stitched together with mattress string by Uncle Désiré during the dark years we had all been through. This poor man's overcoat was the miserable grey flour colour that was seen everywhere throughout the war, made all the worse as my uncle had soaked it in *Panamose*, an old commercial bleach that had somehow been left at the back of a drawer. I looked as grey as a donkey in those clothes, the grey of the rotting flesh I'd seen on

1

carcasses drifting slowly downstream when the Durance is at low water.

At four in the morning in June, the world is like an absorbent cloth. The air you breathe seems like water, but water that is bitter, sharp, noxious and foul tasting. It's water of the night, only just separated from the sky, and tasting neither like sea, nor river, nor fountain. It's water exuded like sweat.

My chrome-tanned leather sandals were falling to bits around my feet. If anyone could have seen me stomping along, with my jug-handle ears and my straggly hair hanging down to my jutting chin, I'd have been the very picture of crucified Europe and its ruins, a picture which seemed to be on show everywhere. But no-one could see me: in June 1945 at four in the morning in the hills around Manosque, even a child could reign supreme.

As far as I was concerned, though, there was nothing lyrical in me or around me. I wasn't thinking, I wasn't musing, I wasn't looking. I had just one thing on my mind, the small ad for anyone wanting to strike it rich, which appeared every Saturday in the our local newspaper *La Dépêche des Alpes*:

> Marius Cases will buy snails
> At ten francs a kilo.

"*Griset* snails," my grandfather had told me ages ago, "*ça bannèje*: their horns are out and they're crawling on the broom bushes from four in the morning in June. By five, it's too late."

I was hurrying. It took about 20 minutes to reach the Sainte-Roustagne valley and we were in the halcyon days, the longest around the solstice.

Ten francs a kilo! In Sainte-Roustagne hollow, where the old men's arms were too tired to stop the olive groves from growing wild, huge bushes of broom – which we call *ginestes* – have completely overgrown the trees, stifling their growth and sending them to sleep until better days. These woods are full of natural green tunnels in the vegetation, enlarged by those who pass through them. Firstly there are the hunters, then the pilferers hiding at the edge of the forest with an eye on the ripe fruit in the neighbouring orchards. Flocks of scraggy sheep make their way through them in the endemic drought, burrowing and pulling out the grass down to the roots. Finally, they are the haunt of lovers who need to hear the murmur of the wind above them as they make love. Even at fifteen I wondered whether it might not be the sound and caress of the wind they would remember in the hour of their death rather than the face and flesh of the person with them. Not that it stopped me from getting down on my knees in their hiding places and sniffing the grey grass for some trace of a strange odour.

Brambles had thrown their tentacles over these leafy archways and re-sown themselves, growing in symbiosis with the broom, so that in the pallid light of dawn, the sides of the tunnels they formed were hung with patches of mist. It was there that the snails gathered, thirsty for the dew.

Did I really like these colourless, muffled mornings, when even the clarion voice of the cock was gagged by the damp air? I don't know. I only know that the all-pervading greyness was something like Henri Gardon's paper, the soft paper he used for wrapping the coffee in the hundred gram packets he sold us. If the only colour I had seen that morning was pearl grey, I'd have called it a rainbow. Fortunately for me, the advertised price of the snails banished any other thought or feeling from my mind.

3

The wild scrub land stretched as far as the farmhouse of Jean Laine who was from Manosque but had died a long time ago. Made of stones from the river bed of the Durance, it was a long, dismal ruin with only two blind walls left standing. Two large fig trees seemed to flourish on the pile of chalky rubble, which was all that was left of the windowed walls. Growing to an enormous size out of the plaster in the debris, they cast a dull grey shadow over the compact masses of fallen masonry, returning them to the earth over the buried memories of happy families. The sections of wall still standing were not, strictly speaking, without any windows at all: two cunningly positioned slits, scarcely as big as the back of your hand, had been cut in a limestone block, the only fine piece in that rough-and-ready wall. Each of the old Manosque farmhouses had them so that the owner could shoot thrushes *à l'agachon* – from a bird hide – while he stayed sitting in the kitchen with his back against the stove and his bowl of steaming coffee held tightly between his knees.

This image made me smile and I was full of joyful anticipation as I watched the happy progress of the snails climbing up the broom bushes. The idea of stuffing these living creatures into my bag one by one, making up kilos at ten francs each, didn't worry me, or rather, didn't worry me any more.

Until I was ten years old, I would often lie huddled on my mattress, horrified at the thought that no matter what he does, as soon as he puts his foot to the ground, man begins to kill – plants, insects, animals – and it only stops while he's asleep or breathing his last. But then I discovered what poverty was, and that state gave me the right to disregard those things.

The bag was getting heavier. From time to time I pulled the top in tight with the shoe lace cord to cut off the gastropods' bid for freedom. Dawn didn't break: it oozed into the sky. The world around me emerged out of the darkness, layer after layer stealthily unveiled and agonizingly beautiful, as if it should take precautions before revealing itself to man as it really was.

From the ruins came the sound of a footstep crunching on the rubble. It was light enough to discern shapes and, from his awkward, waddling walk, I recognized our neighbour Albert the baker. I was annoyed. I had taken pride in being the only living soul up and about at what must have been half past four by this time, and I felt offended by this other presence. It looked as though I would have to share the dawn with Albert the baker.

He had almost disappeared from my field of vision. He was leaning his back against a wall and was fiddling with something in his hands, which, in the half-light, I took to be a kind of walking stick. But now a greyish pink expanse of sky was spreading out from the outline of the mountains, billowing as far as the plain and revealing a layer of stagnant mist hanging over the waters of the Durance. This slow, laborious birth of the morning dampened the sound made by the snails moving in the *ginestes*. Daylight appeared almost reluctantly, and in its first rays I saw the barrel of a shotgun gleaming behind the blank wall. I couldn't make out Albert's head or body, only the barrel of the gun waving and then suddenly disappearing. Then I saw Albert's body and his skinny backside. As far as I could tell, being able to see both sides of the wall, he was kneeling in the rubble, and the barrel of his weapon lay in the slit cut in the wall.

As I was picking my snails like fruit, I vaguely wondered why Albert would be poaching and what he could want to shoot in June. The thrushes had migrated thousands of miles away, the young hares were only two months old and the pheasants hadn't been released yet. But the subject hardly preoccupied me.

My heavy bag now weighed more than 50 francs worth. The snails were beginning their retreat towards the ground. Although the dampness had only just disappeared from the air, the sunlight was already beginning to affect them. I now had to bend down to catch the few that were not already lost in the tangle of the grass.

I was in this precarious position, with my head lower than my backside, garnering the last of my snails, when the shot rang out.

The sound of a gunshot at five in the morning, when even the roosters still respect the peaceful silence of the night, comes as quite a shock. This one was so close that it threw me face down with my nose in the grey couch grass.

I heard someone rushing off, clattering over the stones. I got up. Albert was running under the fig trees among the rubble, clambering over the ruins as fast as he could, heading back the way he had come. It was the first time in my life that I'd seen a hunter not rush to pick up the game he had just shot, but instead rush off in the opposite direction.

The war was still too close for a shot at five in the morning to result in anything but deathly silence. It had taught us not to show any reaction or curiosity on hearing an explosion and to move away from wherever it had happened with nonchalant indifference.

But the smell of gunpowder still hung over the broom, a familiar cheerful smell, reminiscent of autumn and meat roasting on the coals. I was keen to find out what game Albert could possibly have missed, for he wouldn't have left the place without going to pick up his prey.

My grandfather was right: the snails had all disappeared in the twinkling of an eye as soon as day had dawned. If I hadn't tied the cord tightly around the top of my father's *biasse*, all those inside would have made their escape towards the tangle of roots where they went to ground during the day. Well, it was time to make a move, time to go home. I'd turned into a wet dishcloth soaked with dew like the moss on the northern slopes and I had 60 francs worth of snails in my bag. They were heavy and frothing slime. It was time to get rid of them, as I was starting to think of them as living creatures and to feel like taking them out and scattering them in the grass. These are ideas which sometimes cross the minds of poor children and which they have to resist if they want to survive.

I started running down the path, eager to reach the town, when my harvest of snails would finally be no more than meat to be sold in the market.

I was a quick, steady runner, having always had rather short legs. The track, which was easy to follow, turned a corner by a copse of holly oaks. It was there, protruding from the shade beneath the trees, that I saw a man's foot lying across my path.

It was a straight foot with the toe pointing up to the sky. It was a middle-class foot in a good quality shoe. The socks that emerged from it were elegant and probably carefully chosen. Just one foot, one leg: the other was bent back and the second foot was caught under the thigh. It was a long, still, black body dressed in a long soot-coloured raincoat, like a priest's, but he wasn't one. The hat, which was also black with a wide flat brim, had rolled over on the sloping ground and lay upside down, looking harmless and somewhat ridiculous. If I say harmless, it's because for several years that kind of hat was always worn by frightening individuals who never laughed and who despised and oppressed us. When we were in the company of these hats, and without even knowing who was under them, we, the small and insignificant, were scared stiff. We didn't need to know the identity of the ever-changing, domineering heads that wore these hats: whoever they were, they were to be feared, and fear them we did.

The head this hat belonged to was the head of a dead man. Captain Patrocles had been a Resistance fighter from the earliest days of the war, and he had crushed us under the weight of his uncompromising patriotism. We kept our heads down when he was around, feeling guilty of every sort of cowardice for not being as heroic as he was. I was only a child, but in his presence even I examined my conscience.

Here he was in civilian clothes, but even so and even dead, he managed to make me snap out of my usual timid apathy and stand at attention for several seconds, rigid with fear. It was not so much the body that frightened me, as the realization of the difference between what he had been when he was alive and what he was becoming even as I looked at him. So that was what Albert was hunting. Now I understood why he hadn't rushed out to pick up his game: Monsieur Patrocles, whom everyone called Captain.

He should have fallen forward like any good soldier killed by the enemy, but mischievous fate had placed an obstacle on this lonely path: a large branch of broom, which he had been pushing out of the way when he was struck down.

This chance occurrence also concerned me, for if he had fallen face down, I would never have had either the strength or the nerve to turn him over to identify him. As it was, the branch he had been pushing out of the way had immediately sprung back at the moment of his death when his strength failed. It had brushed him aside, throwing him backwards, so that he now lay there on his back with his eyes wide open, his face covered in blood, the handsome features destroyed by the volley of buckshot. In particular, he had a proud aquiline nose I had always envied. He seemed immense, lying there with his head lower than his body because of the steep slope of the path.

Apart from my grandmother on her deathbed (and she still had beautiful blond hair without a trace of grey), I had never seen a dead body. This one was neat and clean, and there was even a whiff of lotion still floating in the air around him, although the faecal smell of the inert body, defenceless against the physiology of death was beginning to overpower it. A busy fly buzzing around this unexpected opportunity was already after its quarry.

So it was Captain Patrocles Albert had just killed, with me a hidden witness. This shocking act, however, changed nothing in the progress of the dawn. The song of the birds as they warbled in the early morning had only been interrupted at the moment the gun went off, and then resumed, soft, tender and joyful.

If you had to stop every time you heard a gunshot ... We were just emerging from a period when, if you heard one, it was better to play deaf than to exclaim and rush off towards it. Having long been confronted with the sound of lethal gunshots, we deliberately maintained a stony impassivity.

It could be many hours or perhaps a day or two in this torrid summer before anyone ventured into these parts. You could be sure that no-one from the two farms nestling in the bottom of the valley would come scouting around to find out the results of the incident.

I could stay there alone in front of Patrocles' dead body for as long as I liked. I was already a reticent, secretive and self-controlled boy. The survival of the poor and insignificant sometimes depends on maintaining this perfect composure. I looked carefully at the man's mortal remains. When he was alive, if our paths ever crossed and he looked at me, I always felt guilty and turned my head away. I said out loud, "But what on earth was he doing here in front of Jean Laine's farm at five in the morning?"

There was no-one about, no chance of a response from anyone or anything. The morning wind was murmuring softly in the top branches of a mournful umbrella pine and a rooster was vainly crowing in the hen house at the next-door farm where the Greeks lived. The only noise came from my bag and the outraged snails bubbling with slime, crazy for their lost freedom. I had to get them to Cases as fast as possible before they broke the cloth bottom of the bag – you can't imagine the explosive force of a thousand snails. But the body held me there like a magnet. I was rooted to the spot. It's a rare thing for a wretch to be able to dwell on the frailty of the great. One usually hears about their death by rumour. Once dead, they are only seen lying in state, embalmed or in effigy. But I had the privilege of gazing at one, in all its helplessness, for as long as I liked.

The sun had not yet risen and the June dawn was cold; the heavy dew was the colour of hoarfrost. The natural surroundings were still much the same colour as the sallow complexion of the dead man, who would nevermore know the splendour of the daybreak that I could gaze at all around me.

And so these awkward mortal remains lying on the dry path in a sense looked slightly ridiculous. This should have inspired pity in me, but the sounds they had made when alive were still too vivid to fade immediately from my mind. What I was studying so eagerly wasn't yet a body: it was still Captain Patrocles, whom I had seen suddenly appear, weapons in hand, on that fine day in August when the underground fighters came out from the shadows. It wasn't so long ago – barely two years. Their faces looked so implacable and so eager that we thought then, and for a long time afterwards, that although their action had kept us safe, it was doubtful whether our lives would be much better for it. At least those are the thoughts that came to the mind of the poor child that I was then, but I took care not to share this sacrilegious opinion with anyone else.

Anyhow, there he was – dead. I had to do something since fate had dumped this body on me. I began to walk around him slowly, wondering what I should do. I remembered furtive, skinny Albert, who had brought this giant down, running off into the half-light. If I'd been a normal, ordinary boy, I should have been horrified. I should have felt a spontaneous revulsion for the assassin. But I wasn't spontaneous, and the only thing this murder had done was open up in my mind a vast field of investigation in which I had to move very carefully. That is why I was slowly walking around the corpse, noticing an insect which had just landed on the collar of the raincoat and was waving exploratory feelers at the abyss below.

It was while I was watching the hesitant progress of that insect towards a world unfamiliar to it – a raincoat collar – that I saw something under the coat where the jacket had fallen open, something made of Spanish leather gleaming softly like a piece of polished furniture. Because of the sharp incline of the body, the object had fallen three-quarters of the way out of the gaping inside pocket. It was a wallet. There was no doubt about it.

Possessing a wallet seemed the height of luxury to me. I'd never owned one, not even a purse. In my opinion, anyone who had a wallet couldn't have a troubled mind. My father taught me not to touch anyone's wallet and especially if you found one in the street. In that case you took it, still closed and intact, to the authorities, who have the right to open it.

"And," my father added, "if the owner then comes and offers you a reward for bringing it back, you shove it back at him, politely but firmly. That's what Father Esclangon taught me at school and that's what I'm passing on to you."

But what if it belongs to a dead man? And a dead man so high up in the world? And dying in such circumstances? I knelt down by the body so that I could get a closer look at that piece of leather shining so mysteriously. I resisted for a few more seconds, then I put out my hand like a cat extracting a chestnut from the fire, and snatched the wallet.

Even today, I can't think of any other words to describe it. The way my hand darted towards the coveted object can't be described in any other way. There was no going back after I'd done that. Till then I'd been neutral, beyond reproach. From that moment when I closed my fingers firmly around Monsieur Patrocles' property, I toppled out of my father's world, and yet in spite of our poverty, it goes without saying that my motive was not money. Even then I wasn't as simple as that and, if I made off with Monsieur Patrocles' property, it wasn't his money I was after, but his now defunct spirit. My heart was beating fast at the prospect of perhaps finding out who Monsieur Patrocles really was, after the way he had always appeared.

A wallet is a secret that you wear next to your heart for a lifetime, something you would never let anyone take from you at the risk of your life. It nearly always contains some apparently insignificant relic, which is the sum of a person's whole being, the revelation that will make all those who know you but who thought there was something that didn't quite add up about you exclaim, "Of course!"

All these thoughts were going through my mind as I broke into Monsieur Patrocles' wallet, opening the two halves like a book. A note fell out of it straight away, landed on the grass and lay trembling in the morning wind, which meant that I didn't have to be so inquisitive and look further. I picked up the piece of paper folded in four and opened it.

It was blue, half-covered with childish handwriting that began a word, hesitated then started it again twice before forming the next. The letter also had a suspect dirty mark across the last phrase. It said:

> My darling, I have something very important to tell you. Come at about five in the morning to Jean Laine's farmhouse where our love began. (Albert will be in the bakehouse.) Love.
>
> Lucinde

So, it was about love. When you're 15 an affair of the heart seems very insipid when compared with all the abominable things going on in the world. You expect fate to come up with something more imaginative. But it was also a dark tale of ambush. Albert, thank God, had made this love story take a merciless turn that would stifle all laughter. A betrayed husband who guns down his rival certainly affects our feelings of pity. Even our formidable punster, Auguste Faux, would not find any material to satirize in that. Foxy-faced Albert had laid low proud Patrocles. Insignificance had triumphed over arrogance. Although I had never encountered Monsieur Patrocles' gaze, I felt avenged for offences that I had never actually endured, as though I had a premonition that my life would suffer from other Patrocleses I could never measure up to.

I was no longer curious about anything else in the wallet I

was fingering. Lucinde's letter with its reassuring aside – "Albert will be in the bakehouse" – was intriguing enough.

I imagined the scene with the scrawny baker dictating the note I held in my hand to his prostrate wife. I imagined him threatening her, brandishing the gun, perhaps aiming it at her, pacing around the closed back room of the shop next to the stove used to warm the yeast.

"Write!"

And she in tears, since the signature was faded, perhaps imploring, perhaps proud, perhaps standing there on her firm legs, flinging home truths at Albert, those you say only once in your lifetime as they pierce the flesh like a dagger.

This short letter fascinated me and I had by now learned it by heart. The sound of the birds chirping around me increased just before the sun rose. Already it was over there in the distance skimming over the Valensole plateau. The steeple bell rang the half-hour after six o'clock. The Gaude siren called the miners to their shift.

The wallet was burning my fingers. I knew I was alone, but I could see myself being caught red-handed with the object in my hand. It would kill my father and I'd get my head cut off.

Luckily I had a handkerchief with me. It was damp and although dirty it was just the thing to wipe my prints from the leather. At 15 I'd read enough detective stories to know what fingerprints are and what conclusions can be drawn from them. I carefully polished the leather all over and, holding it with the handkerchief, I slipped it into the inside pocket of the corpse's jacket. But not the letter; I put that away against my chest between the shirt and my skin. Then I gave a sigh of relief. I had defused the body by stealing the letter. Without it no-one could explain why Captain Patrocles had been there, in front of the slit in the bird hide where Jean Laine used to shoot thrushes, on that particular Tuesday at five in the morning.

I was alone with the blue letter written with violet ink. I was standing there in the presence of this crime as though I'd found treasure. I held a soul in my hands – Albert's, our neighbour the baker. At first it was a rather basic feeling. I could do what I liked with this man's life: I only had to lift my finger to end it. I felt like destiny itself. I was filled with terror, but also with a feeling of power that made me breathe more deeply. I decided then that for the time being I would keep quiet about it. There would be time enough, when I'd had a moment to think, to tell the story to the gendarmes. They would scarcely believe it.

In a few minutes the sun would pop out from behind the hills, dispelling the mystery of the morning and waking up the noisy artisans. I should get out of there as fast as possible.

I ran down the path, the bag of snails banging against my side. Then I went into the *Roumpe-Cuou*,[1] a lane made of a trench dug through the middle of cultivated land and used only by the Gaude miners. It's called that because in winter the ice makes it as slippery as a skating rink. This track ran beneath a tiny aqueduct of the irrigation channel so that you had to double up and bend your knees to pass under it. Apart from the miners, who were used to such contortions, no-one ever ventured into it, even though it came out in the centre of the town lanes, where you seemed to emerge out of nowhere into the shadows.

However, as I passed the old Porte de l'Aubette, where we lived, I met Badasse, wearing his shoes without laces as usual, on his way to piss in the water of the Des Rates creek, in spite of the old signs expressly prohibiting it. He was a hopeless day labourer

1 Neck-breaker (Provençal dialect). [tr.]

who never smiled. He had red eyes and a mouth permanently closed on some blade of grass, which he never opened to say good day. In October he smelled of marrows, and peaches in July. It was pleasant to follow in his footsteps in the height of summer, as he always brought back a sprig of mint between his teeth from the irrigation channels where he was working. It freshened the air around him.

For all practical purposes, Badasse didn't exist. No-one ever took any notice of him. If he ever got up in court to point at me saying, "On a certain day I saw Pierrot coming back to town down Rue Lemoyne," they would only have to ask, "Yes, but what was the date?" for him to be quite out of his depth. He lived season by season, according to the work he was asked to do, and not day by day. I had nothing to fear from Badasse.

I saw Rose Moisson at the end of her yard sweeping up straw in front of the stable, but she had her back to me. Bébé Fabre's door was still closed. He was a second-hand goods dealer at the convent – that's what we called the ugly, mysterious building with austere black walls and few openings, even though it had once been a theatre. I always passed this convent with a certain sense of fear and respect. I could hear the muffled rustling of black and brown robes, whispered prayers. A hundred years of change were not enough to banish the vision of scandalized faces behind barred dormer windows – the only ones – looking down on the street, on Badasse and me. But the secret was safe with these imaginary faces, and after that I was in the clear. Rue d'Aubette was crossed by a curved street bordered with tall houses. On one side it was called Rue Jean-Jacques Rousseau, and on the other, Rue Saunerie. I quickly turned into Rue Saunerie. After that point I could have come from any direction and I started whistling my head off. That was my rallying cry.

The good bourgeois must have turned over in bed impatiently.

"That'll be Pierrot whistling! The devil take him!"

The shop sign, "Marius Cases, Fruit and Vegetables", was as well kept as a notary's plaque and it was sponged down every Saturday. The door of the storeroom by the shop was ajar. Inside, the light was very dim to guarantee anonymity to those who came to sell their produce. There were already four people in front of me, a woman and three men who were as grey as I was and just as ashamed of their poverty. Marius Cases, a good man, had also put on a grey dustcoat to look as much like us as possible.

He weighed and measured with a steelyard that had belonged to his great-grandfather. The notches in the beam were rounded with wear. He could have inadvertently allowed the weight to slip from one notch to the other and rob us of ten sous. He never did it: on the contrary, he put it up two notches for fear of cheating us. He was a man who respected our poverty.

My bag weighed 53 francs 50. As soon as I had pocketed them, I rushed home and grabbed the oilcloth bag.

"Don't forget the *pompes*!" my mother shouted.

They were long bread rolls that could be divided in two down the middle. Everyone in Manosque ate them in the morning, dunking them in their coffee. There were two privileges of living in the town that no-one could take from us: Albert's *pompes* – he was the only one who still kneaded them by hand – and Henri Gardon's coffee beans, roasted twice weekly so that they were always fresh when we bought them. I wasn't likely to forget the *pompes*.

There were 300 metres between the entrance to the old gate in the ramparts, where we lived, and the bakery. I always ran there. That morning the bag in my hand flew behind me, and the clock striking seven had hardly finished reverberating as I wrenched Albert's door handle open. The shop entrance from the lane was down three steps. I landed at Lucinde's feet, having cleared them in one leap.

"Hey there, Pierrot! You're in a hurry!"

That was her. That was her calm voice.

"A kilo of bread and three *pompes*!"

"As usual! Why do you ask for it today? You know that I know what you want."

I said it because I didn't know what to do or say. I said it because it seemed extraordinary to me that Lucinde could be there, without any change to body or soul, while her lover was lying belly up on the path to Sainte Roustagne, and that some inquisitive insect was already thrusting its antennae at that edible, and now harmless, flesh.

Ten times in three minutes I was on the point of shouting out in every possible tone of voice,

"Your husband has killed Patrocles!"

No doubt I was the only one in the shop to know that Patrocles was her lover. I was the only one to see her in a different light from the way she usually was. I admired her, and anyway, even before the event, whenever I went into the shop I was dazzled by her. She was a beautiful woman, cool and controlled, who always seemed to be repressing a lot of anger. She wore skirts made of silky material, which moved in shimmering bronze waves as her muscles tensed when she twisted around to take a baguette or a loaf from the shelf for a customer. I never tired of watching her twirl around. Pretending to be interested in something else, I let other customers take my turn so that I could revel in the vision for longer. There was not one detail of her body that left me indifferent or failed to arouse me.

That morning, as always, Lucinde was frowning, absorbed in putting the necessary weights on the copper tray to balance the weight of the bread. She was wearing a white embroidered collar on her dark purple dress. It was neither crooked nor badly ironed. That morning at about six o'clock, she must have attached it as calmly as can be. But the purple dress had really hit me in the eye. I had only seen the baker's wife wear it once, after her mother's death, when she had worn it for three months. Lucinde always dressed in bright clothes to enhance the way she looked to the customers: floral blouses and skirts with a leafy design pulled in at the waist by wide belts. The purple dress didn't have a belt. It followed the line of Lucinde's body. Rather than just appealing to the imagination as usual, the dress gave it free rein to speculate on the fullness of her hips.

I remember it. There were only three of us in the shop clutching our bags: Julien called Rababè, Jacques – known as Jacques le Beau because of his good looks – and I who kept in the background given the importance of the other two. Lucinde twirled around, raising her arms to reach the bread called *marseillais* on the second shelf. It was then that I saw a nasty bruise on her well-rounded arm, which I always found so attractive. It was just at the edge of the short sleeves and must have been blue, but it was now turning a faded yellow-brown.

So, the letter could not have been written without a fight. The envelope could not have been sealed without threats and entreaties, and it was obvious that Albert was the one who had posted it, slinking out at dusk, making himself as inconspicuous as possible. He had slipped it through the slot at the post-office like someone setting a rat-trap.

I remember it. Lucinde had just told Jacques le Beau the price and he was opening his bag. It was a heavenly moment, too, with

Lucinde leaning over, the top of her dress falling open as she put the loaves of bread in the bag. This was a task she never left to anyone else. The bread was hers until it was handed over to the customer. No-one but she touched it before then. Then I saw her face in profile, suddenly lit up by a slanting ray of sunlight. The same yellowish bruise beginning to fade spread under the skin from cheek to temple. It had been plastered with rice powder and anyone who didn't know wouldn't guess it was there. But I knew.

The aura of my secret should have made me as radiant as an apparition, but my Uncle Désiré's long grey coat camouflaged me as what I was less than two hours ago: a poor boy who had come back from hunting snails.

Now, at the moment when Lucinde turned around towards Rababè to receive his order, a person who was going to change my life drastically entered the shop. The door was pushed so hard that it banged against the wall. I've already mentioned that entering the shop was awkward because of the three steps down from the doorway. Once the door had been struck like that it banged back and forth in the air, and had to be caught and secured between the second and third step. You looked really ridiculous as you tried to get hold of it, and most of the customers avoided doing so by slipping through the half-open door and getting a good grip on the door handle. But the person who entered at that moment was no ordinary person, and slipping in anywhere was not her style. Rababè, Jacques le Beau and I had raised our heads towards the new arrival. Lucinde was the only one who didn't feel a thrill.

Madame Henry made her entrance, fulminating against the door and the people who put up with it. Greetings were also not her style. She usually did nothing more than heave a deep, loud sigh, and we all had to make do with that.

Rababè and le Beau took off their caps. Madame Henry was someone of importance. She, too, had served in the Resistance. She had sung the "Marseillaise" with her sister behind bars in Saint Vincent les Forts, where she had been imprisoned awaiting deportation, and where her sister died. She had escaped by jumping from an eight-metre-high wall into a large bramble bush, which gave way under her, breaking her fall. While they were making a half-hearted attempt to find her (the guards knew that the defeat of their masters was not far away), she gritted her teeth and bore the pain for the whole night. Three years later, she could still show the stigmata on her skin left by the thorns. As my extreme humility made me invisible, I thought I really didn't need to reply to Madame Henry's exasperated sigh. The sight of her always excited me and left me dumbfounded. The first of her attributes to claim your attention were her breasts (not large, but unbelievably firm) and a gently rounded belly, which vied with each other for your admiration. When she turned around, cursing, to shut the door, I could see her behind undulating gently up and down like a fan (and it wasn't the first time I'd watched it). Lucinde was the only one to equal her in those three areas that distracted your attention away from the face. Their faces were equally severe. What's more, they didn't like each other.

But Madame Henry, who was about the same age as Lucinde, was a tigress, while the baker's wife was only a lioness, intent on pursuing her own particular hatreds. Madame Henry, on the other hand, knew all the nastiest things people do to each other. She was always on the watch for what was brewing around her. She had a devastating imagination. If she noticed a tiny detail that did not fit in with an ordinary background, it immediately grew to the size of the Taj Mahal in her mind. That's the main outline of a detailed description of her given to me by my mother, who at one stage was almost her housekeeper.

She applied herself to doing praiseworthy acts so that the word "respectable" would come to mind as soon as she appeared. Her walk was always slow, deliberate and dignified, as though there was a trap somewhere that might close around her ankles. She was like a ship floating on a becalmed sea.

"She has a pensive walk," Auguste Faux used to say.

In spite of his vast knowledge, he feared her like the plague, as she could be extremely cutting in her remarks.

She always wore a snake's head necklace wound twice around her neck. Someone commented to her once that it was a beautiful gold necklace. She corrected the observation.

"It's platinum," she said.

This platinum necklace must have been the only one of its kind in Manosque. For me it had idealized that slightly short neck sitting on shoulders of an amphora-like roundness which belied the inflexibility of character she liked to present to the world. Madame Henry's shoulders were unusual, and I understood in my very unsophisticated mind that they were the distinctive sign of a romantic nature.

She sometimes squeezed gracefully between my skinny person and the counter to be served first. I breathed in the faint odour of her armpits, which seemed to me to have a smell of the forest floor.

"Excuse me, Pierrot!" she would say as she passed in front of me.

On that morning, Madame Henry saw two things: first of all, Lucinde's dark purple dress.

"Well!" she said. "Have you lost someone close to you?"

I saw Lucinde grip the counter with both hands. As for me, slavishly responding to this jest which only Lucinde and I knew to be blindingly true, I couldn't restrain a jubilant cry which came out sounding like something between a cretinous laugh and a goat's bleat.

"What's got into you, standing there laughing like an idiot?" Lucinde exclaimed.

I realized that, since she couldn't attack her important customer, she was venting her anger on me. Madame Henry did not mistake the real target of this diatribe. She was quite capable of freezing a sarcastic remark on the lips of anyone who stared at her. She had permanently adopted a wry smile that played around her mouth from morning till night. She was proud of it – spoke about it all the time.

"When I was 16," she used to say, "my mother was always criticizing me for it 'Hortense,' she would say, 'you shouldn't keep smiling like that. It'll give you wrinkles before your time. You know, the ugliest kind that will turn your full lips into a mouth that looks like a tobacco pouch!'"

She burst out laughing, but it was nonetheless that same laugh she gave Lucinde, who quickly averted her eyes. I was in seventh heaven in the presence of these two marvellous creatures confronting each other, both beautiful but with a beauty that seemed frustrated because it served no purpose. I could have dealt the baker's wife a mortal blow and stopped Madame Henry in her tracks simply by taking the note on blue paper out of my pocket and unfolding it like a holy sacrament, there in the shop with the hot bread still crackling. Everything would have been said in a few minutes, but I had promised myself the delight of slowly pondering the fate of these individuals at the mercy of my slightest whim.

Because of Lucinde's outburst in my direction, Madame Henry turned her gaze on me. Normally it went straight through me, but on that day she saw me. Because I was only 15, I didn't have Lucinde's alacrity in concealing my thoughts. The famous ironic look hit me in the middle of the forehead. I must have blushed, but at that moment the sun rose through the zigzag at the end of Saint-Lazare, between Lauthier's stable and the Marent et Faure building. It passed under the foliage on the plane trees in a blinding sword of light and hit the large front window of the bakery facing the boulevard, obliterating all details in the shop and making Madame Henry's platinum necklace shine. With startling clarity, a surprising tracery of wrinkles showed up in the features of her moonlike face with its enigmatic smile. They exposed her to me there in the most shocking way, as though she were naked (although I hadn't yet learned to read faces). I, on the other hand, had my back to the sun and could blush to my heart's content. Madame Henry would have had to see the sun from the opposite direction for her to detect what I desired of her, as I was not in her light.

It has always puzzled me that Madame Henry didn't realize everything about me on that morning. However, divine mercy had partially hidden me from her sight and from the others, as it had not yet decided if it would save Albert and Lucinde, married before it for better or for worse, or if it would be their undoing. As I was its instrument, Madame Henry should not be able to guess my secret.

But something was starting to stir in her mind and Lucinde would have done well to be wary of it.

"That's quite true," she said. "what's got into you, standing there laughing like an idiot? What did I say that was so funny?"

"I thought you liked to make us laugh. You always say such funny things."

Like all weaklings who do it, I had already learned that it's impossible to toady too obviously to people who like it. Madame Henry relaxed enough to reply,

"It's true. I do come out with some choice things from time to time."

But Lucinde was still standing on the same spot, frozen in mid-gesture with her arms out ready to put a loaf of bread on the Roberval scales. The door from the lane had just been opened with a bang. It was Albert pushing a big basket on rollers, full of crusty bread. This exercise took place three to four times each morning and was something of a miracle: he had to get a boat-shaped wicker basket down three steep steps without over-turning it. Albert had been doing it, not giving it a thought, for as long as anyone could remember. The basket landed behind the counter without making a din or leaving a trail of crumbs or bran dust.

I was standing to attention in front of this weasel-faced little man with his nondescript eyes, who was stretching out his hand between the counter and his wife's flat stomach to open the drawer of the till. He took out a black-covered notebook and a pencil, which he moistened with his thin lips. I held my breath as he felt around between the knob on the drawer of the till and Lucinde's stomach. I watched him write two lines and put the notebook back in one continuous movement.

All this time I had not taken my eyes off Lucinde's flat stomach, which she pulled in even further. She had bent back as far as she possibly could to avoid being touched by a single hair on Albert's hand, but the frightful stillness and stiffness of her body was visible only to someone who knew, and I was the only one who did.

Nevertheless I saw Madame Henry's forehead crease as though

25

she were deep in thought. She was surreptitiously watching Albert.

"Oh! Good morning, Madame Henry," he said. "I beg your pardon. I didn't see you there."

"That's it! Perhaps I'm invisible!"

Apart from Madame Henry, there were two of us in the shop, Jacques le Beau and myself, but Albert, who never greeted anyone, had bothered to address only her. He feared her and her formidable powers of perception. He even held a timid hand out to her.

"It's covered in flour!" she said. "You'll dirty my dress!"

And she took a step backwards. Albert did not insist. His expressionless face was as white as the flour on his checked jacket. His long nose made his thin face seem even sharper and the cigarette butt hanging from the wet corner of his mouth was the only original feature he allowed himself. Turning away from Madame Henry, he put the pencil he had just sharpened behind his ear. He was about to go back to the bakehouse when he changed his mind and, turning to his wife, he said,

"Oh! Don't forget to put aside a dozen croissants for Président Patrocles. He'll pick them up at about ten!"

Later, when I knew how to write, I sometimes thought about that strange imminent resurrection of a dead man by his murderer. Those words, "he'll pick them up at about ten", seemed to me to turn time upside down. That was a strange morning, when we were not ourselves, none of us. The huge shadow of Patrocles was there in our midst, screaming injustice and the loss of all his worldly goods. Lucinde, Albert and I heard him all right. Then there was Madame Henry who was relentlessly sniffing out a secret like a truffle dog under an oak tree. There was Jacques le Beau who wasn't a nonentity either. He had the power to stop water flowing. In this farming region, it was the worst possible curse. One day you'd get up at four in the morning to water your property because it was your turn in the canal register. You'd go out on a bad night to open the sluice gate a kilometre away. You'd be coming back along the channels, following the happy gurgling of the water flowing down to your land, when its joyful song would suddenly die. The bubbling water, which had seemed so full of promise, would evaporate, disappear, sinking incredibly fast into the bottom of the channel and burying itself there for good. Scarcely believing your eyes, you get down into the channel, stamp your feet, calling the water every name you can think of. But that's it! There's nothing you can do. You have to put up with the spell for two days. (Jacques le Beau wasn't mean and he liked farms.)

All that happened because the previous evening at the Workers' Hall, when you were listening to Jacques up on stage singing *Les Vieilles de notre pays* in his overcoat with his cap on and his hands in his pockets, you allowed yourself to burst out laughing behind your hand. Then you'd be laughing on the other side at four o'clock the next morning, when the water stopped flowing in the channel.

Madame Henry had a lovely garden of lime trees where nightingales warbled, and even she treated Jacques le Beau with respect, going so far as to spare him her ironic smile whenever they met.

So there we were, all three of us, carrying the same black oilcloth bag, which made us Manosquins look as though we were in mourning. This was because black was the only colour Stéphane, the owner of the Grand Bazaar general store, could abide ever since he had seen his whole family slaughtered by Turkish soldiers.

Président Patrocles . . . I imagine that in the depths of Albert's mind, the man must have loomed larger and larger as the baker thought about him from every angle, finding to his surprise that he could finally convince himself that Patrocles was really dead.

II

CAPTAIN PATROCLES CAUSED AS MUCH OF A STIR WHEN HE died as he had when he was alive.

His body was discovered, one evening at dusk, buzzing with flies, by a couple on their way to make love on the soft grass of Sainte-Roustagne. The siren at the town hall wailed as it used to as an air raid warning. The man responsible for sounding it, Marcel Sandonnat, was in such a state that he rang it three or four times. If there was one man everyone thought immortal, it was Captain Patrocles. He had escaped from so many traps, successfully carried out so many dangerous missions, killed so many of the enemy at point-blank range, without disturbing his immaculate clothes or softening the severe line at the base of his nose that prevented him from smiling. When he was alive, they called him "the clergyman". He was as implacable as outraged liberty. He was the embodiment of the avenging motherland. How can a triumphant motherland die?

That's what everyone was wondering. People stopped their

neighbours in the street, desperate to stun them with the news.

"You won't believe it! Patrocles is dead!"

"What did you say? Patrocles!"

There were women whose legs went to jelly and they had to sit down. Although no-one could say who it was later, one woman collapsed in the dust there and then and had to be helped back home, as weak as a rag doll.

Our mayor with the bristling eyebrows growled in his bass voice,

"I ask you! With all the experience he had! Turning up alone and unarmed in front of a thrush-shooter's hide! It's clearly suicide!"

Our mayor had been a clerk for 30 years and had kept numerous record books of trials at the court of assizes. At least five times in the course of his career, he had seen murderers who had shot their victims without warning from a thrush-shooter's hide.

"It's a tradition!" he proclaimed. "All the hunters in the *département* know that! Even if you've nothing to reproach yourself with, you must never walk within 300 metres of a shooter's blind!"

It was pointed out to him that Patrocles wasn't actually from these parts.

"That doesn't matter! He was here long enough to know our customs!"

He was annoyed that Patrocles had proved to be naïve. It tarnished the image that the people should keep of a hero. This weakness should not be mentioned in the eulogy at his funeral. He thumped his desk.

"Anyway, that doesn't matter! You had to be a bloody idiot . . . ! How am I going to explain to them that a legendary hero let himself be caught so easily?"

"If I may be permitted to express a modest opinion," Auguste Faux, his deputy, suggested, "if you notice any flagging of fervour at the funeral, you could point out that Napoleon himself at Waterloo had been naïve in counting on support from de Grouchy, who was an absolute ass!"

You didn't need to be present at the private conversations between the mayor and his deputy to find out what they were all about. Early each morning, Auguste Faux held open court in front of the Saunerie Gate and reported it word for word, not neglecting to show himself in the best light. Then he would wink and dig the person he was speaking to in the ribs. It was always some notary or chemist walking his hunting dog.

"And if you look for the person who benefits from the crime," he said, "do you know who the prime suspect must be?"

At the very end of the dark main street, he pointed his thumb over his shoulder in the direction of the town hall square with its shady plane trees.

"Him!" he said. "Patrocles was going to stand against him at the municipal elections in May next year!"

"Ah! You don't say!"

The notary or the chemist would leave hurriedly after hearing this secret, which was best forgotten. "The less you get into, the less you'll have to get out of." No-one would have been sure enough of his facts to guarantee the mayor's innocence, to assert it in public.

Patrocles' importance and the circumstances of his death meant that his body had to be kept for several days, as it was the only piece of evidence those conducting the enquiry possessed. By the time it was handed over, the authorities had had time to organize things so that the people would remember him.

Nalin, the beadle, who sounded his trumpet every evening

on all the street corners, took three minutes each time to list the honours bestowed upon Patrocles, and it was noticed that the sound of his trumpet, which often proclaimed death notices, was particularly melancholy on that day.

"He's making a special effort!" we said as we sat round the table at dinner time.

From three o'clock, all the shops had closed their shutters. There had been groups of young men going around the streets from eight o'clock that morning asking people politely to honour Captain Patrocles' memory by shutting up shop. We remembered these young men very well. Not so long ago they roamed the streets with guns in their hands, looking for some woman who might have slept with the enemy, so that they could shave her head.

At three o'clock the sound of dragging feet, denoting ritual assemblies, could be heard leaving every doorway. Auguste Faux had sighed,

"And to think that we haven't found the murderer yet!"

The weighty significance of these words meant that no family could avoid going to the funeral, for it's well known that a murderer always goes to his victim's funeral. Therefore we all had to be there to confuse the issue.

Nobody laughed in the town that day. No music played in our houses, neither classical or light; from midday onwards we even refrained from listening to the news, it seemed too incongruous for us to have any interest in what was happening in the world.

Our neighbours went out heads bowed as they grappled with their convictions and dressed in their best, expressing all the sadness and fear of death they felt in the clothes they wore. There were mutual condolences as they shook hands.

"Isn't this dreadful?"

"Well, what can you expect? The good always die young!"

"That's true enough!"

Then we went and made sure the crowd at the church saw us. That was difficult: you couldn't be seen by everybody, being only one of the hundreds of people who were squashed in beside the font.

The women were in the nave, their hats rustling as the brims brushed against each other. The men, for the most part, formed a circle around that strange sloping square that tips us in the direction of the church like reluctantly rolling grains of wheat. It wasn't so much a lack of belief that kept them there in groups on the footpath, stubbornly packed against walls or in doorways: it was the awful fear that religion might be true, for if it was, none of us was sure to escape its hell.

I was there, looking shabby as usual, with my hands in my pockets, feeling the letter on blue paper that made me unique among the crowd. Finally I caught sight of the long coffin containing Patrocles, who had just been absolved of all sin through three-quarters of an hour of mass. It was floating above the crowd, carried by ex-members of the *maquis* wearing armbands and basque berets.

This absolution must have also benefited the multitude, for as it fell into step behind the hearse, there arose a light buzz of many voices talking of hope and things eternally human.

"There'll be a few pretty ones crying."

"Yes! And even a few ugly ones too!"

Some laughed discreetly, remembering the dead man's escapades. Some tried to recall his heroic stance, but they were swiftly silenced by those who refrained from being heroic themselves.

"Heroism! Don't make me laugh! He sent others out to fight more often than he went himself! And besides, if he'd been as heroic as all that, they'd have buried him during the war, not today! Listen, as far as living heroes are concerned, I . . . "

"All right! Be happy then. He's dead now!"

Once at the cemetery, it was much easier to be seen. We have the necropolis we deserve: spacious and plain. It's vast and open, crossed with paths wide enough for two trucks to pass each other easily, but you would look a long while to find an ornate tomb. The columns are the same: no lengthy eternal regrets, just regrets. We know they're timeless, and besides, the mason charges by the letter – he even counts the commas – so that the epitaphs are always somewhat terse. Cherubs are not our forte either. There are a few family vaults with small columns, but they were erected in the last century. There are none like that any more, and the white and yellow lichen encrusting their stones only shows that they're solid and not likely to crumble. Nevertheless they're lined up in the best locations: with the heads to the north. I felt a pang at the thought that my remains would never rest in such luxurious surroundings.

However, the sight of everyone jostling to get a good spot for the burial tempered my regrets somewhat. Those leaning over the grave always follow the lowering of the coffin with a kind of sensual eagerness. It's instinctive to crowd around it, as you do when a train is leaving a station. You want to see if it's really true and just stand there in disbelief.

I don't know whether it's the same everywhere, but in our part of the world, funerals are a foreshadowing of hell. Women and men are separated there like the wheat from the chaff: the men in front and the women behind. The separation is just as clear at the graveside, beginning with the huddled, grieving family group. This separation confirms the impenetrable mystery that reigns

34

between one sex and the other, maintained by both as if it were absolutely necessary for the balance of nature, as if it were normal for the two sexes to be forever unknown to each other.

Although I was still a child – though not for long – I knew what all men thought. There was a light twittering of birds hovering ironically over their heads, recalling the morning on the hill to the snail hunter that I was. The men were happy because the others were, although their superstitious fear was still there as they saluted death. You see, Patrocles was the epitome of the herd male. They are dominant males from the beginning, implicitly recognized by females at first glance. Ordinary males can't compete with them, even in the faithful hearts of their wives. This male comes in all guises: he can be a mason or a man of ambition. He doesn't have a plumed helmet, or the pectoral muscles of a wrestler; he's neither tall nor short; sometimes he may squint or have bandy legs. He's not especially handsome or ugly. He just appeals to women. Even though not every woman succumbs to his charms, they would all like to. And that is why, when Monsieur Patrocles died, he took with him the bitter relief of quite a few husbands who were sure at last that they would rest easy that night.

The four pairs of gendarmes who made up our squad knew it too. They mingled with the men – they and a few harmless amateur spies, nonchalantly rolling their cigarettes but with ears pricked to catch quiet conversations.

I was 15, I remember. Never dressed in anything but Uncle Désiré's grey cast-offs, and sometimes a bit smelly, I was always the object of someone's instinctive aversion, leaving a gap between myself and others which allowed me to observe them. Under the lining of my beret, with Lucinde's letter, I had 200 francs earned sou by sou clearing irrigation channels. This was in addition to the pay for my regular work, but I handed all of that to my parents. So I could have gone to Peyrache's shop and, like everyone else, bought myself one of those suits in that sea-green colour which reminded all the migrant children so much of Italy. But I had noticed that Uncle's long coat often inspired a rather embarrassed pity which brought with it quite a few little advantages. They shouldn't be wasted because of stupid vanity.

I had perched myself on a piece of thick marble about six metres from the grave. It covered the remains of members of the Rosallon family, who were not from these parts, which explained the impropriety of their final resting-place: it had a conspicuous base of Tende marble half a metre thick. I had climbed on to this proud monument and from there I could see everything.

The women standing on the esplanade, separated from the flock, presented a potentially scandalous sight. The men turned their heads away or looked down to avoid seeing an excessive devotion to the cult of a hero. But there were also sideways glances looking for a white handkerchief furtively being taken out of a handbag and a face buried in it, ears straining to hear a sob or even a simple sigh and immediately identify it. However, everything was done with extreme decorum; nothing beyond the bounds of simple compassion or reaction to a crime that had struck a man down in the prime of life.

Only the women's clothes were eloquent. Many Manosque women couldn't refrain from wearing flowers, at least in a special hat, so that the sight from my perch was like a bed of black flowers gently rising and falling to the rhythm of their grief.

I saw Lucinde in the distance in her purple dress, also wearing a black hat. She stood as far away as possible when her lover was buried. I couldn't see the expression on her face. She had taken cover in the shade of the cypress alley around the celebrated tomb of Père Jean, which harbours the remains of three dynasties.[2]

The only thing I could tell was that she had not given in. She stood erect, her back arched, her face turned towards the coffin. Because of the wind sighing in the cypresses, she had one hand holding a light hat on her head in a kind of salute.

No-one could be in deeper mourning, however, than Madame Henry, even though she was not in black. She was wearing a puce-coloured suit with a tulip neckline that allowed her to pin her medals in a row across her chest. She was bedecked with medals like a professional soldier. The mocking smile had vanished from her lips. She had washed her face with soap and presented it to the world without a trace of makeup. It seemed as though the expression in her eyes had been permanently filled with patriotic grief. (At least, that's the way it seemed to me.)

I also saw the insignificant Albert slip from one group of men to the other, hand automatically outstretched as if he were seeking condolences. Before that day, I had never really looked at Albert. People always referred to him as the baker. They never called him by his first name. We had quite a number of extraordinary people in the town: Miette-Fume, Jacques le Beau, Martin le Trancheton, Jean le Bleu. There was nothing extraordinary about Albert. It used to quite upset his mother. When he was 21, she was afraid he would never find a wife.

He had come back home with the Liberation Army in '44 as a hero, done up in some sort of weird officer's uniform. His mother had secretly sent it to him before his return with this note: " You'll have some chance of finding a wife with this. Part your hair on

---

2   The tomb of the famous Provençal writer Jean Giono, where eleven people are buried.

the side and wear your cap folded under the right epaulette. It will make you look manly." Though she adored him, she still saw him as he was – small, thin, sly-looking, with a face you forgot even while you were looking at it. The only thing he had which was at all impressive was a marksman's certificate and a bone-handled knife with a notch for every enemy he'd shot. There were nine notches. Sometimes when we were having a drink in the evening, he would point them out one after the other.

I followed him carefully as he brushed past the gendarmes, weaving his way between the different groups, which took little notice of him. They all had various names on their lips directed at close dinner companions, for everyone thought he knew the murderer and gave him a name, strangely enough never the same one. Each had his preferred culprit. Even my mother, who was deaf, had chosen someone who had been disrespectful to her one evening as she came out of the flour mill where she was a cleaner. That very morning she had said to my father:

"It's him for sure!"

As for me on my green marble slab, I was scratching my head through my beret, resisting the desire to take out from the lining the letter I'd removed from the body. It wasn't fear of the outcry that held me back: it was the thought of how much poorer my life would seem when the mystery was over after that brief commotion. At the moment I reigned supreme. With all of my 1m. 58 and my doubtful cleanliness, I was the only one who knew the answer to the urgent puzzle of Patrocles' death. I had never been anything but a negligible quantity, but now fate had dropped this huge gift into my arms: a family secret.

I looked about me as the crowd of people closed in around the grave, seeing their own fate flash before them. First, I saw the brilliant sky. All the old stones of the Mont d'Or tower glistened in the light. It had rained the previous evening, with a summer rain that heralded autumn. Solid things that would ostensibly stand for a lifetime, including the tops of the cypresses bent over in the midday wind, seemed to melt and glow with the pure joy of their own existence.

Below were the men: a strange mixture of attitudes and abilities that never ceased to fascinate me whenever I came in contact with them. At my feet was the hole with its vertical walls. The slight grating of the ropes against the soft stone wrenched the first sobs from the family since leaving the church. The comfort of consolation had faded and vanished between there and the cemetery. Now malevolent reality came creeping into their thoughts and poisoned them.

The ropes were suddenly pulled out, whistling through the air then falling in coils on the mound, leaving the remains of Captain Patrocles in his expensive coffin at the bottom of the hole. Auguste Faux, who was standing closest to the mayor, whispered these words as he looked at it:

"Even he!"

This cry of despair gave the mayor and chief magistrate of the commune the ideal starting point for his funeral oration.

"Yes, comrades! Even he! Slain in the prime of life by a cowardly assassin, when he still had so much to accomplish for the public good! He was killed like Richard the Lionheart: through a gun-slit in a wall! A gun-slit.[3] What an appropriate name!"

He began to describe Patrocles' death, as though he had been there. He touched the hearts of simple people with the well-chosen words Auguste Faux had passed on to him the morning

---

3 The term '*meurtrière*' in French contains the word '*meurtre*', meaning murder. [tr.]

before. While finalizing the order of the ceremony, he had said to the mayor,

"Monsieur, we should observe a minute's silence."

"Two!" the mayor replied, looking his severest.

It was on that occasion that we learned just how long two minutes' silence could be. It was interrupted, however, by a cry from someone in the family group. It was the son, who had not been able to control himself any longer. With his face raised toward the cypresses as if Patrocles was still there, rising slowly between earth and sky, he moaned,

"Don't worry, Papa! I'll avenge you!"

You could also hear the gravel crunching as people who felt they had done enough, shown themselves sufficiently for others to remember that they were there, walked furtively around the graves towards the exit, where they had things to do.

For my part, I really didn't have enough mastery of my senses or enough experience to register correctly all the surprising things my young eyes were seeing.

After the mayor had closed the ceremony with the playing of the Last Post, there was a general exodus like an anthill attacked on all sides. Some, of course, left quickly, while others stood around in groups discussing the whole affair and debating the identity of the unknown killer. Some had watering cans, taking advantage of the occasion to freshen their poor father's grave. Widows stood like black cypresses, as they always did, at the foot of gravestones. I'd have given a lot to know the thoughts that had been awakened earlier and could now have free rein inside their bowed heads.

But instead I'd jumped down from my marble slab and had stupidly allowed myself to get caught up in the stream of people eager to kiss the family or simply shake hands. They were very presentable, all dressed in their best and smelling of violets or vetiver. With my uncle's long coat and my shoes with their toes curled up, I was likely to shame the rest of them, but I couldn't go back against the crowd. I had to follow them and suddenly came face to face with six people dressed in a variety of black clothing, standing like a wall around a tall woman. She was the widow. Under the veil that covered her face and shoulders, she looked ordinary and red-faced. Patrocles must have chosen her for her bovine simplicity. She was sturdy and hardly appealing, at least that's how her form appeared to my inventive 15-year-old mind.

Next to her was a gangly beanpole of a son, not yet fully developed. He must have been about 17. He suffered from even more teenage acne than I did. Pimples came up and then dried on his forehead and chin almost as you watched. Nevertheless, he already had his father's rather haughty expression: an air of self-assurance that convinces others that one is on the way to becoming immortal. It was he who had called to Patrocles right in the middle of the two minutes' silence, shouting that he would avenge him. I was almost beneath his head, pushed there by the crowd behind me who were advancing with their arms outstretched towards those they were anxious to clasp to their bosoms. I kept my fists deep in the pockets of my coat. I didn't want to risk the embarrassment of seeing all those well-kept hands refusing to touch my dirty fingers. I didn't want to risk seeing anyone instinctively recoil when confronted with my poverty. My face had that anxious, bewildered look of some-one who has got on the wrong train. No-one batted an eyelid, except the son with the terrible acne, who bestowed on me what I took to be a scornful look. How could he ever imagine that I would soon become the master of his fate?

I emerged from that trial wide-eyed and red with shame. Staggering from the pressure of the crowd, I nearly collapsed on the wreaths of tuberoses ("To our glorious compatriot, from the grateful people of Manosque") and fled, almost running, towards the gate. I noticed as I passed in front of the rows of cypresses around old Père Jean's mausoleum, that Lucinde was sitting on the corner of the grave, looking further away in the direction of the tight family group around which the crowd scattered and dispersed like dead leaves.

Pretending to scratch my head, I felt under my beret for the letter I knew by heart: "My darling . . ."

"Well, Pierrot, have you got lice? You're scratching your head so much."

It was Madame Henry calling out to me. She had come up behind me. I should have been able to hear her medals tinkling when her breasts rose as she breathed deeply. Actually I had heard them. I just hadn't had time to stop what I was doing. I hastily raised my beret so that she could see that scarcely three days ago Léonce Bernard, our barber, had given me a really close haircut on the express recommendation of my mother. In that way Madame Henry could check that I hadn't any lice since all my hair had been cut off. She was nevertheless looking down on me attentively, bending over my bare head to check what I was saying. I could feel her breath around my ears like the insistent sniffing of a hunting dog.

"Well now, Pierrot!" What do *you* think of all of this?"

She had fallen into step, almost touching me. I bleated like a lost sheep.

"B . . . b . . !"

I was stunned that I should be addressed by this important person, that she was honouring me with a word – she who was so sparing with them. She didn't smell of either violet or vetiver like most of the other women there. A mysterious aura floated around the warm, generous curves of her body. It was one of those perfumes you remember all your life once you have caught just a whiff of it.

"What's this 'b . . . b . . . '? Don't you know what you think?"

I was on the point of lifting the lining of my beret and producing Lucinde's letter, as I was still too young to keep such an important secret to myself. I felt Madame Henry's eyes on me. She had stopped walking and then stopped me. She gently turned me towards her with her lovely hands placed on the shoulders of my cast-off coat. She was looking into my face intently, but such an imbecilic expression covered my slack features that it was impossible to interpret anything beneath it.

Once the first moment of panic had passed, I really enjoyed standing there innocently while those bright eyes gazed at me. I had never seen anything like them: instead of being round, the pupils had an almond-shaped point on the top and bottom, forming a perfect ellipse. This irregularity, which I thought absolutely wonderful, accentuated the mystery surrounding her and gave her a slightly unreal expression very appropriate to her character.

I can still remember it today. There we were, standing in the middle of the crowd that kept moving forward, dividing around the two of us, then joining up again when they passed. We were in front of the modestly impressive flight of stairs leading to the iron grille gate of the small, dull grey private school I would so much have liked to attend, but could never hope to, being so poor. It was past four o'clock and the sun was already beginning to sink towards the west. The light bounced off Madame Henry's medals, making me squint at that conspicuous bosom, the object of all my temptations, which I would have so loved to touch.

43

I would certainly have something to talk about at dinner-time.

"Madame Henry stopped to talk to me!"

My mother would say, "Madame Henry, eh! Why not the Pope? You're such a liar!"

No, I wouldn't tell them about my tête-à-tête with Madame Henry. I wouldn't let my brother and sister smell the places on my uncle's coat where Madame Henry's hands had been, leaving a trace of Chanel No 5. And the only thing I could think of saying to her (it wasn't too bad, at that) after the "b . . . b . . ." of my first answer was:

"You smell nice!" I mumbled.

She exclaimed, "Oh, you rascal! Your mind's already empty and as twisted as an old olive tree! You certainly come from these parts!"

She let me go and began walking again, calling out over her shoulder,

"It's Chanel No 5, if you must know!"

Her back undulated brazenly at my eye-level, as she strode away with that regal walk of hers.

We lived in one of the medieval gateways to the city. These quarters had been given to my father out of charity, when he had come down from Saint-Jurson to work as a road-mender. My mother was holding me in her arms and my brother by the hand close by her side, as he waddled along as best he could on his bandy little legs. She was pregnant with my sister. We were a perfect picture of poverty with the sum total of our belongings fitting into a cart my father was pulling. So people took pity on us immediately. They were all grateful to us for showing them that, no matter how low they had fallen, there was always someone who was worse off than they were.

Apart from a dark kitchen smelling of saltpetre, our home consisted of a former guards' room twelve metres long and eight wide, with a Gothic arch ceiling, badly cracked in the 1909 earthquake. An old organ case from the church had been stored there ("but you'll manage, I'm sure", they said to my father.). There had been no further use for it since Abbé Toine had discovered the phonograph, which he wound up religiously every Sunday to give us some scratchy rendition of "Ave Maria". We used that old organ case as a sort of coat-peg to hang our clothes on. At night the rats composed infernal music in the pipes. All the same, we did have a latrine hole that dropped down vertically on to the des Rates stream. During the spring storms, the sound of the water breaking against the wall drowned out that of the rats in the organ pipes.

I was always on the alert, ready to spring to attention, as the wide cracks under the arches sometimes creaked terribly at night, with cracking noises like the ones I'd heard at the cinema in the Workers' Hall, when there was a film with a ship going down.

I seemed to be the only one who heard it. The thing that typi-fied me and separated me from the other children since I was very young was my worrying tendency to insomnia. My father and mother snored in unison on their straw mattress, she with her nose in my father's armpit and he with his arm under her head like a pillow. My brother also snored, and moaned, worn out by the kicks in the backside he had endured during the day at work. He was an apprentice to the blacksmith in the Soubeyran area. The blacksmith gave him difficult soldering jobs to do, then inspected them in detail, holding them up to the light. When he found one that was hollow, my brother was immediately corrected with a kick that made him arch his back like a crescent moon. They called him Cul-Rouge (Red-Arse) right up to the time he was called up for military service. But thanks to this heartless boss, he developed wonderfully skilful hands. He could make balustrades and guard-rails, that curved as lightly as a puff of smoke floating around a cigar, for the staircases of those inhabitants of our town who had delusions of grandeur. And there were so many of them at that time that my brother was a rich man by the time he was 50.

My insomnia made me into something of a rolling stone. Sometimes I got up and went out to share the night of the town. All you could hear were the owls hooting, the frogs croaking in ponds and that strange, ghostly sound of washing on the line, flapping in the wind.

As I wandered, I sometimes came upon other tormented souls with eyes staring like those of sleep-walkers. There was our watchmaker, a widower whose wife had been a singer, and who imagined he heard her practising during the night, and got out of bed to drown that dream voice with the din of garden frogs. Our mayor also roamed the boulevards in his dressing gown, looking sour and severe, walking down the middle of the road as though he owned it and was simply wandering around his own apartments. Sometimes he would stray in the leafy lanes, listening beyond the gardens for some serenade only he could hear and which brought back painful memories: he had been cuckolded for a long time by the actions of a mistress who had committed suicide for someone else.

I also came across two or three old men who didn't sleep for fear of suddenly dying. They would slink along, close to the wall, and were hard to avoid. I was on the alert, jumping like a cat and heading for the dark as soon as one of them revealed his presence by the swishing sound of his urine as he pissed against a plane tree. Indeed, it would not have been a good idea for me to give these aristocrats of insomnia the impression that a poor child could share their privileged state.

But these wanderings inevitably led me back to Albert's oven. It was at the end of a courtyard, under a luxuriant fig tree, which I climbed to spy on the baker. He came and went from the kneading trough to the oven and from the oven to the wood heap, from which he sometimes took bundles of sticks when he thought it was time to heat the stones. I saw him put the loaves in the oven with his big paddles. When he leaned forward in front of the fire, the blinding light from the red-hot coals etched the lines on his face and showed up his lack-lustre eyes. I tried so hard to read his features, but there was no sign of pain or regret or any feeling at all. Several times during those nights, I had to resist the temptation to get down from my perch and show myself in the right light, exclaiming,

"Well now, what about Patrocles! Hasn't that had any effect on you?"

Now and then he came right up to the trunk of the fig tree to roll a cigarette and breathe the fresh, milky-smelling air circulating among its large leaves. I saw him raise his expressionless face to the stars. It showed just a fleeting hint of disappointment. One night, when he was talking to himself, I heard him murmur,

"All the same ... who knows why they haven't found the letter?"

I realized then that he was astonished to be still at liberty, that he had forced Lucinde to write the note to lure Patrocles, that he didn't care about the consequences when it was discovered, and that perhaps he had even longed to be arrested so that he could finally escape his awful mediocrity. By taking the letter, I had spoiled his greatest achievement.

And so every morning I rushed from our gatehouse to the

bakery with my bag flapping against my legs. Ours was a circular staircase with the steps worn down long ago by generations of soldiers. When it rained, there were numerous little waterfalls, which drummed into the long channel cut in the stone to take away the moisture oozing from the walls. A rope around the pivot was there ostensibly to help descend these stairs. Clinging to that, I flew down them, leaping outside, full of hope and keen to register what ravages yet another night living with that crime had produced on the couple's faces. Nothing was more mysterious to me than to find him still as placid and her still as angry.

When we took possession of the gatehouse as our lodgings, we noticed that Miette-Fume, the last occupant, who had just died, had nailed a dark print from heaven knows where to the wall. It represented three men fleeing before the lashing of an archangel with huge wings and a sword in his hand. Its title was "Justice Pursuing Crime", and the most impressive thing in this allegory was the look of terror on the faces of the three fugitives, their eyes rolling up towards the exterminator.

That was the expression I hoped to flush out in either Lucinde or Albert. They showed no sign of it. They called each other from a distance, from the bakehouse to the shop or vice versa, "Lucinde!" "Albert!" I watched in vain for some failure or trembling in their voices. Hers was always just as commanding, and his just as submissive. They were the usual voices of industrious shopkeepers, who had only ever known one feeling: the one they vowed to each other. I couldn't believe my ears.

III

AUTUMN CAME. ONE MORNING WHEN I WAS AWAITING MY
turn at the bakery, Lucinde roughly pushed me out of her way as
she rushed, hand over mouth, to the room behind the shop. I was
with Bessolote, who was 1m. 50 tall and Madame Chaix, who had
one eye that squinted towards the ceiling. The funereal black
bags swung on their arms, as though to express their surprise.

"Well! What's wrong with her?" Bessolote said.

"Ah!" replied Madame Chaix.

She cupped her hand around her mouth, but I had big ears
that could pick up the rustle of a solitary aspen leaf dangling on
the end of a bare branch. Besides, I had seen my mother make
the same suddenly move as she rushed to the latrine when she
was pregnant with my sister.

"Well! Do you really think so?" Bessolote said.

Madame Chaix nodded her head three times.

"Don't say anything to her," she whispered. "She's got a hard,
eagle eye. She'd know what you were about."

We could hear the sound of a tap being turned on in the back room while Lucinde carefully washed her hands. She came back without uttering a word. Apologizing is not our forte.

"Are you feeling better?" Bessolote asked.

Lucinde nodded.

"I don't know what came over me . . ." she said.

I was the only one to pick up Lucinde's trembling intonation in those few words she spoke. It expressed surprise and fear. It was the only sign she ever gave, the only time she weakened.

I began to think of the nights the couple spent together, imagining the miserable embraces that must have produced this unwanted impregnation: she half-awake and moaning with the memory of Patrocles, and he mistaking his wife's sighs for some moment of pleasure he'd managed to make her feel. No doubt it was dreams, nightmares or fear in the depths of the silent, indifferent night had made them clutch each other with instinctive desire, rather than a deliberate and conscious wish to come together. They were tricked into it by the very fact that they were mammals, blindly feeling for each other in the dark, needing another's warmth. They had deliberately forgotten what was brewing deep down in their dulled minds, normally making them turn from each other in revulsion. But wily nature plays tricks and anything will serve for a belly, so she had immediately taken advantage of this spontaeous embrace, bordering on hatred, to make a child.

This tendency to put myself in another's place, even in situations of extreme horror, unfortunately often came very close to the truth. I carried it within me; it was my constant companion. I didn't need to learn about life, I knew it by heart from birth.

One morning Lucinde wasn't there. We were served by her dull, lethargic sister. She needed three minutes and a pencil to work out the bill by multiplying three kilos of bread by 36 sous. At the end of three days she was completely empty-headed and exhausted. Lucinde came back on Saturday, a little pale and less energetic as she twisted around to shelves where the bread was stacked.

"All the same," Bessolote said as she went out, "she should have been able to manage it. Morning sickness goes after a while."

"What do you expect . . . ?" Madame Chaix replied.

I left, sandwiched between the two women. Whenever I found myself brushing too close to people, I always automatically put my hand on my beret to make sure that no-one was anywhere near the letter.

So, Lucinde had decided not to have the child. I was always looking for some sign of contrition in her and I certainly had one here: she didn't want to carry a murderer's son. I even thought I saw a trace of annoyance on Albert's expressionless face. I'd love to have been there on the Sunday night, to hear the unforgivable things they must have said to each other. I made up all sorts of rejoinders, from insults to declarations of love. In the morning, I scrutinized Lucinde's body to see if I could detect any sign of the violence that must have been done to her, but there was nothing there. Nor was there any difference in the way they called to each other from the bakehouse to the shop.

"Lucinde!"

"Albert!"

These cries were part of our morning pleasure, of our happiness in still being there after the war. I repeated these two names they shouted like a challenge from afar. I clashed them together like cymbals and listened. No! Justice was definitely not pursuing crime in either of their dull consciences, buried deep and undisturbed.

* * *

51

One Sunday morning at about this time, Albert had made the cream puffs and most of the regular clients seemed to be there waiting for them to be brought from the oven, so that there were a lot of customers waiting. When I arrived, there were more than six, taking up all the room in the shop, all of them with those black bags, our funereal emblem, dangling from their hands. I recognized Jacques le Beau, Martin le Trancheton, Bessolote, old Madame Donnet, who was nearly 85 and felt the cold, and behind the exhaust pipe of the stove which was never lit was Blanc, called Rouge to distinguish him from the various 15 other Blancs living in the lanes of Manosque. He was standing there quietly keeping a steely eye on Lucinde's hips. There was also tiny Clorinde Molinas and Martin Cagaïre's wife. They were all waiting for cream puffs. You had to be among the first to arrive and arrive early, for there were never enough for everyone.

I looked down on this group for a moment as I descended the three steps, and then I heard a confused noise like a disturbed hive rising from it. I couldn't tell exactly where the words were coming from, and I didn't understand at first what it was about. I could hear the low voices of the men and the shrill voices of the excited women.

"She was found stabbed with the bayonet her poor father had kept since 1914!"

"It was covered in rust!"

"She had about ten bayonet wounds! It was like the skin of a black pudding ready for the oven. Even the gendarmes turned pale!"

"Come now! What would you know? Did you see them?"

"No, not me. Heaven forbid! It was Odilon, Odilon Testanière who more or less discovered the crime. He was the one who informed the gendarmes when Florence Miane came out of the villa screaming like a madwoman."

"What was Florence Miane doing there?"

"You know. She was doing the housework, like she does every Saturday evening."

"Well! Her employer wasn't very fussy! Getting her housework done by a woman whose father died of TB!"

"Anyhow, a thing like this can only be revenge."

"Do you remember the day when her husband was shot by the Resistance?"

"Well now! The bastard deserved it! He'd sent about 15 people to the concentration camp! And that business at Signes! Do you remember Signes? Martin-Bret and all the others buried alive! He was the one who'd informed on them, for sure!"

"Yes, but do you remember what she said at the funeral?"

"What did she say, then?"

"All of you here will die by my hand!"

"Ah, the poor soul! Her eyes were bigger than her stomach! What on earth could a poor carpenter's widow do?"

"Anyhow," Blanc, called Rouge, muttered, "I wonder what he could have done for her to make her miss him as much as that. You should see the grave in the cemetery! At one stage it was full of red roses every morning! And the dew was still on the flowers! She asked me to cut the grass around the marble slab so that there wouldn't be any moss. And she looked so devout as she kneeled there in the gravel! You could see the marks of it on her knees, and they were bleeding because she stayed so long in that position. Oh! She was a beautiful woman! When I saw her from behind kneeling there, I could have said a thing or two to her!"

So said Blanc, called Rouge, who was the warden of our cemetery and who liked to get an eyeful of our widows when he could. He had an almost lascivious look in his eye as he pictured the coming together in death of such a recent dead body and the other one, her husband, whom no-one would think about much now.

"But still, you can't tell me! Two murders in six months! In Manosque!"

"What are you saying? You forget easily! Hardly two years ago, there was one a week!"

"Yes, but that was wartime."

"What of it? Do you think this is peace?"

That's what Albert's customers were saying as they waited for the cream puffs. At that moment Marius Fouque came in from the door on the main street. He had no nickname as he wasn't from these parts. He was something of a sententious philosopher. He realized straight away from the noise of scandal floating over the assembled company that some new drama had occurred. He therefore enquired,

"Who's dead now?"

"Fulgance Bécarri. She's not dead, she's been murdered!"

I stood there rooted to the spot between the second and third step, my bag dangling and my mouth open. If Fulgance Bécarri had been murdered, it was because someone thought that political enemies had caused Patrocles' death. In that case, the vengeance could be endless: if you counted all those who had something against that handsome man who had assumed the stature of someone bearing the whole of France on his shoulders, and doing it with ease, they were legion.

The letter in the lining of my beret was beginning to weigh on me.

I knew Fulgance well. She was one of those shadows the Manosque night sheltered beneath the arches of its plane trees. She was a sleep-walker. She never saw you, so that you could look at her, follow her, concentrate as much as you liked on what we preferred to think of as a madwoman's strange behaviour, but which was only the endless repetition of an endless sorrow.

Her dull eyes were always raised halfway to the sky and would suddenly become ecstatic as some vision began to appear. Then she would open her arms wide. She beckoned impatiently with her hands, inviting a ghost to come to her arms. She quickly closed them, but not entirely, as if there were a real body occupying that empty space. Then she would murmur these three words:

"Oh my love!"

The voice that came out of her was as dead as the person she was invoking. It wasn't the one we knew when she greeted you during the day or called her dog: it was a voice in tune with death. These were the sole gestures she made and the sole words she uttered as she wandered the boulevards.

I was the only one who could take this meeting of a living woman and a ghost without batting an eyelid. The mayor, the old men, the inconsolable watchmaker all scattered as she approached. They wanted to avoid giving any thought to that extravagant emotion, scared of that love from beyond the grave spilling over from her sleep. Indeed it was shocking. I was the only one who looked death in the face through the intermediary of that woman.

She was a tall, thin, flat-chested woman. She had a long face and there was a fine, thinly stretched film of skin over her nose, so that you could see the beginning of the skeleton that age and decay would reveal little by little. A subtle sensuality trembled over her lips like a wave – the only thing about her that was at all improper.

On that day, between the second and third step of the stairs at Albert the murderer's shop, I could see her pierced by those ritual bayonet thrusts, "done extremely violently", as Bessolote had said, perhaps making it up.

"In any case, this time there's a signature to the murder!"

"How do you mean, signature?"

"Yes! There was a note left beside the body – a note with the words: "From Major Patrocles.""

"Major! He was only ever a captain!"

"On the note it was major."

"Did you see the note?"

"No, I didn't, but Odilon Testanière saw it, and he's no liar. Do you know what he said? He said, 'The note was stuck on the pool of coagulated blood!'"

"Well!" said Fouque, who was rolling a cigarette, " in future her house won't be called 'La Villa Mystérieuse' for nothing."

"Oh? Is that because you think it's for nothing now? There was a famous murder in that house in 1916. It was also a woman who lived there then, the mistress of a naval officer. And she was also found stabbed to death, with but a single blow. And the officer was fished out of the canal."

Fouque shook his head.

"You know a lot of terrible things, Bessolote."

"Yes," Bessolote sighed, "but that one wasn't a murder. It was a love story."

I happened to be looking at the baker's wife when these words were said. I thought her eyes wandered just for a second beyond the counter to the plane tree waving in a silent wind. No-one else there would have noticed it.

Albert was calling to Lucinde from behind the lane door. She hurried over to open it. He appeared laden with two trays, which he put down on the table. The assembled company immediately fell silent. All you could hear was the rustling of skirts crowding around the counter. The murder of Fulgance Bécarri at "La Villa Mystérieuse" was disappearing into the past with the dead leaves.

In three lightning calculations, we had already worked out that, as usual on Sunday, there wouldn't be enough for the eight of us there. What's more, a soft tinkle of the chimes announced the arrival of a ninth. But he wouldn't get anything. Bessolote wanted a dozen, six for Jacques le Beau, five for me, two for old Fouque etc. No, the last arrival certainly wouldn't get anything.

"I was held up!" Madame Henry announced, pushing us out of her way. She was dressed for mass in a suit with a skirt that hugged her figure from waist to calf. Her missal and the little bag hanging from her arm were the only witnesses to her strong faith.

"Keep me six, Lucinde! I have guests! But I'll have my bread first!"

She pretended I was the only one she had noticed.

"So, my poor Pierre! Still just as dirty?"

She had put her hand on my beret, gently feeling it as though patting me on the head. I could feel Lucinde's letter rustling under her fingers. She always called me "my poor Pierre" with that tone of commiseration in her voice, suggesting my advent on earth could only have been a mistake, both for me and others, an unprecedented natural calamity. As a result, whenever I thought about myself, the full weight of that lamentation pervaded my mental dialogue. I called myself poor Pierre with a silent derisive laugh, but without any pity.

The look Madame Henry gave me expressed doubt but not indulgence. She had fine eyes, but I didn't yet know the right word to describe them. On the other hand, as far as their expression is concerned, I had already seen the same one in a dictionary I was leafing through, on the face of a goddess the Greeks dedicated to malice.

Her sudden appearance amongst us all waiting for our share of the cakes had not pleased everyone.

"Did *you* know Fulgance Bécarri well, eh, Hortense?"

Bessolote fired this point-blank question at Madame Henry from the full height of her 150 centimetres, which covered, it must be said, a surface of a good square metre, watching her all the while like a sparrow-hawk.

"Not likely! I've no desire to! She's not worth it!"

"Yes, but by the way, weren't you the one who had her head shaved two years ago?"

"How can you stop a dozen kids from thinking they're saving the honour of their country?"

"Hey! Specially as she can't have been all that bad to touch, with her clothes in the state they were," Blanc, called Rouge, said. "I thought at the time that her head wasn't the only thing they shaved!"

"Yes, but after all, Hortense, weren't you the one in charge of those kids?"

"No. It was Major Patrocles. Lucinde! Look what you're doing! You're putting one in the box on its side!"

I had time to notice the murderous look Lucinde shot at Madame Henry, who had put out her hand to straighten up the cake. Lucinde lifted it out of the way by the wrist.

"No!' she exclaimed. "While the box is on the counter and you haven't paid, the cakes still belong to me. You've come from outside and your fingers are dirty! You can't touch them!"

Madame Henry slowly and deliberately took her left hand away from my filthy beret.

"Oh!" she said. "You're very touchy this morning! You're lucky Albert's such a good pastry cook!"

She paid with short, sharp gestures, scrabbling away in the bottom of her reticule to find change. As she leaned over the counter, her blond hair touched Lucinde's, which was raven black. They looked for all the world like two goats challenging each other. There was no more buzz of voices rising from the group of customers. We were all worried that if they fought, our cream puffs on the tray would bear the brunt and be ruined. But no, the two great cats noticed the silence and straightened up, confronting each other with their proud pointed breasts.

Madame Henry slowly walked through our little group, which gave way as she passed. She stopped in front of Jacques le Beau out of politeness.

"Excuse me, Jacques. You know how it is . . . One's always short of time . . ."

She had just remembered his power to turn off the water supply, and she was fond of her garden.

Fulgance's murder seized the attention of the whole town, especially when it heard about the existence of the note explaining why she was dead.

There were people in the town who had collaborated with Vichy or the Germans and had miraculously come out of it all right, either by giving generously to charity or, when verbally attacked, by highlighting their timid insignificance. They all began to tremble once more. Those who had received a decree of "national unworthiness" and who eked out a living from some inalienable property of their wives' quietly left town.[4] One morning, we woke to find their shutters closed. As for those who were too prominent and too attached to their native soil to leave, they hid themselves even further away in their country properties, surrounded by so many hectares of land that you could see the dust of anything threatening begin to rise a kilometre away.

4 During the "purge" after the war, the official decree of "national unworthiness" deprived a person of their civil rights for life or a number of years, if they had acted "dishonourably", without necessarily having broken the law. [tr.]

From then on, they lived within reach of a gun.

However, they were not the only ones to feel afraid. Our people were very familiar with injustice and they knew from long experience that when the great and powerful fight it out between themselves, they have a habit of doing so by killing innocent people. They recalled some recent stories.

"Remember Raphaël! He was only a notary's clerk, but as his boss was chief of the Légion, it was enough to tar him with the same brush! What's more, he had a big dispute with his father, who was sleeping with his own daughter-in-law, which was a bit awkward while Raphaël was alive. Anyway, to cut a long story short, Raphaël was found in a ditch, riddled with bullet holes. Remember! Remember . . . "

The regulars at the café brought out these stories in an endless stream. They each had one to tell. After Fulgance's murder, they told them to each other past midnight standing at the bar of the Moderne or the Splendid'Bar.

I was trembling too. That letter of Lucinde's, which supplied the key to the mystery, was lying there in the lining of my beret. If I'd shown it in time, Fulgance Bécarri would still be alive and everything would have gone back to normal. If I went to the gendarmes and showed them the letter now, I'd be condemning myself. I couldn't stop thinking about the enormity of what I'd done, or rather what I hadn't done, and I began walking around Manosque with that vacant look, which increased my reputation as a moron. I used to have an appetite like a horse, but now I left half my helping on the plate to be noisily squabbled over by my brother and sister. I no longer even noticed a woman's bottom. I forgot to play with myself. I touched the beret on my head more and more often, almost obsessively. I did it suddenly, with an irrational feeling of panic, as a miser touches his gold.

* * *

A torrid summer was followed by a gentle autumn. One of the municipal council workers died of a carbuncle that turned septic.

"Why don't you go and see about it?" my father said. Up to that time I'd only been a day worker picking potatoes for peasants or removing stones from their land bordering the Durance, or sometimes I hired myself out to the flour mill, cleaning the sieves. I went to see the chief road worker, who felt my calves and biceps.

"All right!" he said to my father. "He's got good feet. He'll be able to pull the cart."

I was allocated a fifth of the town that no-one wanted: from the Saunerie Gate to the Aubette Gate, where I lived. It was the area the flocks went through from May to June on their way up to summer pasture in the mountains, and later when they came down again to the plains from October to November. Flocks of 10,000 head stayed there for one night, then continued on their way, leaving behind 1,000 to 2,000 kilos of sheep manure that had to be removed with the handcart. All the shopkeepers in the area threw up their hands in horror. Customers brought sheep droppings on the soles of their shoes into the shops and businesses of Albert the baker, Madame Gondran the midwife, Chabal the delicatessen, and the Bar de l'Espérance, where the clients scraped their feet on the crossbars of the chairs. Henri Gardon, the grocer, was the only one who saw nothing unusual about it.

"Just pray" he said, "that the sheep will always be there! You have very short memories! In '43, '44 you'd have killed for three lamb chops!"

He was also the only one who gave me 40 sous when I swept his footpath. He's one of the half dozen men I've never forgotten.

You'd have sworn that none of the others had ever seen a goat dropping in their lives. They walked around on tiptoe to avoid them. They called out to me to sweep in all the corners.

"Hey Pierrot! You've forgotten to clean under my stairs!"

"Come here Pierrot! Just clean up my flower bed, will you. My wallflowers will die with all that manure!"

I didn't react. The council secretary gave me my envelope every month, and that's what counted. Now I had 400 francs in the lining of my beret along with Lucinde's letter. The autumn was also the time when the distillers always set up around the Gypsies' wash-house to process the wine-growers' pips and stalks. Then the air was filled with a smell something like a cross between sheep manure and grape pips once the alcohol had come out of them into the chambers of the still.

The smell of vine and manure filled the night air, the high wind churned the plane trees, warning of misfortune, the rushing waters of the des Rates stream swollen by the late summer rains rolled over the pebbles. The old peasants were sitting on benches around the still, waiting for their *blanche* – their warm alcohol. All of that was like a picture of eternity, which delighted me, comforted me and reassured me a little, as I carried my weighty secret around with me.

Standing back from the firelight, far from the acetylene lamp hung in the canvas tent, I spied on life as though I were looking through a keyhole. I could have joined the old men and looked it full in the face, in the light. No! If it was to be remembered, my observer's eye had to define it, and the actors in that peaceful scene mustn't know they were being observed. Their eyes were concentrating on just one thing: the trickle of brandy that I couldn't find the right words to describe, flowing silently into the green-glazed dish beside a bobbing alcohol-measure, a reminder of the rigours of the law.

One evening when I was gazing my fill at these fleeting scenes which delighted me so much, listening to the prophetic wind high up in the plane trees, a hand was placed firmly on my shoulder, a hand that seemed to come down on it rather than pat it.

"What are you staring at so hard, Pierrot?"

It was Madame Henry. She wasn't speaking in her normal voice: she was whispering in my ear. She was leaning towards me as though she wanted to smell me. She must have been on her way back from church, as she had her missal in her hand. I replied also in a whisper.

"I'm contemplating."

"You're contemplating!"

Her voice hissed with indignation. She said those two words the way La Fontaine's ant must have done when it replied, "You were singing!" to its neighbour, the grasshopper.

"Do you know what contemplate means? What do you think gives *you* the right to contemplate?"

Both of us were in the shade, she tall, towering over me, bathed in Chanel No 5, which I then began to doubt was compatible with her regular church-going. She wasn't touching me, but there was so little space between us that when she breathed, the material of her bodice matched the folds of my uncle's coat and made me feel weak at the knees.

"Since we're alone," she said, still speaking softly, "tell me your secret!"

"Oh! What secret could *I* have?"

"Someone who contemplates always has a secret! Contemplating doesn't get you anywhere! Especially at your age and so poor! If you're contemplating, that means you have a secret!"

I felt her eyes following the reflected lights and shadows

flickering over my face from the flames under the still. There was an extraordinary concentration of attention from her to me. It was a big mistake to contemplate without taking precautions, without hiding my true self better. Now someone knew that I could indulge in games usually forbidden to children of the poor, and consequently that I could well be different from what I seemed.

I felt Lucinde's letter on blue paper to Captain Patrocles crackling under the 400 francs in my beret. Fortunately Madame Henry was no more capable of long concentration on someone else than the normal run of mortals nor, in the cold November wind, of looking for long at the picture of four old men savouring each drop of the warm alcohol from the still. There was no mystery in that picture, as far as she was concerned. I was the only one capable of patiently recording that eternal moment, which in real time would last only a few seconds.

"You make me shiver!" Madame Henry said.

Then she left. All the following night I celebrated her in my slow, insistent masturbation, defining details of her body that perhaps she hardly knew herself. Perhaps they didn't really exist, since I dreamed of them so much. I didn't regret not having had enough courage to put out my hand and touch her when we were so close: it was enough for me to imagine doing it.

But reality, in the shape of all those things that had been troubling me, brought me down to earth the next day with the news going around the town: the gendarmes had arrested someone; the gendarmes were questioning someone. I rushed to find out who it was. Tancrède was the one they had arrested, Tancrède the pimply youth, the one in the cemetery who had sworn to heaven that he would avenge his father. The gendarmes had remembered that, had called him in and had asked where he was on the night

Fulgance Bécarri had been hacked to death with a bayonet.

"Hacked to death!" the jurist had emphasized. "Which always points to vengeance. It's the classic sign of that particular crime. You don't kill an enemy with one stab-wound; you go at him till you're worn out!"

Tancrède, of course, had been alone in his bed. The gendarmes had pulled long faces, yes but . . . The house was being replastered and his bedroom door was blocked off by scaffolding. Tancrède had to go through his mother's room to get out.

"I sleep very lightly," she said, "since my poor husband died."

One night the gendarmes, with great inventiveness, had the siren sounded on the roof of the town hall, then came at the crack of dawn to ask the widow if she had heard anything. She said no.

The gendarmes were also troubled by the size of the Patrocles house and the fact that it had two entrances, one on to the square and the other at the bottom of the garden, giving on to a filthy lane.

Patrocles had had that house for a song. It was in the notary's family and when he was declared a traitor to his country, it was sold at auction. No-one had dared bid against Patrocles, with his aura of heroism and his look of determination.

"You must realize, Madame," the gendarmes said to the widow Patrocles, "your son has made threats to kill . . . "

"His father's murderer! Isn't that justified?"

"Of course! And he would be granted attenuating circumstances! But after all, a woman's death is a woman's death! On that night your son could easily have crossed your bedroom without you hearing him."

"But how could he have known that Madame Bécarri was the murderer when you, with all the means at your disposal, weren't able to discover a thing about my poor husband's death? How could my son, who is only 17, do better than you?"

"It's one of the unresolved elements in this case, but we will have to refer him to the public prosecutor's office."

"He's been referred to the public prosecutor's office!"

Auguste Faux whispered these words in Jacques le Beau's ear at eight o'clock the next morning in the bakery. I was there and heard it.

Lucinde said not a word. Her hand, which was manipulating the brass weights, didn't tremble or give any sign of nervousness. Albert came in, pushing his baskets. Nothing worried him either. Of the three who knew, I was the only one to feel disconcerted.

A voice within me, which took no account of my youth, laughed derisively.

"So, you wanted to play god and decide people's fate? See how easy it is!"

When I was sure I was alone, I put both hands out in front of me, palms upwards, raising first one then the other, weighing and balancing, trying not to let myself be influenced by my feelings. I was too shaken to realize an obvious fact: denouncing Albert would not prove Tancrède innocent, since the boy, not knowing his father's real murderer, could well have executed the widow Bécarri if he thought she was guilty. I found myself asking this terrible question:

"Which one is better than the other?"

Tancrède was already on the way to inheriting his father's arrogance and disdain for his fellow man. You could see that in spite of his acne he would turn out to be manly and handsome. He wore glasses, which already made him look serious. He would be first in everything without the slightest effort and, like his

66

father, he already seemed to wear France across his chest like a noble coat of arms, which would be his shield. At least that's how I imagined him, and I wasn't exactly upset to know that he was now at Digne, in a cell which hadn't been painted for a century and where water oozed out of the walls. Between those walls his father had languished and Madame Henry had sung the "Marseillaise" as her torturers kicked her, both expecting to be shot at any moment. Then it was the turn of the torturers themselves, finally brought to their knees, also waiting to be shot between walls that still had not been painted. To my mind Tancrède was one of those privileged people their enemies keep separated from the others to keep them alive.

Compared with this member of a prominent dynasty, Albert would never be anything but a colourless creature with a face you had to make an effort to remember. He would have taken only one risk, which he had already forgotten, in the whole of his miserable life: getting rid of a rival, just as he had once crushed a cat to death between the two doors. One Sunday it had ruined a tray of cream puffs by having a nibble at all of them. The animal's awful cries hadn't stopped Albert from pushing on the door with all his might until the noise stopped. Then he simply threw the dead cat into the rubbish bin and forgot about it. With that in mind, I'd convinced myself that Albert had forgotten Patrocles just as quickly. Two-thirds of the human race are made of up Alberts, and the other third of Tancrèdes. And now I, at 15, had to weigh the fate of those two, as the baker had done for the cat.

However, I was fairly convinced that I was more likely to be with the Alberts than with the Tancrèdes. With a hidden, clairvoyant premonition, I already saw myself as one of the cuckolds of this world. I had all their form and substance, their muddle-headed, awkward clumsiness, their suspicious nature and their shiftiness, their rough hands and tough hearts.

I equivocated, I procrastinated. Time and time again, I resolutely set out for the police station, armed with the piece of paper clutched in my hand. Time and time again, I turned off at the roundabout, lacking both the strength and the courage.

I wanted my nightlife to provide the solution for me. I was walking the streets more and more, unable to sleep. Wearing a balaclava, I braved the winter weather, roaming the boulevards where light snow could be seen falling in the lamplight. The mayor had simply slipped a loose shepherd's coat over his dressing gown. The watchmaker wore gaiters and a hunting jacket; the old men just stood coughing in their ordinary overcoats with their hands behind their backs. The various worries that kept us out of our beds were not going to be put off by a bit of cold weather. I prowled around the Patrocles' house, as if the ins and outs of the house could tell me what to do, as if the imposing house with its several stories could provide the key to my own mystery.

Spring came. Tancrède was still languishing in prison. Time and time again the examining magistrate appointed to the case had slapped the dossier down on his desk; time and time again he put it away, out of sight. He paced up and down late at night in his office by the green light of his lamp. Auguste Faux said that he had judge's cramp and that it could last for ten years.

Now one night when I was walking around the lanes as close as possible to the Patrocles' house, I saw the big windows on the mezzanine floor lit up and bare of curtains. I was at the bottom of the garden, which was separated from the alley only by a low wall. These windows were the finest casements in the building, looking into a drawing room. The shutters were never closed, because they were too heavy to move. The windows in the Patrocles' house were usually shielded from prying eyes by long curtains with a design based on La Fontaine's fables, but it was spring-cleaning time when Manosque washed its curtains. My mother brought basket-loads of them from middle-class houses to wash at the brook.

Suddenly Madame Henry sailed into the room through a door-curtain that had been pulled back for her. The light was dim and the dark, heavy furniture emphasized the idea that life was meant to be grim and earnest. She was wearing a provocative hat I'd never seen before, probably pink, but with an extended shell-shaped front brim, a brim that could hide her rather sharply chiselled features from the light. As it was past midnight, it occurred to me straight away that she might have come through the streets, walking close to the walls, and that the hat was there to keep her in the shadows. She must have known that the mayor, the watchmaker and the old men walked about at night, tortured by a host of anxieties. She wore this headgear with wonderful theatrical panache. I'd have burst out laughing at anyone else in that hat, but looking at her, I was silent. When that beautiful woman entered the room, with its dull colours made darker still by the tarry tones of a grim painting in a gold frame, she lit it up like a fresh flower. This time there were no decorations on her lavender blue suit. I imagined her holding a pair of gloves for appearances and to emphasize her gestures, but her hands were bare, without any rings, apart from a dull gold wedding ring, indicating her widowhood. None of her movements was in any way excessive or exaggerated. I think it was that restraint which made me fall in love with her that evening.

The red-faced woman I'd seen under the heavy black widow's veil at the cemetery followed her. Although she was trying to appear haughty, her bearing couldn't compete with the stage presence of her visitor. She nevertheless had a certain beauty, with her full hips and proud bosom. I pitied her as I thought of the severe privation she must have been suffering since the death of her Patrocles. Anyone who is a careful observer of changes in thoughts and feelings could read it in her eyes. In spite of being only 15, I constantly watched for all the expressions of passion that I came across, be it a bird singing or a woman moaning, even inaudibly; I lay in wait for life and all its turmoil. Nothing about myself was of any interest, but everything about other people fascinated me.

And so, without a moment's hesitation, I jumped over the low wall around the vegetable garden into three rows of leeks just beginning to firm up. The dim light from the table lamps on various pieces of furniture guided me to its source.

The mezzanine floor was low. I took the precaution of keeping well out of the light in the blind corner. It was a useless brick addition with decorative accentuation on the supports, an architect's flight of fancy.

I was looking at Madame Henry from below, as though she had been raised up on a stage. She paced up and down with her lioness's walk, in front of the red-faced woman, who said nothing to begin with, but watched her with a look of suspicion, or was it distaste?

Madame Henry spoke without a break for a good three minutes. Unfortunately the windows of the drawing room were originally a notary's windows, therefore well sealed to keep private talk secret. I had ears attuned to catch the slightest sighs that nature proffered during my night walks around Manosque and I could also make out what other people were saying, even when they were talking softly. However, here Madame Henry was talking to Madame Patrocles side on to me as she walked slowly across the floor, almost like a teacher dictating to her pupils, stressing each sentence with a short, sharp movement of her hand.

She finally stopped, hiding the other woman completely. I noticed the almost imperceptible sign of oppression in the visitor's shoulders, the restrained gesture that accompanied every inaudible sentence. My frustrated curiosity was torture. Something vital I knew nothing about was taking place before my very eyes.

At that moment Madame Patrocles finally replied. I noticed then that her contralto voice came through those tightly sealed windows more easily. That music came to my ears like an indistinct hum without words.

The widow had slowly moved around to the side, wanting to put some distance between herself and the visitor, so that they were now both standing in profile. They seemed ecstatic. Two or three words had just relaxed the shape of their mouths, which I desperately tried to read to catch their feelings. Then Madame Henry slowly turned around. Her silhouette was between the window and the lamp standing on a snake-patterned carpet. She was wearing light clothes for the early spring weather and, as soon as she had stopped moving, with the lamplight behind her, I could see the curve of her legs and hips outlined beneath her skirt. As I gazed at her, the different colours and graded shadows revealed the panties and stockings. That sight was enough to make my mouth go dry and make me forget that I was there solely to discover a secret. Fate produced this unexpected vision which distracted my attention. I'd already seen women's legs moving under the obliging material of a dress in the sunset, but that was just a glimpse, and I pretended not to notice, living in fear of being seen doing it. But here I was comfortably installed, sheltered by a big rambling rose rustling in the shadows behind me. I could spy on her for as long as I liked. I forgot the lips and the inaudible words. The most important thing was there at eye-level, the silky glow darkened by the two sides of the skirt around that marvel – a woman's legs. I tried, successfully, to draw a half-real, half-imaginary mental picture of the sight that enthralled me: a tense body with taut skin trembling imperceptibly when Madame Henry held her breath, thinking she'd caught the hidden meaning behind the words Madame Patrocles was saying.

Then, with three decisive steps, the woman who had become the centre of my world that night escaped from my prying eyes and became once more just a disappointing, uniform shape with no mystery at all. She had just waved her arm in the air in a decisive gesture and raised her voice so that I could now hear her.

"Come now, Marguerite-Marie, have you forgotten he's my godson?"

"And he's *my* son!" Madame Patrocles retorted in the same tone of voice. "No! And that's definite! I won't let you spread that disgusting story!"

"Disgusting story! If all you have to do to save him is simply admit that he spent the night under my roof?"

"In your bedroom! In your bed! On your body!"

Her face turned redder still as she stamped her heel forcefully on the parquet with each statement. Her eyes were flashing with barely contained anger as she held Madame Henry's gaze. For a moment I forgot she had a red face and began to wish that she would also stand in front of the revealing lamp, but it didn't happen. The two women were talking head to head, their eyes full of hate, confronting each other in combat over the possession of a teenager scarcely older than I was. Suddenly Madame Henry had had enough. Her gestures were no longer controlled.

She waved her round arms in the air helplessly and her voice became shrill.

"You're nothing but a silly idiot! Well then, let him rot in prison! And I hope it kills you!"

She turned away and walked towards the doorway, roughly pushing back the curtain on its rings. The padded door closed silently, but I heard the door at the carriage entrance in the Rue des Marchands slam shut with a bang.

I resisted the mad desire to follow this fury through the empty streets to her house. I imagined her running from one plane tree to the next, and wondered what would happen if one of the tired-eyed old men came across her and greeted her quietly but fervently when she was in such a state.

I resisted because I was much more fascinated by other people's pain than my own desire. From the shadows in which I lived and the humble station that was my lot, the sight of suffering was a feeling I was keen to experience. Seeing torment develop in someone is even less common than coming across two lovers exhausting themselves in pursuit of pleasure, and I was at the age when they seemed equally mysterious. I had fleetingly tasted pleasure, but I couldn't imagine suffering. I had to experience it through someone else and, I must admit, on that particular night, I was not disappointed.

I had to stay crouching in the shadows until it got too cold for me. During all this time, Madame Patrocles kept pacing up and down her expensively furnished drawing room. Her hands were clasped and she twisted her fingers uncontrollably, as though wanting to hurt herself. She tripped on the carpet, tottered, stood up straight again, staggered once more. She walked about aimlessly like a fluttering moth caught in the light. The sound of her small hurried steps reached me in spite of the sealed windows. Her face reflected everything that was going on in her heart. New, indelible lines appeared from one moment to the next, making her ugly for the rest of her life. Sometimes she would put her hand across her mouth and there was panic in her eyes. Sometimes she bit her nails. She would also collapse into an armchair or throw herself on a couch, head back and black hair dishevelled. Three times I heard her scream at the top of her voice.

I was terrified. It seemed to me that this woman's grief at Patrocles' graveside had not been as keen as it was now. And she must have been suffering every night for a long time, in fact ever since her son had been in prison at Digne. As a result of seeing her so distraught, I promised myself never to have children.

That night I went back to our slum of a home with my back bent under the weight of a whole new load of different emotions, but the dominant one was suffering. I asked myself, "Would you be capable of it? Could you bear so much unhappiness?"

I had absolutely no awareness that my life of poverty could also contain an element of suffering, for I had exemplary parents who had never dwelt on my state or theirs. They were humble, they were close and they were happy. My father was silence itself, the embodiment of resignation. His only attitude to those above him was polite indifference. "You're rich? That's good! May God go with you!" His hovel, his wife and his children were enough for him. Earlier on at Saint-Jurson his living had been even more precarious. As for my mother, she warbled all day long. She had crooked legs like my brother, and used to rush out of the door at five o'clock in the morning, clutching her dirty missal in her mittened hands, waking the neighbours by singing love songs out of tune:

Don't send them mad, the men and boys!

To you their hearts are only toys.

She stopped singing as she timidly entered the church by the little door on the Rue Voland with the respectable women parishioners. In the beginning she used to go straight through the great Saint-Sauveur gateway like everyone else. However, she quickly noticed that seven or eight women – and not the most infrequent attenders – carried humility to the point of slipping in by the side door in the Rue Voland, so that no-one would notice they made the morning sacrifice of getting up at five to hear the first mass. As far as humility is concerned, my mother could teach anyone a thing or two. From that time on, she never went in at the front entrance of the church in full view of the people of Manosque.

Her even temper reigned in our dilapidated home, keeping the five of us in an atmosphere of peace and calm. She had been deaf since a thunderbolt had stunned her when she was looking after the goats at Saint-Jurson. She laughed about it a lot.

I thought it would have been wrong of us to consider ourselves unfortunate, since we had escaped the war and we had work. Consequently, any suffering I noticed in the world seemed much worse than ours and essentially more noble. The anguish Madame Patrocles had suffered that night troubled me considerably. Although I continued unconcernedly to sweep my areas of the town with my big birch brooms, I was always on the watch. My steps led me more often than not to Albert's bakery, where I could reassure myself that the couple quite happily accepted the fact that Patrocles' son was in prison.

I slept less peacefully than they did, and while I was awake I often thought of them. I pictured them sleeping quietly at night; Albert's alarm clock going off at three in the morning, calling him to the bakehouse; their bed at dawn, scarcely ruffled, with the two hollows in the mattress quite separate from each other. When Albert wheeled in the batches of bread hot from the oven, he sometimes said to Lucinde,

"Did you think of telephoning Moullet for the flour? When are they coming?"

And Lucinde would reply calmly,

"They're coming on Friday."

Could intense hatred and terrified collusion become so deeply assimilated that nothing showed on the surface? In any case, they seemed to accept Tancrède's arrest with the same self-control as Patrocles' death.

They began to get rich. It was the time when Manosque thought it could go back to cosy pre-war living and forget the rest of the world. But suddenly hordes of people from Marseilles en route to the mountains for winter or summer sports landed in town. Albert had greased some palms on the council so that the Saturday and Sunday coaches to Le Dévoluy and Barcelonnette would go along his boulevard rather than that of his rival Duranton. From seven o'clock on, they all wanted bags of croissants. When the Marseillais had gone, there was nothing left in the baskets but a few poor specimens mangled by all the gloved hands that had rummaged about among them.

"They've squashed them all!" Lucinde would say.

Her laugh was rather joyless. The money still managed to cheer her up. The drawer under the cash register had to be made bigger. On Saturdays and Sundays it still wasn't big enough. Albert's reputation for rolls and Viennese bread and buns went beyond the town gates. That murderer had the lightest hand for croissants, and the aristocratic d'Autanes sent their chauffeurs from Forcalquier every morning to get a basketful. Albert's reputation, the influx of the Marseillais, the situation of the shop all contributed to make the bakery prosper. Fate mocked them by giving them everything to make people envy them. They had just bought a car and went out in it every Monday, treating themselves to dinner in a country restaurant, where they sat facing each other, bored stiff. They bought a large block of land. They had a house built. People said,

"The Alberts are doing well!"

But I had that note in my beret and I knew their real worth. I couldn't stop thinking of their nights, before the shrill sound of the alarm. I thought of that beautiful woman denied all pleasure by a gun-shot, suddenly cutting her off from that source of inner joy, which is the most constant sign of happiness. I thought of her warm, graceful, rounded human form, brimming with frustrated desire, lying awake rigid and tense beside that thin man with no imagination, who had neither the words nor the hands to properly caress those sublime curves and valleys.

As I stood there every morning holding my bag, my palms were sweaty from imagining myself taking Albert's place in the conjugal bed. Since the misadventure with the unwanted child, Lucinde must have got so far away from Albert in the bed that she nearly fell out, as so many poor women have done.

And now, as well as Patrocles' dead body, there was the innocent young man languishing in prison, and there was Patrocles' avenger, who wouldn't stop there when it was proved that Fulgance was innocent. Someone capable of stabbing his victim twelve times wouldn't be likely to forget or restrain himself.

The Alberts must have felt the threat of that uncertainty every night, and even if they put such a brave face on it during the day, how long could that last? How many more bodies could their common decency withstand? When would they fall on their knees in the middle of the bakery and beg forgiveness? One for having killed Patrocles, and the other for having sent the letter.

I hoped it wouldn't happen when I wasn't there, so, using my work as an excuse, I arrived earlier and earlier. More and more often I was there alone with Albert and Lucinde, waiting for them to finish weighing out the yeast for the next day's baking. It was a task they carried out like a communion, with their heads almost indecently close together over the scales and their hair intertwined.

That was also the time when, as often as possible, Madame Henry would arrive, quietly entering the shop behind us. She was very clever at stopping the chimes that tinkled when the door was opened. You suddenly felt she was there behind you, breathing down your neck like a wild animal scenting its prey.

As soon as I came into possession of the secret, I should have realized that from then on, I had to regard other people as enemies ready to tear me to pieces to discover it. Therefore, I should never give the slightest glance nor let any unusual expression appear on my face when anyone else was present while I was waiting in the bakery. But I still had too much to learn about real wild animals to be able to hide everything.

On several occasions Madame Henry must have caught me gazing at the couple, with perhaps a look of surprise or fear or curiosity or desire. One day she asked me,

"Tell me, Pierrot. How would you like to come one Sunday and gather up the leaves from the plane trees on my path and in the pond? You'll see! I won't be *cochonne*!"

That sentence actually meant that I shouldn't expect to be paid a huge amount. "Not to be *cochon/ne*", in our part of the country, means to have both an open mind and an open wallet. The person who makes that boast, however, always reveals at the same time that he's not what he claims to be – anyway, that's how we understand it, and on that subject we're rarely wrong.

Lucinde was astonished to hear me accept the offer, as we both knew the plane-tree walk at Madame Henry's house. It was nearly 200 metres long, bordered with big trees, which shed their leaves like tears for weeks in autumn. The task of sweeping them up had something of the myth of Sisyphus.

Lucinde couldn't know that I'd been wanting to get into Madame Henry's house for some time, even if it had to be by sweeping. I nonetheless arranged that it would be in November, after the last flocks had come down from the mountains. On every occasion after that when she met me at Albert's she reminded me of my promise.

During that time, the name of Tancrède Patrocles was heard as high up as the Chancellery, thanks to the efforts of his lawyers, who emphasized who he was. The bits of information spread by Auguste Faux and others reached my eager ears and ignited my imagination. "The Chancellery". I had to look it up in a diction-ary in the municipal library. It was a dusty place, jealously guarded by a former teacher who chose what I should and shouldn't read. When I finally found out that it was the Ministry of Justice, I conjured up a world I would doubtless never know. I imagined an office with a huge desk, like those I had seen belonging to the rich and powerful in films at the parish cinema. A host of servile, attentive little men carrying boxes stuffed with papers came and went around it. Sometimes they would take one and open it with a bored gesture. That's how I imagined Tancrède's dossier had come under the eyes of some uncon-cerned functionary, who had sat up and asked,

"Tancrède Patrocles! But, tell me. Isn't that the name of the great patriot who rendered such signal service to the Resistance?"

"Yes indeed!"

"Get rid of that dossier! Give me a brief résumé of what's in it and refer the matter to me!"

The dossier must have snapped shut in the hands of the subordinate thus addressed. Some time later, Auguste Faux brought us the news one morning at the bakery.

"It's the judge who said it: there's no case to answer!"

I felt a great weight lifted from me, and I saw from the way her breasts rose that Lucinde felt the same.

The time for the flocks to go up to the mountains and come down again had now passed. I had promised Madame Henry that I would do her work in November. One evening I started out for her house. With the birch broom over my shoulder, I must have looked like a scarecrow. She lived in a big villa with a four-sided roof and a metal weather-vane in the shape of a rooster on the top of the ornamental motif. Many big casement windows adorned the building. I had always dreamed of having a house with a four-sided roof and a long plane-tree walk. Poor people's dreams are always out of all proportion to their state! Oh, those tall trees! They were all I needed to feel happy, when they were all I had.

The iron gate at the top of this path hadn't been closed for decades. The dead leaves, then their leaf mould, had blocked up both sides, and grass had grown on them. Rust had finished the job, so that the gates to the Henry house could never be closed again. I went in by this monumental gate supported by two pillars topped with two large stone pine cones. The gravel on the path had disappeared under the carpet of dead leaves. Further away, in the grove of tall cedars, I could see the outline of a small separate building with a balustrade. I immediately imagined a deceived lover there, coming out on to the balcony in the evening and peering into the darkness.

The wind was blowing but the rain that had just fallen made the thick layer of sycamore foliage stick to the ground. I set to work slowly and patiently. I spent my Saturday or my Sunday there rather than at the cinema or the café. This curiosity of mine was not normal. I hid it from the people I knew (I had no friends), pretending to take an interest in their toys, the football and the Tour de France to avoid their hostility. But to tell the truth, I preferred places like Madame Henry's plane-tree walk and the small empty building with the closed shutters, where I felt a sense of the past. Fortunately I was shielded from my own mediocrity, as though I were wearing armour. No-one else wanted a share in these worthless possessions.

I swept patiently, stoically, not even complaining when a gust of wind destroyed the result of half an hour's work by scattering my piles of leaves. I was fortunate in that I'd been influenced by elders who were even more resigned and lowly than I was. Thanks to their example, I was a past master in the art of making little fires in heaps of dead leaves, which burned slowly without spreading or growing too big.

There were rainy days when I worked twice as fast, and windy days when suddenly I had to start all over again. The small building behind me merged into the November mists and in the distance I could see the outline of the main house with its big windows where the reflections from a lamp sometimes flickered in the last rays of daylight, as I put my broom back on my shoulder. Having the excuse of estimating the extent of the task, I could have begun by walking the whole length of the path and discovering there and then both the path and the house. But I was one of those voluptuous souls whose only notion of pleasure is something that is slow to reveal itself as such. I preferred to discover it gradually, for going up to that house was a pleasure and I was happy that my job as a sweeper permitted it.

One evening when I'd stayed later than I should because I was standing there with my mouth open, listening to the wind in the high branches, I saw a man walking towards me, preceded by the smell of American cigarettes. I recognized Victor, the slaughterman at the abattoirs. Every afternoon he was dressed to kill, sporting a soft felt hat and a sharp crease in his trousers. He didn't dare wear gloves, but the Lucky Strike he held between his first and second fingers in a V shape was enough to show that he was striving after elegance. He had a short torso, but long legs, and he was as supple as a cat. Silence was his constant companion. He spoke so little that people thought he was dumb. I knew very little about Victor except, for example, that in a drawer in his bedside table he had 15 watches taken from the bodies of German soldiers he had executed during the war. He put a different one on his wrist every day.

I was crouching near a dying fire I was trying to revive, so that Victor passed very close to me without noticing I was there, and I certainly didn't want to meet his shifty eyes. When he looked at people, he seemed to wipe them from the face of the earth, as captive tigers do when they look straight through you into the distance, knowing they can't get at you. In the same way, Victor never looked at anyone.

What was Victor doing at Madame Henry's? The path was long enough for me to watch the visitor go right up to the house. He walked along nonchalantly, in familiar territory, like someone coming home for dinner.

I leaned on my broom as I watched him move away from me. Seen from behind, he looked like a convicted murderer, with a short, animal neck, leaving very little space for a buttoned collar between his shoulders and the back of his head. He had very long earlobes that almost touched his collarbone, and the vertebrae in his neck seemed to be tightly and economically packed together, as if his skull would one day refuse to be separated from his body by the blade of the guillotine. At least that's how I saw him, as the dead leaves whirled up then dropped back on the ground behind his disturbing figure.

What was Victor doing at Madame Henry's? I could have followed him and tried to find an answer by spying on him, as I had done that other time at Madame Patrocles', but I was sometimes overcome by inexplicable scruples. These scruples grew out of fear. The killings Victor had committed remained in everyone's memory, however legitimate they might have been in the war. He'd first of all been fêted as a hero, but now on reflection, people transposed the proverb "who steals a box, will steal an ox" and applied it to him, without any extenuating circumstances: the box being the traditional enemy and the ox being any one of us. With our trusty common sense we thought that if he had killed 15 Germans out of duty, he could well start again on a few French just for pleasure.

Auguste Faux used to make us shudder with these wise words,

"Once a person starts killing," he said, "if he can't do it any more, he gets bored and restless."

So I let Victor the slaughterman walk away into the dusk.

IV

HOWEVER, AS THE WEEKS WENT BY, THE PATH BEHIND ME was cleared and I was drawing closer to the house with the weather-vane. The days were getting shorter. The shapes of the plane trees stood out against the black sky and their skeletal branches knocked together in the wind with a dull, ominous rattle. One evening I finally emerged on to the clean, treeless court in front of the house; the lights were on and it seemed to be waiting for me, watching for me, welcoming me.

The house itself was Madame Henry to a tee, as I dreamed of her during my steamy nights. Its low and compact construction suggested her firmness and determination. It had a wide staircase leading to a raised single storey, and a terrace running the full length of the house with a line of holly bushes, their red berries a permanent reminder of Christmas. This hedge was set off by a row of ragged hydrangeas with faded blooms still blowing in the November wind.

That morning in the bakery, Madame Henry had said,

"Pierrot, come and get your pay."

It was an order. I'd cleaned myself up a bit: that is to say, I'd swapped my filthy dirty pants for another pair that smelled of washing powder. A strange feeling slowly came over me, but it was nothing like joy. Yet everything looked beautiful: the house, the lawns, the plane trees behind me singing in the wind, the weathercock squeaking like a coffee mill and, behind a blind waving in the breeze, Madame Henry coming and going, soon to appear before me, alone.

The thought that I held the fate of Albert and Lucinde in the palm of my hand had given me a childish feeling of power, but here among all that opulence, I was helpless before my own fate.

"If you open that door," I thought, "it's your own life that's suddenly going to fall in on you! You had nothing to worry about hidden away behind your poverty and your ugliness. You're going to learn that there are other forms of suffering just as unspeakable!"

I felt like rejecting this choice of action and running away. I remember beginning to turn around to go back to Manosque and my gatehouse with its Gothic arches, but I heard the sound of a door being roughly pushed open.

"Is that you, Pierrot?"

There she was, standing in front of me, alone, just as I had imagined. She'd pushed the door with such force because it always stuck and would open only when hit hard.

"Come in!" Madame Henry ordered.

She flattened her bust and stomach slightly, as if she feared that there was not enough space between her and the doorway for my thin frame to pass.

I found myself in an anteroom with a high ceiling, furnished like a small sitting-room. The walls were blood red. There were tapestries going right around the room depicting some colonial massacre; all that was missing was the noise, but you could imagine it. There were spahis shouting at the tops of their voices, and Arabs with clenched teeth trying to exterminate each other to the last man in a tangle of ladders, bayonets and scimitars. Bodies being ripped open tumbled down the wall partitions, a Zouave with his throat cut lay dying behind a Louis XV swing mirror and a white horse stared at its own entrails in front of a hidden door. A bayonet was being plunged into a sheik's chest under the torch of a silver wall lamp.

It was sumptuous, horrible and in bad taste.

"My grandfather was a major in the Second Spahis in North Africa," Madame Henry explained in martial tones.

I had already seen this pitiless slaughter in an encyclopaedia. It was called "The Capture of Constantinople". But I had no time to linger over it, as Madame Henry was moving away from me with that swaying walk of hers. I could see the straight seams of the smoke-coloured stockings, which moulded her calves and stopped at the hem of her skirt. She opened the door, where an oblong of light suddenly took the place of the dying sheik. As she went in through the doorway of a well-sealed room, I was hit in the face by both the disturbing perfume of Madame Henry's armpits and a musty smell like a tomb where ten generations have lain.

It was a room filled with ghosts, as if they'd been crushed in a crowd on fair day. Each one had left his stamp on it with an object or a piece of furniture, which would last ten or a hundred times longer than a human life. There was an initialled goblet with a dent on the side and a piece of ladies' handwork with the bobbins still hanging over the cane circle, which an ancestor might have been embroidering when she breathed her last. In the corner stood a whist table strewn with cards on which every picture had been touched countless times by the moist fingers of an idle old man or woman looking at the rain falling on the cedars and feeling the endless boredom all around.

It was a very large room, but the plethora of furniture reduced its size. I had stopped in the middle of it behind Madame Henry, whom I had been following, not missing a quiver in the regal swaying of her hips. Something I'd become aware of as soon as I entered, but hadn't yet registered, checked then stopped my lustful flights of fancy, banishing the hope that I'd be able to masturbate shamelessly to my heart's content with the indescribable picture of Madame Henry moving in front of me.

On a table in front of a mirror, to the left of the fireplace, I could see the orange-coloured horn of a gramophone lightly dancing on a record. The end of it opened out wide like a hunting horn. The sounds that came out of it into the rather dusty air first rose up into the coffered ceiling, before cascading down on me like a prophetic, absolving, compelling sign of God's presence.

I was transfixed. I'd read somewhere that someone had been changed into a pillar of salt just for turning around and then seeing the face of the Almighty at work. I didn't even have to turn around; the face of the Almighty filled me utterly, but it was through my ears, in an incomprehensible communion of my five senses in harmony, which even included the sight of Madame Henry's regal figure as she walked in front of me. Until then, apart from "Si j'étais roi" played by the municipal band in the town hall square on the Feast of St John in summer, I'd never heard music.

In this room, where even the ghosts had faded into insignificance, the music that had nailed me to the spot was sweeping through me with the same quiet steady rhythm that I'd used to sweep up the dead leaves. With a brutal, blinding light, it suddenly tore away the veil of appearances. Yes, I was nailed to the spot. I've looked for other words for it in the course of my life, but I've never found them.

"Come on! Don't be afraid! It's only an Empire drawing-room, you know!"

With a wave of her slender hand, Madame Henry dismissed the antiquated treasures that might have intimidated me.

"Sit down!"

She moved about then picked up a wallet from a low table. I should have realized immediately that it would show me a very different side of Madame Henry's character, but I was transfixed, unable to take a step. I was incapable of pretending to be interested in anything else but that music. Despite rendering me powerless to move, the music transported me. It precluded any other passion.

"Well!" Madame Henry said. "What are you doing standing there like a log?"

"What is it?"

"What's what?"

"That music?"

"It's Bach! That won't mean much to you! How many hours did you work?"

How could she dare to speak so loudly and with such assurance while she could hear what I was hearing?

"How many hours did you work?" she repeated, as though she were calling to me from the bottom of the garden.

"Well . . . "

"What do you mean 'well'? Don't you know how many hours you did? It's incredible! Make it up then!"

No, I didn't know how many hours I'd done, and added to that, the sudden silence that had just fallen after the Bach had made me come back to earth and see Madame Henry in all her glory again.

"Couldn't you take off your beret?" she said. "You should take off your beret in the presence of ladies! I'll have to teach you manners!"

I made up a hasty lie out of the blue, with the considerable presence of mind that has protected me all my life.

"It's my cousin Raymonde!" I exclaimed. "She said that as I've got ears that stick out, I should never take off my beret and they'll go back if I keep them tucked in."

Madame Henry shrugged her shoulders.

"It's much too late!" she said. "You should have started when you were two! And anyway, it'll give your unremarkable face a bit of character!"

She opened her wallet and pulled out one note, two, and hesitated about a third, which she finally put back.

When I'd seen her parsimoniously getting change out of her purse in the bakery, I'd guessed that Madame Henry was careful with money. When she handed me the two 100 franc notes saying, "There you are!" her casual manner made me realize that she had hidden passions more destructive than avarice. Two hundred francs! As much as I had in the lining of my beret with Lucinde's letter, representing 20 kilos of snails for Marius Cases. I'd been so accustomed to getting miserable pay that this generosity immediately made me suspicious.

I glanced at Madame Henry surreptitiously when she wasn't looking at me. She suddenly realized that the gramophone needle was making a scratching noise on the wax. She stood up quickly, then came back towards me, holding out the record in its sleeve for me to look at.

"There you are!" she said. "Have a look, since you seem to be interested in it."

In the centre of the wax platter I saw a fox terrier with his head on one side, listing to a gramophone exactly like the polished mahogany one on the table at the far end of the room. Underneath in black letters on a red background, I read these words:

"J. S. Bach. Cantata BWV 140, *Sleepers Awake!*, Choir of
Saint Thomas of Leipzig. Orchestra of the Gewandhaus
of Leipzig under the direction of Günther Ramin."

Every word on this label was part of the same magic as the vision of Madame Henry in her own home, where she was showing me a very different face from the one she presented at the bakery and everywhere else in the town. Here in the drawing room with the green plants and the hangings that matched the aspidistra, Madame Henry's violet eyes never gave a hint of the play of little lines that was part of the belittling, mocking smile she gave us in public.

At first I had the impression that, in the presence of a person as totally insignificant as myself, she shed her usual persona as you might leave a coat on a peg that is too heavy to wear. Nevertheless, her back was straight as she sat down in the wing chair facing me. She examined me closely, looking suspiciously at every detail of my face. I realized then, that in spite of seeing each other every day in Albert's bakery, Gardon's grocery, Chabal's delicatessen, on that day we were seeing each other for the first time.

She leaned over and literally snatched the record from my hands.

"You'd never heard Bach before?"

I shook my head.

"You lucky little bastard! You've still got all of that to discover!"

I felt her eyes on me as though they were looking down on a prey of some sort, but a prey that would be awkward to manage and indigestible. I had to restrain myself from constantly putting my hand on my beret with that tell-tale, automatic gesture reassuring me that Lucinde's letter was still there.

"You've got a secret!" Madame Henry exclaimed suddenly. "And it's a secret you don't even know yourself!"

I enjoyed at last, and for the first time, being able to look her full in the face and to feel the exchange of our eyes meeting directly. That was something I'd always found dreadfully difficult. It was second nature to me to look away, because I was always ashamed of the thoughts going through my mind when I looked straight into someone's eyes. Another human being's face had the same effect on me as the sun: I couldn't look straight at it, and I didn't know how. I'd also noticed that whenever I didn't lower my head when facing someone else, that person immediately resented it hugely, as if I'd broken into his cupboard or desk at home, stealing his most private letters. It actually took me weeks and weeks to get over a confrontation like that.

I never think of an answer until it's too late. When someone was looking at me, the blinding truth about them that I saw in their eyes before they went blank, took an age to get through to me and convince me it was true. That revelation was never of any use because I had no faith in my own judgement.

In Madame Henry's case, the first thing people saw was her mocking mistrust. It seemed obvious that I would never know anything about her and she would never know anything about me. It seemed obvious that there was only one possible relationship between the important middle-class lady who was decorated, perfumed with Chanel No 5, and who wore stockings with smoke-coloured seams, and myself, a poor day labourer with worn-out shoes, who had come into the house only to be paid: that of master and slave.

But here we were, and Madame Henry wasn't happy. She'd

seen me standing there stock-still in the middle of the room like a stubborn mule, not moving forward, glued to the spot. And all because, in spite of me being there, she had thought herself alone and had been foolish enough to wind up her gramophone to hear a part of Cantata No 140. She could have kicked herself. It was obvious. How could this wretched youth be enthralled by the same things as she? That's what I read in her angry stare. I should have done nothing more than just tried to please her and, as a precaution, only show her what she always saw: a spotty youth, with his beret pulled down over his ears, dirty fingernails and one shoulder slightly higher than the other. In my poor man's cast-offs and my hobnail boots turning up at the toes, I would still have been invisible to her.

But no! It would happen that I couldn't control my emotion when I became aware of that music I'd never heard before. My usual caution failed me.

An unnatural silence reigned now between the two of us. Madame Henry had got up and was walking about in front of me. I was still seated, discreetly admiring the curve of her hips. As I was thinking how much I'd like to see her in front of the low lamp, her clothes transparent as at Madame Patrocles', I noticed some rich brown shadows I'd taken for panelling, going up and down the partitions on the wall. They were strangely compact but hard to make out, as the green lamp was not strong enough to light that vast high-ceilinged room. By looking at it really hard, I finally worked out that it was a whole wall of books. Although I could see only their spines, I'd never seen such an inviting display. The ones at the municipal library looked awful, and those that looked at all attractive were so high up that I would never have dared ask for one. Besides, the old watchdog of a librarian would never allow me anything beyond Victor Hugo or Chateaubriand, whom he considered quite enough to beguile a poor man's dreams. But here, the books gleaming mysteriously in the shadows all seemed to me to have a spark of life in them, and their disturbing presence was calling me to investigate.

"Where are your thoughts now?" Madame Henry said brusquely. "Do you really think you can forget yourself like that! Look at me!"

"I'm looking at your books."

"They're not mine! They belonged to my grandfather, my father and my uncles. Dead, all of them!"

She turned her back to me and walked over to the shelves. She took down a volume close at hand, which I thought she'd chosen at random.

"They've been the salvation and the ruin of me," she said, "and more ruin than salvation! Can you read?"

"Of course! I have my primary leaving certificate!"

It was the only time that evening she gave me the mocking smile she used so often in public.

"So, you have your certificate and you can read! All right, read that. Perhaps it will teach you a thing or two."

It was a volume that had often been read but was in very good order. On the cover, a young priest was on his knees kissing the hand of a lady in a crinoline. Stark moonlight bathed the two people and made them look unreal. I eagerly took the book from her hands. I would read anything. The imaginary world of books always consoled me for my grubby existence and I realized very early that in my world, reading was a largely disdained privilege that scarcely anyone wanted to contest.

Up to this point, I had wrongly interpreted the significance of my meeting with Madame Henry. Now the music I'd just heard and the book she'd just handed me made me think that there was a mysterious code and I had the key to unlock it, and that, deep in our subconscious, we had taken a clumsy, hesitant step towards each other.

I was transformed, ready to go back to our slum with a load of lead to be changed into gold. If happiness had been my goal, I'd have been in seventh heaven.

"Off you go!" Madame Henry said briskly. "I'm expecting company. But," she added, "I have four beds of blue hydrangeas that need pruning. Come next Sunday. I'll show you how to do it."

As I left, I passed Victor looking as handsome and elegant as a store dummy. For a moment the cigarette he was smoking prevented my heart from melting in the pungent smell of the tall trees. His eyes looked over my head without seeing me.

As I left "Villa Eden", which was the name of the property, and went out on to the boulevard, I almost bumped into our mayor who was slowly passing by the gate looking disgruntled. He was a man who held his head high and counted his steps when he walked, making him look as grave as an oracle. The eyebrows beneath his pensive brow were unreal, enormous, like theatrical false eyebrows that had to be taken off every night. He didn't seem happy to see me suddenly emerge from "Eden" and gave me an icy stare. He was my boss, so for him I snatched off my beret and said, "Good evening, Monsieur le maire!" loud and clear. An indistinct mutter was all I got in reply.

I knew the essential bits and pieces of the mayor's life from Auguste Faux, who had the privilege of being his second-in-command. We, too, had the privilege of being part of the group, including Auguste, who waited every morning at the bakery for the *pompes* to arrive in the shop. Albert made only 50 and Lucinde wouldn't keep any aside for you for anything in the world. You had to stand there and wait patiently. Auguste Faux would make the time pass with his jokes and puns. On the subject of the mayor, he had whispered to Bessolote, who had asked him for some information,

"He has a Semiramis complex . . . "

He said it loudly enough to be heard by all. When I got home I opened the battered dictionary that had belonged to one of my grandfathers. I learned to my astonishment that Semiramis was queen of Babylon and that she had been responsible for the laying out of the hanging gardens, one of the seven wonders of the world. I looked up the other six at the same time. That was always another thing learned.

"One Saint-Pancrace evening," the deputy had said on another occasion, "he surprised the woman he loved – and it wasn't his wife – astride a fellow on a seat in a dark corner of the municipal gardens. Ever since then he has been putting so many lights in groves of trees that you can see everything, or else he is planning to get rid of them and turn them into car parks."

These important revelations made conversation buzz at Albert's. Bessolote commented that she had noticed it was becoming more and more difficult to find shade to walk in, as the trees were disappearing. Of course! I'd also had the impression that transferring the war memorial to a place where plane trees had to be cut down in order to make it more visible was not dictated by piety alone, any more than was his acquisition of the old disused convent, where so many big pines had been knocked down. He was a man who hated shade. We'd all noticed it. He was now installing central overhead lighting under all our plane trees and on the vaulted ceilings of all our public washing places, where so much mystery had always lingered with the smell of dead embers and soap. The light cast by the caged globes got rid of all that, making the water in the troughs reflect a mournful colour never seen there before.

Auguste Faux allowed himself to enlighten us about our mayor's deepest secrets because he knew his audience well. His whispered confidences sank into each one of us as into the silence of the tomb. No-one divulged them. We were a community of reticent people who liked to know everything but tell nothing. And we were all the same; which explains why Lucinde's note could lie there harmlessly in my beret until the day I died, if it was necessary. That secret gave me an advantage over everyone, which I'd lose as soon as it were known. Rain or shine, my life was always rainy-grey, like that of the other 3,000 inhabitants of this country town. If we didn't have that bit of mystery of our loves and hates, we would soon have died of boredom, in spite of the profusion of natural beauty in the countryside, which should have been enough to satisfy and fulfil us.

Like everybody else, I carried around the mayor's secret with so many others, so that meeting him as I left Madame Henry's house seemed a bad sign. However, I didn't linger over it. I hugged the book I'd been lent to my chest, sniffing it from time to time as I walked along. When she took it and held it in her hand, the spine and cover retained something of Madame Henry's own particular identity concentrated in the Chanel No 5 she used to be different from other women.

It was really only the hazy memory of a perfume. The wind blowing over the book had disinfected it from all its past. No-one could have opened it for half a century. I'd read the title in the light of a street lamp: *The Red and the Black.*

I hurried home, hoping to find my parents already asleep. I went up the spiral staircase two steps at a time, holding on to the rope. Everyone was snoring and my sister was happily dribbling like the contented child she was. Some remains of the meal had been left out for me. I wasn't hungry. The surfeit of new things I'd experienced ruined my appetite: the house with the weathercock, the 200 francs, the library, Cantata 140, Madame Henry's perfume which I hoped to smell on me from the book she'd handled. I was *gonfle*, as they say in our part of the country, that is I could have wept for not being able to capture everything I'd just seen and heard. No-one had yet told me that one day, memory would make these things a thousand times clearer than today, when I'd only just experienced them. It was all enough to make hunger seem commonplace and of secondary importance.

I had a small light by which I could read without waking the whole family. That night, it suddenly went out, but I'd had enough time to take an instant dislike to Julien Sorel. I found this insufferably proud young man quite obnoxious. He prided himself on looking death in the face, but had never felt the slightest hint of it in his soul. I hoped to see him humbled, which he never was in life or in death. From the very first, Madame de Rénal seemed thin and bony, which Stendhal never suggests at all. Mathilde de La Mole didn't seem real or any more fulfilled after Julien than before. I tried in vain to picture her thighs, her belly, her breasts, her face. Even her eyes escaped me. So, there was no flesh to her. When you're 15, you sometimes make these dogmatic judgements. The strange thing is that after reading it ten times, I've never changed my mind.

I went back to Madame Henry's the following Sunday morning. The door was locked. I was about to go away disappointed when I saw her at the end of the path walking slowly and sadly with her head down, for she thought she was alone.

I looked at her until she came level with me. When she raised her eyes and caught sight of me, I saw at once that she had an expression of unhappiness on her face I'd never seen before. The arrogance and disdain, her mocking smile, everything that she did to intimidate us in the bakery had disappeared.

"I told you Sunday!" she sighed.

"But . . . it *is* Sunday!"

"Oh yes . . . it's Sunday morning . . . Well, since you're here, come in."

She was holding her missal and wearing a coat that looked black over her pink blouse. Thank goodness she didn't realize I'd been watching her. There was nothing in my clothes, my naïveté or my poverty that could make her imagine that I was an observer. She could see me only as someone amusing.

There was a smell of veal blanquette through the house. That was a dish we could have only twice a year. I could see a dining room adjoining the drawing room through an open door with glass panels. The table looked festive as though set for a wedding feast.

"I'm expecting the mayor," Madame Henry said.

She sighed.

"And his wife! And his youngest daughter and the bishop, if he doesn't miss his train as he did last time. He's so absent-minded!"

She threw her missal on to the sofa followed by her hat. She began to take off her coat.

"One of these days," she said, "you'll have to learn how to assist ladies."

"Do what?"

She gave a mirthless laugh.

"To take their clothes off!" she said.

She moved forward and called out,

"Antoinette!"

"I'm here, Madame."

I saw a young woman standing straight against the wall between two potted palms as though she were waiting there in ambush. She was wearing a regulation black dress and a white, lace-edged apron. It was the first time I'd ever seen a servant. My mother had no need of a uniform in the households where she worked.

I understood straight away that Antoinette was Madame Henry's shadow and that she faithfully followed her around the house. What's more she had the same shaped body and posture, but a slighter build. She was almost as supple and she had the same mocking smile, but as she had no sense of proportion, she wore that smile all the time, like a caricature of her mistress.

She saw me and summed me up immediately. Her smile vanished and she became tight-lipped. My uncle's coat was a Nessus' tunic capable of repelling the most courageous hearts, and my hobnail boots would make anyone tremble for the fate of their parquet floor. Madame Henry's was inlaid like a piece of antique furniture.

"You'd be mistaken, Antoinette, if you thought this boy was of no account!"

Madame Henry said these words in a calm, even tone as she loaded her servant's arms with everything of which she had divested herself, including the missal. She looked intently at Antoinette. I felt she was warning her. With a gesture which was now almost a tic, I had to reassure myself that my beret was well down over my ears and firmly set on my head.

"I was returning the book," I said, "and you'd asked me about the hydrangeas . . . "

"Yes, yes, I know. The hydrangeas can wait. So, have you read the book?"

I knew right away that caution demanded I say nothing more than some modest banality. I replied that yes, I'd read it and liked it very much and that I thanked her and if she had any others . . . I liked reading very much. She nodded her head at each of my replies, while stealthily watching me closely. I felt she was more intrigued by me than enthusiastic about the dinner she was giving, or about her guests, including the vicar-general from Digne. I guessed that my naïveté disconcerted her and increased her distrust.

I'd realized very early that naiveté is the great weapon of the poor, and I used it shamelessly. The idea of being (as opposed to appearing) naïve came to me while I was looking at the portrait that my mother had had taken by Bizot, the family photographer, when I was scarcely six months old. I was frightened by the piercing blue eyes I had even then. I began refining that baby look when I was at home alone, looking into the only mirror we possessed: a mirror leaning crookedly against the wall. It was probably taken from the dilapidated wardrobe, in front of which everyone did their hair.

But creating my naïve persona stopped me being on my guard against the traps involved in all the new things I was discovering here. I hadn't been on my guard when I'd heard the music Madame Henry called Cantata 140 in the hall; I'd stood trans-fixed before the books in the library, and I'd listened too long to the grating of the weathercock on the four-sided roof. That was enough to puzzle Madame Henry.

If Madame Henry appeared different to me here from what she was every morning in Albert's bakery, I couldn't expect that she would see me exactly fitting my image of the poor boy, happy and naïve, going to fetch the bread for the family. In spite of her decorations, her position in the world, and the erotic pictures I had of her during my nocturnal erections (when I no longer saw her face), I realized that I too had taken her to be of no account, to use her expression to Antoinette. I also realized that it had never crossed my mind she could take me for anything but a sweeper of dead leaves.

"Come!" she said. "I'll show you what to do with the hydrangeas."

I followed in her wake. The sky was black and I remember that the wind was sighing, but we knew that it wouldn't rain and that the sky would stay black until evening, enclosing the long rattling branches of the plane trees in its November shroud.

The bed was a metre wide and encircled the whole house.

"There you are!" she said. "Look, you cut them short. You see these things protruding here? They're buds. Leave two on each branch, no more, and you cut one centimetre above them. No lower!"

She had suddenly crouched down and her skirt had pulled up above her knees. They seemed enormous in that bent position. As I leaned over to follow her instructions, I found myself with my nose on a level with her neck and wafts of Chanel No 5 combined with the smell of well-turned earth.

"I grow the best blue hydrangeas," she said as she stood up again. "It's not easy here, but I've got a secret technique."

For the first time since I'd arrived and seen her sadly walk up the path, her sardonic smile reappeared, but only for a moment.

"Yes, Madame!" I said.

I took the secateurs and, as she had shown me, I set about cutting off the spent flowers, being very careful to leave two buds on each stem.

"You're a quick learner," she said.

"As long as it's easy!" I said.

She told me to leave the secateurs on the verandah post, turned around and walked away. I heard her joyfully greeting a large clergyman approaching the front stairs. I couldn't make him out very well, except for the fact that he was very fat. The mayor, his wife and a tall thin girl arrived after him in a black pre-war convertible with a noisy engine. They all went into the house uttering exaggerated cries of joy, as if each of them were afraid of not appearing happy enough to be there. They had to show how honoured they were to be the invited guests of Madame Henry, the owner of that beautiful property called "Eden": three hectares on the edge of the town, its box walks as tall as a man, its romantic paths hidden from prying eyes, and its curved green seats waiting to receive lovers whose whispers echoed the dreamy murmur of the wind in the cedars.

As I made my way around the house, increasing my black piles of dead hydrangeas ready to be burnt, I listened to the muted hubbub of the party behind the windows. Inspired by the smell of blanquette wafting out from a ventilator, I could see it all in my imagination, and that was food enough for me.

Naturally self-absorbed, like the good bourgeoise she was, Madame Henry hadn't realized when she set me this long task that it was midday and I hadn't had any lunch. A straightforward person would have pointed it out to her and come back in the afternoon. But I wasn't straightforward, and my father and mother had taught me to be available to a prospective employer at all times.

"Remember," they told me, "people must always know that you're a hard worker, ready to lend a hand and conscientious! And being conscientious towards your boss means never noticing that he's stealing your time. You should never be hungry or thirsty or want to scratch yourself or need to pee. That way you'll get work and they'll want you before anyone else. And then you'll get on in the world!"

I had two big advantages in life: just as I was prone to long periods without sleep, going without food was no trouble to me. I could just as well skip two meals as spend two hours stuffing myself. That may not sound very impressive, but very few men can do it frequently. I never boasted about it, as this unusual ability was only an advantage if no-one knew about it.

And so, I could quite happily go about my work that afternoon. I'd made a little fire on the gravel forecourt, which I kept feeding with dead hydrangea flowers. That meant that I could see the dining room where the festivities were in progress as I went back and forth to the fire. The room was in the corner of the house and lit by bay windows with large panes of glass surrounded by wrought iron in the style that was popular around 1900. As I carried my armfuls of dead flowers, I could glance at the people around the table, who were drinking each other's health with increasing enthusiasm.

The mayor and his family left at about four o'clock with endless expressions of gratitude. They were still calling them out towards the house from the lowered windows of their car as it disappeared into the dim light of the drive. Night was beginning to fall.

The vicar-general stayed longer. When I passed in front of the drawing-room windows with my arms full of rubbish, I saw this man of the cloth warming a small glass of liqueur in his plump hands. He was engaged in a long consultation with Madame Henry, who was sitting in front of him with her head down. Sometimes the bishop's coadjutor casually extended his hand towards his hostess's and patted it gently, with that gesture that everyone does to show there's no need for such distress, no matter what the cause.

Knowing how arrogant she was in the bakery and how secretive she could be when she knew someone was looking at her, I found it extremely disturbing that Madame Henry accepted this absent-minded, superficial consolation. What comfort could she need and why?

At nightfall, when the flames from my fire were hazily reflected in the drawing room windows, the vicar-general finally took his leave. I could hardly hear him. His muffled tread didn't crunch the gravel. Madame Henry stood there at the top of the staircase, watching him disappear down the path. I took the opportunity to go up to her and say,

"Madame, I've finished. I don't know whether I've done the right thing, but I found a hoe in the shed and I used it to do a bit of hoeing around your hydrangeas. It was dry."

She looked at me as though I was someone from a dream taking place in front of her eyes.

"Come!" she said.

She turned around smartly and preceded me into the house. Nothing in my life would ever be as good as following in the rustling wake of a woman of that age confidently striding ahead. It was the second time since the morning and it made my day. Her perfume also preceded me, fading as she went, bringing a host of false memories to my mind.

She'd left her bag lying on some piece of furniture. She opened it and asked me,

"What do I owe you?"

"Um . . . I don't know."

She held out a 100 franc note.

"It's Sunday," she said, "and you did the right thing to hoe my flower beds. Do you want some books?"

"If it's no trouble."

"Which ones?"

"Oh, whatever you want to give me . . . "

"What *I* want . . . And what do *you* want?"

"Oh, I never want anything."

"Fancy that. You know how to use negatives properly?"

"I try to."

I saw the mocking smile reappear on her face. Without thinking, I pulled off my beret, the way I usually did, to slip the 100 franc note into the lining with the 400 already there, kept warm by Lucinde's letter.

"So that's where you hide your treasures, is it?" Madame Henry said.

She put out her hand towards my bare head, which Léonce Bernard the barber hadn't shaved for some time.

"That's a pity," she said, "you have nice hair."

My hair looked dreadful, making my face seem as foolish as those of the Chouans[5] in Year II after the Revolution: theirs fell from their hats to their chins, making a frame around the dull planes of their faces. My hair had tufts like a field ravaged by a storm.

"My cousin Raymonde told me that I . . . "

"Ah yes indeed! Your cousin Raymonde!"

She held out three faded books, lightened and darkened in turn by sunshine and shadow. The titles were in red on a cream background. I closed my eyes. I didn't want to see the titles straight away. I was only capable of savouring one pleasure at a time and Madame Henry's eyes trying vainly to catch mine was enough for the moment.

"Antoinette!" Madame Henry called as she turned to the back of the room.

5 18th-C. counter-revolutionaries from the west of France. [tr.]

"Yes, Madame."

"Antoinette, would you put the remains of the blanquette into the big milk tin and bring it to me."

I heard a voice in the wings.

"All of it?" Antoinette said, quite scandalized.

She appeared in the kitchen doorway. "All of it!" Madame Henry said. "It's for a large family."

I left the house with my arms full of gifts. I'd jammed my beret back over my ears and was hurrying away as the storm rose above the tall trees. They seemed to be in a noisy huddle over my head, trying to decide my fate but unable to come to an agreement. They were all trying to give each other orders with me as the object of their commands.

I heard steps hurrying up, then passing me. Antoinette stood there in front of me with her hand out to stop me.

"Don't get the wrong idea!" she said. "Madame belongs to Victor and you hardly measure up!"

"But, I only come here to sweep and cut the hydrangeas."

"All right! Be content with that! And this!" she replied.

She pointed a disdainful finger at the aluminium milk tin I was holding in my hand. She turned her back on me and disappeared into the gale. I knew who Antoinette was. Her mother was the newspaper seller and they had been swept into France by the war in Spain, like a hundred thousand others. She was as poor as I was and that's why she was trying to put me down.

I had no time to waste over Antoinette. I was dying to know the titles of the works Madame Henry had put into my arms. I was dying to get back to our poor dwelling and put the gleaming milk tin, filled to the brim with blanquette, down on our table. The Galice family was in for a feast tonight. It wasn't often we could stuff ourselves at our place. It was lucky the bread was good, for it was our staple food.

That evening the blanquette was treated as though it was being served at a grand table where the guests held their forks properly instead of clutching them like weapons, and as they ate they all naturally praised the quality of the meat in whispered tones. The aroma of the subtle, creamy sauce with its hint of capers was enough to inspire respect. It made us eat less greedily, more carefully, and we were better able to savour what we were consuming. Although my three-year-old sister's chin was dripping with sauce and my brother furiously wiped his plate clean, we all sat there rather prim and proper before the steaming pot to which my mother had added some rice.

My mother never stopped praising Madame Henry, whom she had only crossed in the street and who only ever replied to her greeting with a grunt. Thanks to the blanquette, she had become this good person who was so charitable to those less fortunate than herself. My father languidly nodded his head in agreement.

I was longing to get back to my mean bed to find out the titles of the books I'd hidden between the mattress and the blanket as soon as I came in. One day my mother had said to one of the ladies she worked for, in what she thought was a whisper,

"And you know, he reads!"

I'd heard her, as she was deaf and always shouted when she spoke. Since then I never read in front of my mother and only put on my lamp once I heard her snoring, which didn't take long.

For me reading was a very personal matter. No-one should interfere with that mystery. I was quite onanistic regarding the few pleasures that life allowed me to glimpse in secret. I didn't want to share them with anyone else for fear that someone might breathe on them and they'd blow away for ever.

During that day, I'd been so close to a beautiful woman, had become full of her presence and been able to feast my eyes on her and even imitate her voice in my head, that the urge to immerse myself in thoughts of her that evening seemed more delicious than the pleasure of reading. But then I found that Madame Henry would no longer respond in the way my erotic fancies dictated. I was about to slowly remove her underwear when a vision of Antoinette and her skinny legs suddenly planted itself between her mistress and me. I could hear the dreaded words, "Madame belongs to Victor!" This obstacle thwarted my desire and my cock went limp.

On Sunday I put my books under my arm and climbed up the Mont d'Or, where there were so many overgrown olive groves, regretfully left untended by so many men killed in the war. An unruly mat of wild grasses grew more thickly underneath them every year, preventing the rain from reaching the dry tree roots underneath. I hid myself in the couch grass, to which we give the much nicer name *groussan*. I began, as usual, by running my fingers over the edges of the books, the colour and the paper. I opened all three of them. A dried four-leaf clover fell out of one. I thought of the person who must have happily put it in there years ago. The books were more than 20 years old. Someone had occasionally underlined a passage in pencil. I read Claudel's *L'Annonce faite à Marie, Le Pain dur, Le Père humilié* without understanding anything, fearful but enraptured. The words rolled between the sun and the page like grains of wheat into the mill. A light wind accompanied them, blowing one page over on top of the last, as a gentle invitation to read on. The phrases went round and round in my mind like leitmotifs, each one gathering momentum from the last and passing on its strength to the next. I examined them like prehistoric objects unearthed in a newly ploughed field, turning them this way and that. They seemed sealed and impenetrable, the author caring little for the person who would read them: "Jesus, thrice heralded in Mary's heart."

During that time I came to God without thinking about it, because Claudel presented Him to me as proud and threatening, like a stage character. For a long time thereafter, He was at my side in a totally heretical way, similar to the Greek theory that the pagan gods began as humans. There was neither respect nor love, only wonder tempered by fear.

It took me three weeks to screw up enough courage to return Claudel to Madame Henry. I was so apprehensive that she'd ask me what I thought about it. She only said,

"Do you want some more?"

I had the impression that she chose daunting works especially to test me. My evasive answers and my hopelessly foolish expression when she questioned me about my reading gave her no hint of my progress, but she could see it in the way I was changing. One day I timidly reached out my hands towards her shoulders to help her out of her coat.

"That's good!" she said. "You're learning."

Unfortunately for me, she'd been out and her fur had that very strong honey smell of Lucky Strike.

"Do you want some more?"

And she kept filling my arms with all the treasures kept in the shadows on the mysterious shelves. Madame Henry wouldn't let me choose the books myself any more than old Berlie in the municipal library, and I read whatever her fancy dictated. I absorbed the knowledge contained in those ill-assorted, haphazardly chosen books like blotting paper, thanks to my prodigious memory.

Madame Henry now watched me constantly. I could tell she was flabbergasted by the enigma I had suddenly become to her, what with Uncle Désiré's long mouse-grey coat, my noisy boots turned up at the toes, my beret pulled down to my eyebrows, because of my jug-handle ears and cousin Raymonde. Once or twice I noticed that she had put some tiny objects in between the pages of the books I borrowed. She wasn't sure I really read them and wanted to find out.

From the time she asked me to sweep her path, I no longer heard her voice addressing me in the bakery. At most, she sometimes patted my beret when I passed within her reach. If that happened, when I got home, I'd pull it off my head and look at it as though Madame Henry's face or the shape of her hand could be seen there.

The beret was filthy with accumulated dirt and the leather strip around it that was supposed to keep it in shape was so dirty you could literally scrape it with a knife. I soaked it for a whole evening in the soda crystals we used to wash the dishes. Then I wrung it out and left it to dry in the air that came in from the garret window looking out on to a roof lower down. In the morning it was still damp, so I didn't put my 100 franc notes and the envelope containing Lucinde's letter in it.

I went off to the bakery wearing this headgear, now more or less navy blue. Lucinde was the first to notice the change.

"Oh, Pierrot! Have you washed your beret?"

"Well I never!" Bessolote said. "It's just as well! Any longer and it was so stiff it'd wash itself!"

That particular morning Madame Henry had refrained from massaging my head, but when she heard all the women around her laughing and making fun of me, she shook my head as though it was a game, her fingers lightly feeling the empty crown of the beret.

I was served before her and when I went out she was waiting for me at the doorway leading to the lane.

"Well, my poor Pierre, have you lost your fortune?"

Until then I'd been Pierrot. Now I was "my poor Pierre". This condescending and commiserating form of address contained all the pity you feel for someone who will never get the good things of life. I guessed that when she felt my hat, she realized there was nothing in it, whereas she usually felt paper crackling under her fingers. I proclaimed hurriedly,

"I gave everything to my mother!"

It wasn't true. For the moment I'd hidden the 500 francs and the letter on the floor under my mattress.

"That's good," Madame Henry said, "you're a good lad."

But the way she looked at me made me think straight away that she hadn't been fooled and that she knew now that I was hiding something else besides money in my beret. Nevertheless, I looked her straight in the eye, something I always found difficult. The only time I've ever managed it with a woman is when I've tried to let her know the erotic thoughts she made me feel. In this situation, I've always been believed.

"Come on Sunday." She said. "I'll be bored."

That was the Sunday of the greatest adventure of my life, the one I've never forgotten, the one that made me what I am.

V

I CAN REMEMBER IT. WINTER HAD COME LATE AND VERY suddenly, with a nasty burst of snow and ice. The old city gate where we lived was dark and miserable. It was also as cold as an icebox, the only heat coming from our own breath, which changed into mist as soon as it left our mouths. Fortunately we all had iron constitutions. My father had tried to fix the stovepipe, but it crumbled into dust, and the coal from the Gaude mine we were given smelled like a death chamber where sulphur is burned as a disinfectant.

When I was making my way to "Eden" on that Sunday at about four o'clock, I felt the cold as sharply as toothache. There was not a single erotic thought in my mind. There I was, as usual, wearing socks with holes in shoes with the soles coming apart, wobbling on their hobnails and stiff with cold. Uncle's coat was as pitiful as a scarecrow's. I was carrying a book to return to Madame Henry under my arm, a book like marble, which was part of the reason why I felt frozen to the bone: Pascal's *Letters to a Friend in the Provinces.*

When Madame Henry opened the door, I felt as though a big, warm coat had been put on my shoulders wrapped around me down to the knees. Only my feet reminded me of winter snow sparkling outside.

"I bet you've never seen a fire burning in a fireplace," Madame Henry said.

I shook my head. I was as cold as a bird on a bare branch, and I wondered at that moment how they all managed not to die, having nowhere to shelter in the winter weather. I felt the weight of the book in my hands before handing it over to Madame Henry, and that book seemed beyond any question a freezing man should be asking himself.

"You didn't find that very entertaining, I imagine?" she said, taking the volume from my hands.

She didn't insist on a reply. She'd taken a firm hold of my head through the beret, where the papers I carried around there were also crackling with cold, and was drawing me towards the far end of the drawing room. A fire of live coals took up the whole space in a sombre black stone fireplace and beyond, hurling its silent curse against the cold into the room. I turned my back to it immediately, as that part of my body needed it most.

That beautiful woman and I stayed there without speaking for more than a quarter of an hour, gazing at the tongues of flame darting straight up towards the black flue. I couldn't think of anything but the cold. I looked through the window at the garden. There were still some black traces on the snow-covered lawns of the half-burnt hydrangea stems I'd piled up a few weeks earlier. A whole quarter-hour spent together watching evening draw in, without a word, a sigh or a movement; watching the fire glow red, and me breathing in that Chanel No 5 perfume, changed somewhat by the warmth of the room.

Lying back in the deep armchair where I'd curled up, I began to get an erection from the feeling of total relaxation and well-being. The thought of going back to my gatehouse, where my family was holding out against the winter, seemed more than I could manage, now that I'd experienced comfort.

Madame Henry stared at my thin trousers, where my cock was happily erect.

"Wait!" she said suddenly.

She got up and left the room. I waited for so long that I eventually got up and wandered past the shelves of books gleaming in the flickering firelight. At eye-level, the reflections shone blue and gold on a whole length of books of the same size and same appearance. They were in much better condition than the rest of the library, as though someone had not had the time to read them all before some major occurrence. I pulled one out at random, with some difficulty as they were so tightly packed together. It felt soft and slippery, with a lot of thin, slightly creamy pages, which promised me long hours of delight.

There was a blue ribbon attached at the spine going through the book, which opened automatically at the page with the book-mark. Without thinking, I began to read:

> This prince, on his way to Meudon the day after Easter, as I have mentioned, came upon a priest at Chaville carrying Our Lord to someone who was ill, and he got out to kneel and worship it with the Duchesse de Bourgogne. He asked to whom they were bringing it: he learned that the man was sick of the smallpox. There was much of it about. He had had it but lightly, fleetingly, as a child. He was mightily afraid of it.

I raised my head. What I'd read took my breath away: "He had had it but lightly, fleetingly, as a child."[6] None of the writers I'd absorbed until then had been unconventional enough to write this graceful, compressed turn of phrase. I went through all of them in my mind: no, this writer was really the only one.

I was standing there awkwardly perched on one leg against a stool, the book which I'd closed feeling slippery in my hand. I don't know why I'd closed it: perhaps to protect myself from being dazzled for too long, perhaps to keep my eagerness intact for other times when I'd be alone.

I began to scratch myself furiously. Just reading those few written lines made me feel as though smallpox was beginning to break out all over my body. It frightened me. I could see the showers of dust blowing in Chaville that day falling on the imaginary carriage. I could see those two people of great importance in the world, Monseigneur and Madame la Duchesse de Bourgogne, leaning forward with backs bent, then suddenly sinking to their knees on the stony road, contrite, devout, their necks bared to the world's ills. And there, in front of them, glittering gold: Our Lord. It was the first time I'd seen these words used in the sense of the Eucharist, but I'd recognized them straight away, and it was indeed in front of that golden circle surrounded by rays of light that I saw those two great names, Monseigneur and Madame la Duchesse de Bourgogne, bow the knee.

I had just heard the same warning bells as the other day when I was crossing this room and had been stopped in my tracks by a Bach cantata played on a gramophone.

I now began to look at the portrait on the dust jacket. He was

6 *Il ne l'avoit eue que légère, volante et enfant.* A most unusual and grammatically inventive construction. [tr.]

a self-confident man with a forehead falling straight from his wig to his eyebrows, expressing outraged integrity at the villainy of the age. The only quality that showed through in his eyes was the strength of character of a man who is sure of his rights and the surprise of a proud, perpetually outraged victim.

I stayed there for a few minutes gazing at that portrait which told me nothing of the long-dead man it depicted. I felt the weight of the volume, ran my fingers over it with sensual pleasure at the strange, slippery contact with it. Then suddenly a new feeling I couldn't understand began to stir within me, a kind of inexplicable confusion, which grew so strong and oppressive that it quite overcame me.

The text I'd just read had impressed itself on my mind for ever – every word, with its punctuation, its prophetic tone and even the strangeness of the language when *avait* used to be written as *avoit*. It brought a feeling of emptiness not only to the pit of my stomach, but also to my view of the world. It made the winter fade into the background and my wonder at the fire in the hearth seem banal, even though I was experiencing that for the first time too. It would have made me feel even more insignificant if I hadn't already been thoroughly convinced of my own worthlessness.

I feverishly tried to think of something to which I could compare it. Thanks to the books I'd been reading – I'd never have managed it without them – I finally realized, without actually being able to give it a name, what this unexpected feeling was. One night in a wealthy part of town, I'd seen a man climbing on the gatepost of a low wall to try and look through the shutters on one of the windows. They were not quite shut, but were sufficient to stop him from solving the mystery: knowing if another man was taking his place in his mistress's bedroom, which he'd just left.

It was the sublime author of those pages who finally showed me what was disturbing me in that way: it was an unusual, acute form of jealousy, a jealousy whose nature, origin and purpose I did not understand. Until that moment I'd never even said the word or thought about it. I'd never envied or been jealous of anyone. The rich were rich and the poor were poor. The things everyone indulged in or tried to didn't excite me. I was as contented as I could be as long as I had work, provided it was manual and didn't interfere with my thoughts, came home to a bowl of soup in the evening, and was allowed to wander where I pleased in nature and in my dreams. As for happiness itself, I was suspicious of it. Seeing what happened to those who thought they'd achieved it, I was inclined to believe that it was transitory and I'd do well not to go near it. Even Victor meant nothing to me although, according to Antoinette, Madame Henry belonged to him. He had a felt hat, smoked Lucky Strikes and was 1m. 80 tall. He'd die one day, he'd be cut down to size and would have to share most of the torments of my miserable state. So? Why Victor? What could that really mean "to belong to someone"? No. Not even Victor.

On the other hand, here I was gazing at that indignant face of one of the great ones of this world, who had dared to write those stinging sentences and so many thousands more my jealous heart would have to endure. I would have given half my life merely to have written one of them.

Just then I heard Madame Henry coming up behind me, letting all the things she had in her arms fall on the floor. She yelled at me, "No! Not Saint-Simon![7] I don't want you to read him!"

---

7 Louis de Rouvroy, Duc de Saint-Simon (1675–1755), famous in France for his *Mémoires* dealing with life at Court 1694–1723. A haughty, perspicacious but cynical courtier, his portraits and descriptions of Court intrigues are written in an original, sharp, succinct style. Syntax is sometimes bent to reflect the immediacy of the way he sees and thinks. [tr.]

She rushed at me like a fury and snatched the book from my hand. She put it back in its place with the precise, anxious movements one might use to close a safe when someone else has almost discovered the secret it contains. She stood with her back to the shelves to prevent me having access to them. She had even stretched out her arms to make doubly sure that I wouldn't approach them again. I managed to ask the appropriate question.

"But why?"

"Because you're naïve!" she cried. "And because you won't be any more if you read him. You'll know everything about human nature, you'll know all about the ways the passions work if you read him! But what good will that do you? You'll never have the strength to wield that sword! You'll never have the shrewdness to use what you've learned! You'll have a key but no lock."

Her arms fell back to her sides in a gesture of helplessness. She sat down heavily on the couch, showing more of her legs than I could take without getting an erection. I had to think really hard about death to stop it happening. Madame Henry pulled down her skirt without thinking about it. She pointed a tired hand towards the pile of clothes she'd dropped on the carpet.

"There you are," she said. "See if there's anything that suits you. They belonged to my poor husband. They'll probably smell a bit of mothballs, but still . . . You can try them on in my mother's room. It's there. The door next to the aspidistra."

"The what?"

"The aspidistra! The potted plant."

People with more pride than me would have declined the offer with wounded dignity, but I'd decided long ago that dignity was beyond my means and that I couldn't afford such a luxury. I'd decided to take life as I found it, to be adaptable and ready for any eventuality. The winter wind was blowing outside and I was well aware that my clothes could no longer protect me from its sting.

I gathered up everything lying on the carpet, went into the room she had indicated and closed the door again. Someone long ago had died in that bedroom and had suffered there. All the air closed in by the four walls was still heavy with that suffering.

I scattered the spoils from the late Monsieur Henry on the floor as I did with my piles of dead leaves. I discovered two or three striped articles which looked like the short pants I wore when I was a child for the Saint-Pancrace fair when my mother dressed me in white pants and a little shirt with a jabot. I'd heard that people who were well-off wore underpants under their trousers, but it must surely be unhealthy to use a dead man's. I found it strange to let my private parts come in contact with material that had contained others, which must have closely fitted against Madame Henry's form. But the material felt so silky and sensual against my skin, I could no longer resist the pleasure of getting into one of them. Next to the underpants was a shirt, still folded and smelling of lavender. I could now change my jumper, which was fraying at the wrists. I threw off Uncle's coat, then the jumper.

The trousers were much too long, but Monsieur Henry must have been thin, for they fitted perfectly at the waist. I turned up the legs quite a way, intending to pin them later. On the other hand, the navy jacket with the gold buttons fitted my shoulders as though I'd always worn it. In a dull mirror standing in front of the tapestry, I saw the image of a poor wretch touched by a fairy's wand. I felt wonderful in the warm softness of these materials I'd never known before.

Two more priceless objects still lay on the red and blue carpet: a pair of shoes and a jacket lined with lamb's wool. I went for the shoes straight away. They fitted, neither too big nor too tight. I admired them on my feet, hardly believing my luck. They were solid, waterproof and had hardly been worn. I looked at the old clothes and worn-out boots I'd just taken off. Was it possible in just a quarter of an hour for winter raging outside to become a friend and not an enemy?

I came out of the room as embarrassed as if I were naked. Madame Henry hadn't moved from where she was sitting. She had only leaned forward with hands clasped and fingers tapping. We were both still shaken: she for having snatched Saint-Simon away from me, and I for having discovered him.

"That's fine!" she said. "Leave your old rags. I'll put them in a bag and we'll throw the lot in the rubbish bin."

I protested.

"No! They'll still do for work!"

"All right. I'll put them in a bag and you can call for them tomorrow."

She hadn't finished with me yet. She was looking at me with a quizzical expression I found hard to interpret.

"Now you look human!" she said. "Take off your beret."

I did what she asked, taking care not to spill the papers inside it.

"My goodness! If you had your hair cut short, you'd look almost handsome!"

There was mockery now in her rather set smile. It was the only part of herself she could not always control. She suddenly turned away from me and walked to the door of the anteroom. Next to the door was an upright stand with two umbrellas and a red cloak that Madame Henry took down when the air in the garden became chilly at dusk. There was also a black hat with a ribbon, similar to the one Patrocles was wearing when he died.

Madame Henry walked slowly back towards me holding the hat she had just taken down from the peg.

"Here you are!" she said. "It's a rain hat. If my dead husband's shoes fit you, the hat will too!"

I had instinctively backed away as she offered it to me, for Madame Henry was holding out her empty left hand for me to make an exchange.

"And you'll do me the pleasure," she said, "of taking off that unspeakable beret I dislike so much and throwing it in the rubbish bin. Antoinette will empty it tomorrow."

I was in a tight spot. Then I had one of those lightning reactions I always seem to have when I'm in a fix.

"No!" I said firmly.

"Why?"

"Because I don't want to look like Victor."

I realized from her sudden silence that I'd managed to throw her off track. The hat faded into the background.

"How do you know anything about Victor?"

"I come across him everywhere with his felt hat and I've passed him on the path. Don't take it the wrong way . . ."

"Oh, you've passed him on the path?"

"Yes. Twice."

She looked thoughtful and her hands no longer invited me to give her my beret in exchange for the civil servant's hat. She repeated my words.

"Twice . . ."

"Moreover," I said, "I washed my beret less than a week ago!"

"Moreover!" she sniggered. "There wouldn't be four people in Manosque who could use that word properly, and here you come from your wretched ruin of a home as though you'd been using it all your life. I certainly did the right thing not allowing you to read Saint-Simon!"

The sky was dark when I went out, warmly wrapped up in my

jacket, walking for the first time in shoes that didn't let the water in. There was a new confidence in my step.

It was late and so cold that life seemed to have come to a halt. I was tempted by a nasty habit of mine. When I left a place where I'd been with other people – even those who were dear to me – whenever possible I would creep back again to find out what they were saying about me (there's nothing like it if you want to really know yourself, and there aren't many who have the courage to do it); or else to check how that dear person I'd just visited acted when alone (there's nothing like it for really knowing other people). So I pretended to leave, but came back down the dark path. The only light came from the windows of the house, where the curtains hadn't yet been drawn. I stayed at the edge of the darkness, peering into the well-lit drawing room. Madame Henry hadn't moved. She hadn't drawn the curtains. She was otherwise occupied. She was weeping like someone who had been doing it for some time and often. I remembered the day I'd seen her walking so slowly and sadly along the path. Why?

Still wondering about that question, I took the long way home to our gatehouse, but instead of hugging the walls as I usually did from a feeling of shame, I took pleasure in making my heels ring on the asphalt in the streets. I'd become a well-dressed man; until then I'd felt naked.

That night I spread the dead man's jacket over my bed as an extra blanket. I curled up in the warmth for the first time that winter, but I didn't fall asleep. When Madame Henry had snatched the book out of my hands, I still thought that I'd be allowed to take it home and lose myself in it for some time to come. For want of that, I just kept repeating the sentence I'd been able steal before being interrupted: "This prince, on his way to

Meudon the day after Easter, as I have mentioned . . . ". I was frustrated at not being able to go any further. I didn't even think of pleasuring myself with the memory of Madame Henry collapsing on the couch and showing her legs, and neither her tears that I'd seen when I went back to spy on her, nor my new status as a man who wears underpants, distracted me from my discovery. I was obsessed with Saint-Simon.

The next day, having taken back my things which Antoinette had given me at arm's length, her eyes full of the disdain she felt for me, I worked the whole day thinking over an idea I'd had. In the evening I went to the news agency at La Saunerie, the most affluent place in Manosque. As soon as you arrived, you felt naked, as everyone's eyes seemed to strip your very soul.

I changed clothes after my day's work. The light was fading and several people, both children and old men, after passing me without taking any notice, suddenly stopped in their tracks, not believing their eyes. Yes, it was Pierrot with his beret, but beneath that he was dressed in his Sunday best! On a Thursday evening! What's more, he'd never been seen in Sunday best. I had the impression they were stunned, and then they suddenly took off in their own directions to spread the news.

With my heart thumping, I set off towards the only place in Manosque where the printed word was sold. It was a tiny bottle-green shop squeezed between the Grand Café Glacier and the Restaurant du Grand Paris run by Léonce Alivon. All the windows had been whitewashed to man height, so that you couldn't see those who could be accused of being readers in this agricultural town. Every time I went in my heart thumped and I felt the same sense of shame as if I'd been caught at the entrance to our brothel, the Villa Robinson. The manageress was sitting on a high chair behind the counter. I'd never approached her without feeling a mixture of timid humility and brazen desire. Her name was Mireille, but she was in mourning, all dressed in black as shiny as a beetle's back. Her lustrous lips were carefully made up and always looked as though they were lusting after some tasty titbit. It was almost indecent the way her transparent pink nostrils quivered the moment that face framed in blond hair registered something new and interesting. She had a husband with a brick red face, for he was a drinker, and it was hard to imagine them together. Auguste Faux was so much in love with her that he'd knock against the postcard stands as he went out, having made sure not to stay longer than the two minutes it took to buy the paper of his choice and leave. He never managed to say a single witty remark to her, though he was full of them.

That evening there was a buxom woman standing guard over her. As the proprietor of the kiosk and the building, all 80 kilos of her balanced on tiny feet in fur slippers, she was often there breathing down her tenant's neck. They both gave a start when they saw me come in. I was wearing the lined jacket over the blazer with the gold buttons and the trousers my conscientious mother had immediately altered to fit me.

"Oh, Pierrot! Did you break the wardrobe mirror?"

They looked at me with exaggerated admiration and it became harder and harder for me to say what I wanted. I normally only came here to get *Harry Dickson*, a badly written serial that cost 1 franc 50 and was worth no more, but it was set in London and there was a time in my childhood when London seemed like the promised land.

I wandered around the shelves pretending to be trying to make up my mind which book to choose from the inviting covers. People came and went, which increased my embarrassment. Mireille was watching me suspiciously. Perched up there on her high stool especially for the purpose, she was always hoping to catch a pilferer red-handed. It was an obsession with her, but while she kept her eye on poor children, it was the rich old men who were cheating her. The got in the way on purpose and pretended that newcomers were bumping into them, even vociferously cursing their lack of manners. Then, as people's attention had been diverted, they slipped a dirty magazine under their overcoats. On the other hand, a poor child, even dressed up as I was, remained trapped under her eagle eye for some time.

That whole performance paralysed me. I trembled more and more with shame for what I was going to ask. I don't think it could have been worse if I'd dared whisper in Mireille's ear the question I'd been thinking about for such a long time:

"Are your knickers black too?"

The two harpies weren't smiling. Their cruel hens' eyes were trained on me as I walked towards them almost hypnotized, like a sleep-walker. I realized that they were nonplussed by my unusual appearance and that their minds were working overtime trying to explain it. Having reached them and their cloud of warring perfumes, I heard myself say these never-to-be-forgotten words:

"Would you have a book by Saint-Simon?"

They immediately forgot I was wearing a blazer with gold buttons.

"*Voï!*" said the tub of lard. "*Qu'èsaquo* Saint-Simon?"

"Where on earth did you get that idea?" Mireille asked, frowning.

I realized that my question about the colour of her knickers could not have scandalized her more. They both looked at me wide-eyed with shock and confusion.

"Tell me, Monsieur Faux, you who are so learned! *Qu'èsaquo* Saint-Simon?"

125

Auguste Faux had just entered and as usual was making for his weekly paper with the right money in his hand, so that he wouldn't have to linger in front of Mireille, who could have detected the love he felt for her at once. As he'd been addressed directly, he was obliged to stop and reply, but he did it with his eyes averted towards the dirty magazine section, not really seeing a thing.

"Which one?" he asked. "The Count or the Duke?"

The ladies behind the desk were quite taken aback, unable to answer the question and regretting having caused Auguste Faux to ask it. Then I raised my head towards my fellow customer in the bakery and said to him quite firmly,

"The Duke!"

"What!" he exclaimed. "You're the one who . . . "

He was also taken aback by my new appearance and the startling questions it raised in his highly intelligent mind. All this, together with the sight of Mireille panting and rapidly licking her full lips in that special, charming way of hers convinced him that he just had to get away from that atmosphere where if he said anything else, especially to her, everyone would see he was in love.

"Well then! If you're the one who . . . "

He turned and fled, waving his newspaper in the air.

The shop had emptied, as if by magic. I was alone with the 80-kilo lady and Mireille who featured delectably in my night thoughts. Both of them were laughing heartily at my discomfiture, seeing me so disconcerted by Auguste Faux's last rude remark. They were also relieved that they now had no need to reply to me since he'd done it so well for them. They didn't even wait until I'd left the shop before bursting out laughing,

"What do you think about that? Saint-Simon! Him!"

The 80-kilo lady slapped her thighs with merriment.

* * *

I went and hid my disappointment at the end of the boulevard overlooking Madame Henry's "Eden". A flight of steps, flanked by spindle trees, still incredibly green in spite of the icy cold, led down to the continuation of the promenade, which kept the same name as the boulevard. There were 60 steps in all, so that I could look down on that haven called "Eden" which housed the forbidden Saint-Simon. The cedars in the garden all swayed and moaned in the north wind. I was alone. The memory of that page Madame Henry had snapped shut made me feel like a bashful lover reading a letter his beloved has written to someone else, beginning "my love . . . ", and then seeing it snatched away when he had only just begun to suffer.

> This prince, on his way to Meudon the day after Easter, as I have mentioned, came upon a priest at Chaville carrying Our Lord to someone who was ill.

The pangs of mortal jealousy (which I thought quite groundless) urged me not to give up. I even thought of getting into Madame Henry's house at night and taking the books that had such an attraction for me. The only thing that held me there on the edge of the grounds was fear of the terrible Victor.

I was huddled in the shadows, rueful and wretched, when I suddenly saw the door of "Eden" down below open and stand out against the darkness. It carved a corridor of light in the gloom, striking the cedars, the spindle trees and the hundred-year-old box walk. Someone was standing in the doorway, then moved forward and closed the door again. I realized that it was Madame Henry. After pushing the door shut, she disappeared into the darkness.

The path bordered by bare plane trees and the green gate were always lit *a giorno* by the lights in the street outside. But Madame Henry was not walking towards the boulevard. She had immediately gone out into the night under the tall trees and the darkness had swallowed her up.

The appearance of Madame Henry from the top of the stairs was a great surprise. Framed briefly in the doorway when she opened and shut the door, she seemed ten years older than when you saw her face to face, protected by her arrogant attitude and her self-control. A silhouette has no arrogance and Madame Henry's seemed slightly stooped. I think she had also thrown a shawl around her shoulders, making them appear narrower, and clasped her arms around her body, as though it needed comforting.

I stood there bitterly cold, with my feet as frozen as they used to be in my leaking boots. The moonless night made it impossible to see into the mysterious groves of trees. My first thought was that Madame Henry was going to meet Victor. That was absurd. She was alone, a widow and free to do as she pleased. What's more, it was so cold that there wouldn't be any prying eyes in the area. You had to be obsessed with the feminine psyche like me to withstand it. There was no sign of Victor along the boulevard as far as the eye could see. He could have come through the terraced gardens from the abattoirs, but each garden was separated from the next by a wall three to four metres high. The ground in them was hard and cold and the gates to the outhouses were carefully padlocked to prevent anyone stealing the tools. Besides, I'd seen Victor strolling up the path holding his Lucky Strike between two fingers as a gentleman should. No, Madame Henry was not going to meet Victor.

Standing at the end of my balustrade, facing the Hôtel Pascal in darkness, inside the iron railings I had the company of the bronze greyhound, which we've known for so long, hiding there behind its box hedges. In spite of my frozen feet, I thought of nothing but finding out what was going on. That didn't stop me appreciating the soft, warm lining of the late Monsieur Henry's jacket, pressed into service once more in this biting winter. This was another compartment of my mind always on the lookout for new experiences to enjoy.

I also took pleasure in the sight of Manosque huddled behind closed doors. It hadn't yet taken peace for granted – in fact it was still trembling from a sickening war and the awful feeling of fear that had not really disappeared.

When I was alone late at night in the silence of Manosque, all the sensations I felt came to my mind in harmonious phrases of fine, precise words, exactly rendering what I thought. But far from being delighted or proudly self-satisfied, at 15 I felt crushed by the burden of this gift. While I tried to spy on the invisible Madame Henry; while I pictured Manosque, bed after bed, street after street; while I listened to the clock tower striking nine o'clock; while I remembered sensual Mireille's arms and full lips (having forgotten her insulting attitude to me for the moment); while I was doing all that, I was thinking: You have a lucid mind! Those words applied to me froze me with anxiety, the cold notwithstanding.

The grounds of "Eden" were square, like the house. Madame Henry's ancestors had cherished them like a child so that they reflected their own finely balanced minds for generations to come. It wasn't a big area – three hectares at most – the same measurements on all sides and one section following the other. Half was covered with very tall trees and box bushes in staggered rows, sternly kept in their place by yew trees in the shape of ladies in green crinolines, with round heads that looked as though they

had been clipped by a hairdresser. The other half was surrounded by a walkway with square columns, shaded by nettle trees.
Manosque had held its fairs and guild festivals there. Half the
love stories in the town began in the dust of dances held at
"Eden" in the lazy, warm summer evenings.

On the edge of the boulevard, built up against the wall of a
semi-detached house, was a large pond. It was full to the brim,
and in the summer the silence was broken by the rippling calls of
frogs. In the light from the street lamps, the white ice covering it
this winter made it look like a dull, blind eye.

Looking down over these grounds, I was leaning further than I
should have over the railing that curved for 200 metres along the
avenue. I was trying to see what was happening in the darkness
of the groves of trees where Madame Henry had just disappeared. Suddenly, a feeble light shone through the whole of
"Eden" and the thick groves of trees bristled with points of light
outlining trees and hedges.

I've already mentioned the small building nestling under the
cedars, with its balcony around the first floor. Dandelions had
self-seeded in the accumulated dust in front of the doors on the
ground floor, indicating they had been closed for a long time.
The balcony on the first floor had a wrought iron arch overgrown with an enormous wisteria that had twisted the metal.

Madame Henry, who had been invisible until then, must have
climbed the wide staircase – far too grand for this little folly –
gone inside and turned on the lights. There were shutters over
the windows, and the light shone through the slats on to the
trees. That light drew me like a magnet.

I was quite alone. Not a soul had ventured out into the icy
night air on the boulevard from the time I began my looking
down over the end of the guardrail. Only old Esclangon had

come out in a balaclava to put his rubbish bin away under the stairs, placing a large stone from the Durance on the lid to keep it down. It fell on the metal with a terrible clang. That was a good half-hour ago, and since then, nothing. Just the street lamps and me.

I rushed down the stairs at risk to life and limb, as the ice had built up on all the steps. I crossed the boulevard, but instead of going down the main path from the entrance to "Eden", I turned right and took the small hidden staircase to where the labyrinth of clipped box bushes began. They were head-high, but I knew where the small house was and went towards it with no hesitation. Every step of the stairs to the circular balcony was piled with several seasons of dead leaves Madame Henry had never asked me to sweep. I went up them with my heart pounding as though I were going to break in. A handsome door with copper fittings hid the mystery of the pavilion, and I wouldn't have dreamed of trying to open it, but I longed to do so. I imagined myself suddenly appearing in front of Madame Henry, wanting to know, ready to know, perhaps ready to help her, for when I saw her silhouette I had the distinct impression that she was weaker than she thought.

Anyhow, I wanted to be clear in my own mind about it, and so I crept along the balcony, my back flat against the wall, my eyes riveted on the gaps in the shutters. Unfortunately they were at an angle, and no matter how I twisted my body, I saw only a bit of the ceiling with a sparkling chandelier. All the rest was hidden by the angle of the slats.

There I was, standing on tiptoe against the icy-cold wall, but to no avail. The ceiling and the chandelier were all I could see. The silence was so complete that I had the opportunity to imagine all kinds of noises. For that reason, it took me a long time to recognize one I wasn't even sure was coming from inside the house. It sounded like a quiet sob, but perhaps I was imagining it. I heard this sound, something like a hiccough, while I was looking at the chandelier. Its crystals glistened merrily as if defying me to find out the truth. Perhaps it was even inviting me to forget propriety and break in, appearing suddenly just as I was to Madame Henry, naïve and compassionate, self-conscious and ultimately useless. I was so good at imagining bodies writhing with passion when I was all alone at night, but I'd have been quite unable to cope if Madame Henry's had suddenly fallen into my arms.

For a long time I fought against my shyness and the rules of propriety which told me to know my place and not interfere with fate. I even went up to the door several times and touched the softly gleaming latch in the shape of a woman's hand.

"Who are you to think you can influence a destiny that's been decided once and for all?"

It was a question I often asked myself or someone asked me impatiently to stop me doing something, so that the road to hell remained paved with good intentions.

I've often wondered writing this, sucking the arm of my glasses thoughtfully, what would have happened if I'd gone into the house and suddenly appeared before Madame Henry, awkward, ineffectual and out of place. I'd have risked her anger at being unmasked like that. But who knows whether a secret once aired might not lose its power, its harm and its attraction? I may have been able to defuse it, as I'd done for Patrocles' death by taking Lucinde's letter, and perhaps then . . .

I couldn't do it. I didn't have the nerve to lift that latch and boldly walk in. But on that night it was always too late. Suddenly I heard the sound of the lock opening beside me as the light was turned out and everything went dark again. The clock tower was striking ten. I must have been pussyfooting around those walls, trying to make up my mind, for almost an hour. It was much too late. The door began to open and stuck half-way. Madame Henry gave it a kick to free it. The light from the torch she was carrying swept the stairs. She held a white handkerchief screwed up in a ball. She was sniffling unashamedly, thinking herself quite alone in the dark.

When she turned around to lock the door, the light from her torch outlined her silhouette against the night. You could see in her now, bent over, what she would be like one day as an old lady. She looked so fragile that I all but stepped forward to help her down the icy steps, where she could have slipped.

But it was an illusion on my part. Her energetic steps could already be heard on the gravel, scattering it in all directions. I held my breath. The icy air was moaning through the cedars. Years and years later, the sound and feel of that air lingers softly in the night around me now, as if those years were still to come, still untouched.

I saw the door of the main house open and Madame Henry disappear into another pool of light. Now I was alone again, cautiously going back up the box tree paths smelling of cat's pee towards the street lamps on the cold, misty boulevard.

I'd only just gone out the main entrance gate when I suddenly saw our mayor standing alone and deep in thought in the middle of the road. He hadn't given up his night walks. He'd simply thrown a green Inverness cape over his shoulders on top of his dressing gown, which hung down over his heavy shoes. The picture of the woman he loved caught unawares on top of another man one summer evening in the gardens at the Saint-Pancrace fair came to my mind whenever I saw him. I wasn't present, but I could imagine it better than those who claimed to have been there. The smell along the paths of arching spindle trees is so pungent that even the colour of the leaves reminds you of it. I could smell it so strongly that the man's pain still affected me, while he had no doubt forgotten it. Not so! He could not have forgotten it! Whenever he met people who lived in Manosque raising their caps with a deferential "Good day, Mr Mayor," this tragi-comic picture rose up in the collective memory between the polite greeting and the councillor. It was like a trap that automatically snapped shut at the slightest approach. The person speaking always had the image in his mind and projected it on to our mayor, as though he had spat at him. No, the mayor still had that knife turning in his heart.

Some coincidences can be like a death warrant. Having twice been surprised at the dead of night at almost the same place by a man who must have dreamed of Madame Henry as a balm to his wounded heart, I was sure I'd made a mortal enemy of him. And yet, I immediately wanted to call out to him, to throw him this incredible piece of news.

"Do you know that she cries? Do you know that she's capable of crying?"

I restrained myself, too afraid because my living depended on this man and I could see his beetling brows and beneath them the nasty look in his eyes, determined to avoid me. He passed by scarcely five metres away, his shoes crunching on the black ice which formed and melted according to the weather. He'd no doubt decided to ignore my presence and I to refrain from greeting him so that his ruminations would not be interrupted. That's the explanation I'd have given next morning if he'd reproached me for my lack of courtesy. He passed by and continued on his way. For quite some time I watched his high, slightly rounded shoulders disappear down the street and into the bitter night. He hadn't reacted in any way, but he was smoking his pipe spasmodically, angrily, it seemed to me.

I was only 15, so I didn't give any thought to the apparent contradiction in that man taking a dislike to me because he'd come across me leaving the house of a widow he could well have consoled, but preferred roaming the streets of Manosque night after night in despair over the immense hole in his life left by the memory of that woman, still strong after three years. I didn't know then that a man's body and soul could play on several different registers.

VI

I WENT BACK TO OUR GATEHOUSE, MY HEAD BUZZING WITH the new mysteries that had followed my footsteps on that eventful night. Yet I still felt disappointed: Saint-Simon was further from my grasp than ever. I kept repeating the sentence that haunted me: "This prince, on his way to Meudon the day after Easter, as I have mentioned . . . " It seemed to me that for a child of the poor, every discovery was a new source of suffering.

I had one hope left: Bébé Fabre. This man's place in my life was of epic proportions. He wasn't tall, 1 metre 63, and he walked with a measured tread, head down, pince-nez on his nose and his eyes trained on his little paunch. He was, however, master of the convent I've already described, where I used to imagine the scandalized look of the nuns as they peered at me through the iron bars on the spy-holes in their doors: they knew I spent my nights in frantic masturbation.

This convent was my Aladdin's cave, as I could explore its mysteries only in my imagination. It occupied a large area of its own, with buildings going to rack and ruin at each end. They were black houses where the rain fell through stained ceilings on to disused beds, because the roof tiles had been blown about by the wind and no longer fitted together properly.

Bébé Fabre wandered around the centre parts, solitary, pensive and shivering with cold even though he always wore a short cape that came down to his navel. He sold second-hand goods in the convent chapel, which had been turned first into a theatre, then a shop. Under the small oval window that once held a leaded glass pane, the words "Old Wares" painted in black, took up the whole of the façade.

It was the first time I'd ever opened the big, heavy door with its dirty panes of glass. It stuck, just like Madame Henry's the night before. This time I wasn't wearing my blue blazer. I was dressed just as usual in Uncle Désiré's long flour-sack coat, my beret pulled right down over my ears, and was dragging my feet over the cobble stones in the old hobnailed boots.

The "Old Wares" shop in the chapel was huge. Two centuries ago, 300 unhappy nuns spent their lives in that convent. I always thought I could see them prostrating themselves on the flag-stones of the shop with the miserere sounding in their ears. The smell of incense still lingered in the place. The white ceiling consisted of three Gothic arches that leap-frogged from one vault to another. Just a whisper of these nuns I insisted on seeing as women would have been enough to keep me standing on the doorstep, my conscience tormented by all the harm that must have been done to them. Luckily I had a good excuse: that morning I was replacing a fellow-worker who had the flu. I usually did the area including the town hall square, the Cour de Corbière, and the Rue d'Aubette. I had to sweep his sector as well as mine.

I entered confidently, giving the door a kick, as it was the only way to move it. I'd seen people do it so many times before. However, I must have been a bit too enthusiastic, for once inside I heard a grumbling voice reprimanding me,

"Hey there! Hey there! Go at it a bit more gently or you'll have my door off the hinges!"

It was Bébé Fabre hurrying out from his shambles of a shop, just as I've always known him and just as he must have appeared when he left this life 60 years ago. When he saw me looking like a scarecrow, with my broom over my shoulder, he took off his pince-nez with surprise.

"Oh. Is that you, Pierrot? What do you want?"

What I wanted was harder to ask for than love from a woman at eight in the morning. Nevertheless, I felt some comfort in the fact that my audacity was backed up by the 600 francs salary from Madame Henry hidden in my beret.

I said, "Do you sell second-hand books?"

"Well, yes ... some ... Some people leave them with me to sell and then I occasionally get some that have been part of an inheritance. Why? Do you want a book?"

"Oh! More than one!"

"Do you want to start a library?"

"No. I want to read."

"What is it you want to read?"

"Saint-Simon."

He gave a start, then looked me up and down as though he was seeing me for the first time. He stared at me, trying to see something that wasn't the youth he knew, beyond my old grey coat, the dull eyes, the brow made even lower by the cretinous beret pulled down over my ears on the advice of cousin Raymonde. He asked the same question as Auguste Faux,

"Which one? The Count or the Duke?"

I replied with a sigh, "The Duke!"

"Ah! The Duke? The Duke . . . "

Bébé Fabre was nodding his head sententiously. Without asking me to accompany him, he turned around and walked with his usual little steps towards the apse painted with blue flowers and gold stars and a banner that neither the former theatre proprietor nor the present owner had had the heart to rub out:

Stella matutina, beatrix consolatum, virgina martyrum.

Underneath this protective sign was a huge jumble of dust-grey books, like a junk cemetery. Hundreds of books that no-one would ever read again for centuries to come were piled on rickety shelves. The books were falling to pieces and many were without covers, titles, authors' names, or the first section.

Bébé Fabre said to me while still walking,

"But my poor Pierre, what do you hope to get from the Duke? The Count, perhaps, but the Duke?"[8]

"I want him to teach me how to write."

"But you already know how to write! Your mother told me that you had your School Certificate."

There was a slightly mocking drawl in his voice as he said these words. He reached the books and felt around among the volumes with his little fat hands, mumbling to himself,

"Saint-Simon . . . Saint-Simon . . . Louis de Rouvroy . . . Duke de Saint-Simon."

He bent down and reached under a table for a box, pulling it towards him with some difficulty.

"Just a moment! This should be it . . . "

He swept various second-hand objects off the round table to

---

8   Claude Henri, Comte de Saint-Simon (1760–1825), was a member of the same family and an influential philosopher and economist.

make room for the things he was searching for in the box. He took the books out one by one and lined them up on the oak tabletop, banging them together and making the dust rise and scatter in the first ray of sunlight appearing through the oval window with no glass.

"Monsieur de Loth gave them to me *baylés* just before he died," said Bébé Fabre.

We use the verb *bayler* discreetly. It's a compromise between giving and selling that can only be expressed in the dialect and understood in the minds of my people. There's no equivalent in French.

"How much do you want for them?"

I was impatient to hear the verdict, even though it might put Saint-Simon beyond my reach for ever, but Bébé Fabre was in no hurry to give it.

Still mumbling and cursing the dust, he kept lining up the volumes, piling them up and pushing them together to make them take up the least space possible. He stood up at last, moaning because his paunch made bending his knees a painful process

"How much have you got?" he asked.

"Six hundred francs."

He shook his head.

"That's a bit short of the mark. It's the Boislile edition and there are 41 volumes."

"Could I pay off the rest in instalments?"

During the whole of this negotiation, which was such a critical one for me, I'd been frantically clutching the handle of my birch broom, and the tone of what I said rather than the content revealed such fervent longing that Bébé was quite startled by it. At the same time I began to notice there was a struggle going on inside him between the shopkeeper and the art lover. It was ten years now since he'd received that box of books.

"Get what you like for them," Monsieur de Loth had said to him.

There was something about this street sweeper who had arrived on his doorstep at eight in the morning looking like a scarecrow that disturbed Bébé Fabre's composure. It made him remember a vague creative impulse he'd toyed with years ago, but which would never have come to anything because he was so hopelessly faint-hearted. He'd have blushed to the roots of his hair had anyone accused him of trying his hand at any sort of artistic work. This kind of strange behaviour was not acceptable in Manosque, but some regret still lingered in Bébé Fabre's heart, for he was essentially a good man.

The outcome of these bitter thoughts was in the sigh he gave me. He pointed to an old wicker basket whitened by the washing it had held for decades. It had been left to someone by a poor washerwoman, sold for ten sous, and ended up there in the shop.

"All right! Grab that *banaste*. The bottom's falling out, but we'll tie it with rope."

He began to pile the volumes into the basket, complaining to me,

"Ugh! Come on, give me a hand! Make yourself useful!"

When the works of Saint-Simon were all in, three-quarters filling the basket, Bébé Fabre ferreted about a bit to find some washing line, which he tied in a cross to hold the bottom together.

"There you are!" he said. "Take it away! It's been cluttering up the place for ages! Don't talk about payment, but come and see me now and again, and tell me what you've discovered in your Saint-Simon!"

I stuttered out my ineffectual thanks as he helped me put the basket on my shoulder.

"Leave your broom there!" he said. "No-one's going to take it. Come and fetch it later. Now, take all that home, and much good may it do you!"

He opened the door for me.

"But . . . ," he said. For it had just occurred to him that he'd done a good deed and something deep in his shopkeeper's heart slightly resented it.

"But," he repeated, "when you've got some free time, you must come and do some sweeping under my plane tree. My house-keeper draws the line at that, and they really pile up as there's no wind in my courtyard."

I was starting to quiver at the thought that my wish had been granted. By asking for a payment of that kind, Bébé was still making me a present of it. The tree in his courtyard extended over the whole of the vast coach entrance on the Rue d'Aubette. It gave so much shade that darkness set in there for the whole summer as soon as the leaves came out; and in winter its sturdy skeleton was so thickly intertwined in the light that a stagnant green shade never left the place. The tree itself covered 100 square metres, taking up the whole space in the courtyard of the old convent building and extending over the wall of the priest's garden. An enormous twisted branch looked as though it was kneeling on the top of the wall and, because of its weight, played castanets with the rubble work, slowly wearing it away.

There was a double door hidden behind this colossal plane tree with its strong, pale, smooth trunk, but it was never opened because Bébé and his customers always went through the shop. It stood at the top of four worn steps and was guarded by two huge tin torch stands with torches that rattled in the winter wind. You heard it if, like me, you took the trouble to slip into the shadows of the coach yard, but your heart was beating at the thought of being caught there, for what else could you say to someone who might appear and ask the question, "What are you doing here?" but "I'm listening to the wind blowing around the torch stands."

No-one would believe you. Nevertheless, that's precisely where my first ideas came to me. Bébé Fabre didn't know that by asking me to come and sweep under his plane tree he was opening up as many avenues to me as giving me Saint-Simon to read.

I went off, bent under the weight of the *banaste* full of books. Climbing the old stairs in the gatehouse, I banged the wall at each step. I hastily dumped the books down at the foot of my mattress, as I was worried about leaving my work and anxious to go back to Bébé Fabre's to pick up my broom and start sweeping again.

The door had carelessly been left half-open, so I could hear Bébé's slow voice in the echoing space of the shop. He had probably not got over my sudden early-morning appearance, as he was mumbling to himself,

"Saint-Simon! What do you know about that? It might give him delusions of grandeur! One should always think twice before doing a good deed for someone."

"Come now!" a toneless voice replied. "How much longer are you going to stand there reproaching yourself for doing it?"

Through the opening in the door, where I'd bent over and pressed my face against it like a servant listening at the keyhole, I saw the rather ghostly form of Madame Peltier wandering around the piles of furniture and utensils. Everyone called her the sister-in-law and no-one ever knew her first name. Likewise, we had no idea whether she'd been ugly or pretty, as we were never at close enough quarters to see her as anything but a shapeless, insubstantial apparition. She seemed to trot aimlessly around the vast rooms and courtyards with a huge ring of keys hanging from her belt, jingling as they hit against her thigh, the only material sign that made her any different from a ghost.

She was short-sighted and you couldn't see her eyes behind her glasses. Always dressed in mourning, she groped her way around the whole convent, looking for little tasks which she never finished, and always seeking a plausible explanation for the misfortune that had struck her. She'd been a widow for more years than she could count, but the moment she heard the news was still as fresh in her mind as the May morning when old Michel, who delivered parcels in the town, had thrown a huge badly wrapped package at the door of the shop. It made no sound as it fell.

Old Michel was always in a hurry. He shouted, "Hello! Anyone there!" to let them know, then disappeared in the noise of his van pulled by two big, strong, plodding horses.

That day they'd both heard him, so Bébé and his sister-in-law emerged from the shop together.

"What could it be?" Madame Peltier said.

Bébé shrugged his shoulders.

"Another of those useless knick-knacks my brother sends you from his beloved Africa."

They both dragged the parcel into the shop with enormous difficulty and opened it up on the stone floor of the chapel. A huge fur popped out, unfolded and spread out from the wrapping that had held it prisoner. It was a whole lion's skin including the proud head and mane and the lashing tail, still giving an angry twitch whenever the skin was moved. An envelope containing the following letter was pinned to the beast's forehead:

Dear Madame,

Your husband was eaten alive by this lion, which he

144

unfortunately missed. However, we, his faithful companions, are sending you this skin which contains something of your dear husband's noble soul. (He often spoke to us about you.) Please accept our sympathy and sincere condolences.

It wasn't signed and from that time on Madame Peltier began to wander around the convent, walking with small, slow steps, dressed in black, diaphanous, like a lady long dead. One evening she pulled the bell connected by a wire to her brother-in-law's bedroom down the corridor. He finally arrived after the fourth ring, having first put on his ermine coat. He knocked at the door and was asked to come in. Madame Peltier was sitting on the side of her bed, modestly dressed in a stiff nightgown and frilled nightcap, with her bare feet buried deep in the fur.

"What do you think?" she said.

The lion's skin, spread out flat on the red tiles with the feet extended, made the ordinary room look like a royal bedchamber.

We didn't know whether Bébé and his sister-in-law were lovers on that occasion or any other. We had too much respect for them to ask the question, and we also knew that they'd been struck in the past by other misfortunes which now lay deep in the silence of their hearts.

Now, I had permission to be there sweeping leaves under the plane tree, and these were the very workings of fate I was so interested in. I wanted to sense them and let them permeate my memory and imagination. When you're young you love to learn about the unhappy fates of others, not so much out of curiosity as from a kind of high excitement, as though misfortune was one of life's trophies you had to attain.

That same evening, I started the first page of Saint-Simon, deter-mined to go on to the last without coming up for air. The days were simply hours to be filled before I could experience that happiness every night. I did my sweeping, energetically, meticu-lously, leaving no corner untouched. No-one was to know that my mind was elsewhere. Each morning at the bakery, the other habitués were a little surprised, but just in passing, for I was of no importance as far as they were concerned. They could see no grounds for my inner joy. I was just a sweeper with holes in his shoes, living in an old ruin. What right did I have to the happiness they could see in my face?

Madame Henry was the exception, affectionately touching my beret where the money and Lucinde's letter crackled under her fingers.

"Have you forgotten me?" she said softly if I went out the side door with her.

She studied me closely. She was the only one who could stop me looking away. When she did, I was filled with an exciting kind of panic as I tried to convey how much I desired her. But in spite of all that, I managed to reply in the same tone.

"There are no more dead leaves on your paths and your hydrangeas are ready for spring."

She bit her lip. It seemed to me that she would like to have given me a sharp reply, but self-esteem prevented her.

In the evening, as soon as I'd had my soup, no matter what state of cold my feet were in, I got under the dirty sheets on my mattress where bits of straw poked through the unbleached canvas. (My mother washed so many sheets for others that she could only rarely see to ours.) I spread out the lined jacket given to me by Madame Henry and, with chin in hand, I entered the king's court.

These tomes gave off a strong smell of mould. Their covers were the faded blue of an old cart. It was the same blue but so washed out that it had turned grey, apart from the cover flaps, which had kept their colour. But as soon as I started to read, Versailles with all its dazzling gold came to life in front of me, as fresh as an Easter morn. Splendid, sordid Versailles, peopled with dwarves one foot high, famous men martyrs to gout, hobbling hunchbacked princes with noses eaten away by syphilis. There were duchesses with dainty armpits, and finally the huge, pathetic king missing some teeth, a poor man drifting on the tide of his misfortunes. The Duke always hated him and frequently mocked him, yet he felt an enormous compassion for him, and had to admire him in spite of the way he was treated.

They all loved and feared God with a deep faith, without the shadow of a doubt, and yet their passions were so strong, their pride so overweening, their vices so ingrained that they ignored it and Saint-Simon showed me them ignoring it. It was a magnificent and a frightening revelation. I almost reached the stage of thinking that they would never get to heaven and that the cynical Duke was presenting me with a hunting picture of the damned.

Never had a world so sparkling with life been presented to my imagination and become part of it. As I read I sometimes whistled the central motif of Cantata 140. I'd heard it only once but knew it by heart. It seemed to me a perfect analogy of ends and means could be drawn between Bach and Saint-Simon. It gave me a feeling of extraordinary exhilaration.

I began to work out how much it would cost me to go to Versailles where I could revel in that empty theatre and fill it easily with faded ghosts. Then I realized how much it would look like the Basses-Alpes, Manosque and the people who milled about in my wildly active but sharp imagination.

Because of Saint-Simon I no longer felt like playing with myself. It took three or four days for the build-up of my wasted youth to make me do it. Then images of Lucinde or Madame Henry, whom I now shamelessly called Hortense in my erotic fancies, would appear in the sky over Versailles. Sometimes it was even Mireille, the newsagent, with her smooth, straight stockings.

When these enticing women appeared to me like that, they always did it laughing loudly. I could see their tongues moving in their pink open mouths and their teeth, gleaming in the light, looked like shimmering lace I despaired of ever being able to describe. This laugh is the secret expression of a mystery known only to women. I've always felt that, in them, it's the most revealing expression of joie de vivre in spite of everything. It blots out the world, despair to come, unspeakable misfortunes that may have just befallen and must be forgotten at all costs.

Then this laughter I thought was endless would be stifled and transformed into those faltering words of love I'd never really heard, inspired or honoured. But as soon as this shadow of desire was satisfied, I'd come back to Versailles and Saint-Simon. At the bakery, Auguste Faux looked at me strangely. When we went out of the shop together, bag against bag, he said to me in confidence,

"I'm not curious, my poor Pierre, but what on earth could you do with Saint-Simon?"

I didn't reply, but hurried away feeling as ashamed as if he'd just told me to my face that he'd seen me masturbating. Then Auguste Faux called out to me.

"Do you know what Sainte-Beuve said about Saint-Simon?[9] His writing is slapdash, but it will last for ever!"

This remark struck my heart and remained eternally engraved

9 Charles Augustin Sainte-Beuve (1804–1869), writer, critic and literary historian, best known for his *Portraits littéraires* and *Causeries du lundi*. [tr.]

on my memory, even though I'd heard it only once, like the central motif of the Bach cantata. As soon as I lay down, watching the dormice silently skittering up to the ceiling, and opened one of the blue volumes, I would quietly murmur those words: his writing is slapdash, but it will last for ever. I'd immediately taken down the old dictionary without a cover, which didn't have all the words, to look up the name of the saint Auguste Faux had mentioned. Now I knew who he meant, I felt reassured. A hundred years had gone by between Saint-Simon and Sainte-Beuve and 200 between Saint-Simon and me. That was ages to come, that was forever. A new man, new images, and yet they're 200 years old.

One day when I was lying in the grass by the side of the castle tower, thinking myself hidden from prying eyes, a shadow fell between me and the open book. It was Auguste Faux.

"So, you little rascal!" he said. "You've finally got it!"

I was so surprised that he managed to snatch the book out of my hands.

"And the Boislile edition to boot!" he exclaimed. "You sly little devil! Where did you manage to pick that up?"

"In the rubbish bin," I mumbled, in a voice that sounded as though I'd like to throw him in it too.

I was in the process of creating an erotic object with the Duchesse du Lude, whom Saint-Simon had crucified with his vicious words.

"I followed you!" Auguste said. "I wanted to know what was going on."

His eyes narrowed as he looked at me. My mouth was as tightly shut as an oyster that had just been thrown into the basket. I saw before me a tall man wearing a tie, standing elegantly at ease in fine socks showing under the impeccable crease in his dark trousers. Although there must have been many more exciting people with whom he could have spent his time, he'd taken the trouble to sneak out on this Sunday afternoon and get his polished shoes covered in dust on the steep path up to the Mont d'Or. He'd gone to this trouble to find out what a spotty youth who had hidden himself away to indulge his vice could possibly be reading.

But I was surly, secretive and touchy. I smelled like a donkey, on purpose, to avoid any kind of intimacy. I didn't appreciate Auguste Faux's intrusion into my hidden spot in the grass, primarily because to me he was always the deputy mayor, a confident, rich man who spoke with ease and grace. He always said "I don't know" instead of "Don't know" like the rest of us.

He tried the velvet glove approach, talking to me as a human talks to an animal he wants to tame. He tried to convince me that with Saint-Simon we were equals. I wanted to be alone with Saint-Simon and took umbrage at this promiscuity. When he saw my inscrutable expression and my determination, Auguste Faux stood on his dignity.

"Why on earth should I waste my curiosity on an insignificant creature like you?" he said angrily. "What could there possibly be about you that nobody sees? I'm an idiot! I came as a friend . . ."

He turned on his heel and left. I saw him disappearing into the distance waving his arms and talking to himself as he passed by some old women of our region who were knitting socks. There were six or seven of them in a line on a gentle slope, comfortably enjoying the sun, as though it were the last they would see in their lives.

They'd seen me go by, they'd seen him go by. Their white heads with long knitting needles stuck through their buns nodded in time, expressing their disapproval or perhaps their complicity.

Their silence was also eloquent as was the glance they gave me as I walked in front of them on my way home, intoxicated with Saint-Simon and the strong wind on the mount.

Auguste Faux had braved their conjectures to come and offer me his friendship, but I had no need of friends. To me, male humanity was a bear pit. I only liked men who had been dead for a long time. I was old-fashioned, out-moded, obsolete. I'd have preferred to hear nothing but the horses' hooves under the shade of our boulevards or the dim light of our streets. At 16, as I was then, I was determinedly turning my back on the future. It didn't interest me, because at some time I'd cease to be a part of it. Actually, I'd long ago acknowledged the fact that I wasn't normal and had accepted it quite easily.

Women were the only things that fascinated me. They had so much more depth than men, even the most frivolous of them. They were so much more in tune with nature and the joy of living; they were so much more adaptable and more able to deal with hardship, so much better equipped to control it, forget it and transcend it.

Even the old women sitting on the slope, watching me go by with a knowing look on their faces and sniggering silently to themselves (for they remembered having seen the navy jacket I now wore every Sunday on the late Monsieur Henry's back), even these harpies seemed more capable than any man of understanding life and making it bearable for all those in their company.

No, I couldn't allow anyone, even Auguste Faux, to come close to the confusion in my heart and mind, to which I had added Saint-Simon. I was absolutely full of wild contradictions between my instinct and my hopes, between what I thought was my duty and the reprehensible lapses into which my deceitful nature constantly led me. I had one safeguard I clung to like the rope in the well of our circular staircase in the Rue d'Aubette gatehouse: it was my work as a street sweeper, which I did to everyone's satisfaction. Those who didn't call me Pierrot or my poor Pierre, said of me, "He's a good lad", watching me with approval as I swept the droppings from the mountain flocks into the gutter.

But I wasn't a good lad at all. Undecided as ever, I had an idea at the back of my mind that grew, then withered, then sprang to life again, lost its intensity only to come back and haunt me, making me panic-stricken. My legs felt weak at the thought that one day I'd set out for the bakery, that I'd confront Lucinde's irritability and, taking off my beret, which I'd never pulled off in front of her, I'd say,

"There you are, Madame!"

Taking out from the lining the terrible letter that could send her to court and unfolding it before her, I'd add,

"Don't worry! It's a secret between the two of us. I don't ask anything in exchange. I'm simply returning it to you."

But it would have to be on one of those awful Sunday afternoons when the bored women serving in the bakeries hope that a late-comer, on his way to afternoon tea with friends, might come in out of the blue and buy up the five or six odd cakes left over from the Sunday morning rush.

Yes, that's what I should do. It would be one Sunday afternoon. Albert would be snoring upstairs, sleeping the sleep of the unjust. (That's what I called it when I thought of his apparent equanimity.) I'd be on the other side of the counter, watching Lucinde rereading the short note Albert had made her write. That would have to be at least two years away, for I couldn't risk it until I was 18, if I was to have any chance of being taken seriously and not simply be treated like a kid.

I'd also have to use my extra earnings to buy one of those green suits from Peyrache I envied so much on the boys of my age and, if it was winter, put on a tie and overcoat. Turning up at Lucinde's, beret in hand, wearing a tie and with my hair parted on the side and slicked down with Roja brilliantine, would give me the greatest possible satisfaction.

Then there would be something new between us, for good or for ill. Perhaps she might wrench the Roberval scales from their base, rush out from behind the counter and hit me with them; then again, perhaps she might collapse on the counter sobbing uncontrollably.

That would be the moment to put my hand on her shoulder and say,

"Don't be afraid. I'm here!"

That was a phrase I'd read countless times in books. It's the very picture of human helplessness, since when misfortune strikes, no-one can suffer it in your place, take it from you or you from it.

Anyway, it would be something new! It would release the two of us from that terrible Sunday afternoon boredom that can only be escaped by those capable of making love then and not ending up just as bored as ever on a Sunday afternoon.

But there you are: I was only 16 and on Sunday afternoons in winter I would jauntily passed by the shop window to sneak a look at Lucinde at the back in the pretty-pretty pastoral decor. Lucinde was there alone, biting her nails, the radiant beauty of her thirties inexorably fading now and continuing to fade for 20 or 30 years more, denied love, the property of a man who left her tragically unfulfilled. Patrocles had been taken from her like a noisy rattle from a child.

And I was 16! At that age you can't go to a woman of 30 and say point blank,

"I think of you every night! I get terribly aroused when I picture you. I know what your skin feels like without ever having touched it. All last night I called you 'my love.'"

I endured that long wait from being a child to becoming an adult with a mad rage that made me want to make time go faster. Today, of course, I want to hold it back. Whenever I find myself under the plane trees on the boulevard, where the winds change with every season, I can still see that window before me, even though it doesn't exist any more, that shop now something else. I see that 30-year-old woman, her feet impatiently tapping on the bar across her stool; I see her legs, the shape of her plump knees at the hem of her skirt and then, further still, the mystery of her hidden flesh. That woman of 30 is now nothing but dust, and my wallet no longer contains that terrible letter, although I remember every word and the way it was written. I suppose it's still blue. For a long time now it has been lying between the minutes of a file marked "Cases Closed".

VII

AT THAT TIME, QUITE BY CHANCE, LIKE A WEATHER-VANE veering wildly in a storm, something catastrophic happened that was to change the direction of my life.

First of all, a terribly hot summer caused fires around Manosque in the broom bushes, which had already been looking like candelabra for some time before they became flames streaked with black rising ten metres high, as if some madwoman were running over them, her hair loose and streaming in the wind. They crackled furiously and uncontrollably – so much so that the sudden noise bursting from these bushes as they caught alight almost panicked the firemen, who tried to stop their ears. Since there was no more water in the ponds, they went from one blaze to another with nothing but useless brooms to try to extinguish the flames.

That summer remained in our memories. It had taken root in the drought of a winter when there was neither rain nor snow, only violent winds. When you walked on the asphalt in the streets and boulevards it felt as though you were wearing soft slippers.

The peasants winked as they weeded the vines where the tight bunches of green grapes held the mystery that would turn them into good wine or bad.

"It'll be at least twelve!" you could hear them say. They were talking about degrees of alcohol.

The springs had almost dried up and the last of their water lay hidden deep in the dark folds of the earth. Even so, cracks in the zaffre rock went down like tongues lapping the edge of their transparent, ever-diminishing pools. Above ground the streams dried up. Swarms of flies drank the last drops through the wilting moss.

That summer had us all in a state of torpor by 15 May. I was exhausted from carrying the hoses on my shoulders from one tap to the next, to clean the streets in front of the houses. Our middle-class citizens watched me anxiously from behind their bead curtains while the precious water imitated the almost-forgotten rain on their stretch of road.

"He's a good lad!" they said with quavering voices.

They dragged their slippers and their chairs from one draught to another in their long corridors. As a result, several died of pneumonia.

On 24 August, St Bartholomew's Day and my mother's birthday, I was awoken at five in the morning by a sound I thought I'd never hear again: rain falling on the trees in the boulevard and on the ground of our old gatehouse in drops as big as coins, leaving hollows in the dust. On the first day we welcomed it with cries of joy. On the second, the thundering storms that accompanied it began to die down, and soon they were a faint rumble in the distance, leaving the driving rain to make all the noise.

People grumbled. The beans had stopped drying and were turning black. We began to fear for the vines.

On 1 September it was still drizzling. We thought it was going to stop, summer would return and we'd put our straw hats on again. We were delighted that a second crop of lucerne after the June harvest had grown in a week.

But then, one evening around 14 September, the bells worn by the rams in a flock of sheep were heard tinkling mournfully. It was a *scabot* flock come down from the mountains. The flock spread out on the Promenade de la Plaine, right in front of the same wealthier citizens, who were shocked because they believed they still had a month to go before the front steps of their houses were soiled with droppings. They questioned the *bayles* – the head shepherds.

"What's going on? We didn't expect you before October! What happened to you? Isn't there any more grass up there on the mountain?"

"It's under snow," the *bayles* replied.

"What difference does that make? It's not the first time that's happened! It'll soon melt!"

The *bayles* shook their heads.

"No, this lot won't! When we left there were easily 15 centimetres and it was still falling. You can imagine we stayed as long as we could!"

They were almost apologizing. The whole *scabot* had stayed quietly at the end of the Esplanade behind the goats that led it, as if waiting for permission to move. The worthy bourgeois took cover, raising their arms to the heavens. The *scabot* spread out quietly. Madame Dépieds came to see what was happening, her prying eyes peering through her pince-nez. Her face had that look of disgust typical of her in a bad mood.

"They've never been so dirty!" she said, quite revolted at the sight.

She went inside again as the rain was starting to fall once more. This *scabot* looked almost mouldy with damp. Even the late lambs, hardly four days old and being carried in haversacks, were dirty with rain like their parents. Henri Gardon gave coffee to the unsmiling shepherds. They said they'd come down from the Col de l'Agnel above Saint-Véran and that the marmots up there were already in their burrows. It had been snowing since 25 August. It snowed, then melted, it rained, then it snowed again, but the snow hadn't melted since the 30th. It had kept on snowing since then with the north wind. In conditions like these . . . They shrugged their shoulders.

"It happens. In '23 . . . "

Slowly, at the rate of about two a week, the *scabots* came down to the plain a month earlier than they should: the ones from l'Ubayette, la Cavale, Parpaillon and Thorame. By 1 October, there were no more flocks in the mountains.

In our area, the beginning of September was heralded by a sickly sun that went behind the clouds at midday every day. From 15 September it began to rain on the grapes, which should have been ready to pick, but half the bunches were still partly green. Some growers walked around the rows in the rain with their spray cans over their shoulders, vainly spreading Bordeaux mixture on vines as green as virgin forest. Their leaves hung down like bats' wings absolutely soaked with water streaming off them, making the bursting vines swell and absorb even more water. These poor men tried desperately to save their crop. Our more inquisitive citizens watched their efforts standing under big umbrellas, shaking their heads. They even brought their children along.

"Now son, you'll remember that in such and such a year . . . "

The wine makers went to harvest with black armbands like widowers, their brows furrowed, their looks gloomy. There were no songs in the vineyards, as they harvested in downpours of rain. The grapes were the same colour as a whitlow. They were piled into the vats more out of habit than anything else. Everyone knew the wine should be thrown away. We also knew that we'd drink it anyway, for whatever it was like, we would know as we drank that it was the fruit of our vines, our land, and it was the only way we had of communicating with it, even if the sour taste of that verjuice set our teeth on edge.

On the whole, you would have to say that autumn was frightful. The trunks of the maples were bright green and bursting with sap, so that the leaves quickly turned varying shades of red then died. They were scattered through the forest, looking like magic lanterns swaying in the wind, beckoning to the traveller from the side of the road, then all the light went out of them.

The gentle des Rates stream now roared along like a mountain torrent. It sounded like a hunting horn as it blew up the holes in our latrines. A spring suddenly burst through the bitumen at La Burlière with a huge, swelling mushroom of water. Everyone came to see it but no-one looked terribly happy. Albert's bread turned soft and children made marbles out of the usually springy texture of his *pompes*.

The elements had such a depressing effect on us all that Auguste Faux was no longer witty and the mayor almost caught his death of cold walking at night in the wind and the rain. We didn't think he'd survive. One morning, the lane beside the bakery turned into a stream of rushing water. It splashed down the three steps, came under the door and under the wheeled basket, then flowed across the floor, finally escaping out the front of the shop on to the boulevard.

Nature became omnipotent. It was impossible to ignore: its omnipresence stifled any feeble attempt we might make to organize our lives.

There was a new noise filtering through in the night when the town was quiet. It was the sad, muted roar of the Durance, four kilometres away, sounding like an animal resigned to die.

My mother rushed hither and thither with saucepans, not knowing where to put them as there were so many cracks in the ceiling arches. Water was silently flowing in sheets down the walls of the gatehouse. That silence was sinister. We'd always looked on the waters of the des Rates stream as harmless, but now their roaring at the bottom of the latrines seemed threatening.

While I was mentally reconstructing Versailles from the pen of Saint-Simon, the fissures in the ceiling running from one arch to the next became deeper and the edges further apart. Outside it was like the Flood.

I'd spent 30 francs to buy an umbrella, for if water happened to get into my beret, it would turn Lucinde's note into blotting paper and then the scenario I had dreamed up for her would come to nothing. As an added precaution I'd bought a replacement at Stéphane's, insisting on a leather lining to protect Lucinde's note from contact with my head. Stéphane chose one from a shelf, scattering the others on the ground. He put it on his own head, pulled it down to his ears and went to judge the effect in the big wardrobe mirror. He took it off and as he handed it to me, said in passing,

"*A-quéou ti pinta*! (this one's really you!)"

Which meant that I had to take that beret or offend the seller. I went quietly after putting twelve francs on the counter.

* * *

I remember, it was 20 October. My beret still smelt new and I'd just whipped it off respectfully as I came across a hearse unexpectedly passing by. I normally had enough time to hide behind a plane tree precisely to avoid having to do this, but that evening I was deep in Saint-Simon, as I often was at that time.

I remember. I'd just swept up half the droppings left that morning as the last *scabot* moved off, the rams noisily snuffling the water slowly dripping from their noses. Work was finished, evening was falling early and I'd whipped out the volume I was reading from Uncle's grey coat. That was when I came upon the funeral procession, where some, seeing me with a book in my hand, shot me a reproachful look as though I were engaged in some sacrilegious act against the consumptive man who had died of the damp.

I remember. I can see the Boulevard Mirabeau as it was 60 years ago, that is, just as it is today without the cars. When I was 15 I'd try to put my arms around the trunks of the trees, just for fun. It would take only a finger's width on each side for my hands to join. Last year, 60 years later, I did it again, at night time so that I wouldn't be seen. Now you'd need a whole hand for the arms to join.

The trees on the Boulevard Mirabeau are still young, but I'm old. I remember it perfectly. The funeral cortège had just started up the steep slope of the Boulevard des Tilleuls, with Aimé the hearse driver giving a discreet crack of the whip above his two horses to encourage them to pull harder.

I remember that I'd been laughing heartily at this phrase of Saint-Simon I was savouring:

"Moreover he knew much Greek, whose morals he had also learned."

I heard something that sounded like a big bone cracking. I

was ten metres away from the medieval gatehouse that served as our home. I could see it quite clearly. It was grey, a dirty stone colour, with four rows of round tiles under its Florentine roof. The first thing I felt was a shower of black ash pouring out from the tiles. It was debris from old swallows' nests breaking up under the tiles. It occurred to me that the rows of tiles were out of alignment and that they were hanging rather dangerously over the wall. I stepped back five, ten metres. The gatehouse seemed to follow my retreat, throwing itself forward to catch me in its deadly embrace.

I saw a crevasse zigzag across the wall like a silent flash of lightning, cutting diagonally across our small window, and suddenly the perfect rectangle collapsed on one side into a diamond shape. The two parts of the high wall broke, parted, then opened out wide like a book. In an instant I saw the inside of our miserable home like a pomegranate cut in two, with spots and streaks of various colours: our ragged clothes.

The two parts of the gatehouse began to disgorge their contents like a belly, ejecting their entrails of Durance stones held together by lime long since dead, stuck with tufts of straw and bits of worm-eaten wood. A thousand years after it was built, the true nature of the gatehouse was finally revealed: it had been built forshow, to reassure the nervous burghers on the cheap.

The huge noise hit me as I fell on my knees: my father, my mother, my sister! I knew my brother was at work with the locksmith, but my father, my mother and my sister! . . . My blood ran cold, but through the pain I felt an even stronger concern which would override even the love of my family: my basket with the volumes of Saint-Simon lay under the rubble beside my mattress. I would never be able to read them again! There I was kneeling in the mud and the manure left by the horses pulling the hearse just before they started up the slope, and the fear of finding myself suddenly without a family was being swept aside by that of finding myself tomorrow without my books. The catastrophe suddenly made me realize the depths of my self-interest and my face contorted into a grimace of despair.

I cried out, "Oh God!", which expressed all my anguish; an "Oh God!" which made nonsense of the unthinking atheism I'd lived by until then. I must have stayed there on my knees with my hands clasped, uttering one "Oh God!" after the other.

The rumbling had stopped and the rain had started again. The des Rates stream flowed even faster with its newly acquired roar of a mountain torrent. The sound of human voices and activity began to grow louder. It was the end of the funeral cortège half-way up the Boulevard des Tilleuls that had heard the noise of the walls collapsing and had run back to find out what had happened. Their pity for the dead man had not been able to compete with their curiosity. The only ones remaining behind the hearse were the family, the immovable clergy and the four returned soldiers who were the pall bearers. The rest had rushed back down the hill, all ready to exclaim and sympathize.

I must have had a recorder in my head that wouldn't stop or take notice of my distress or my physical pain, for I was crying "Oh God!" with my mouth full of the plaster spreading over everything like a sheet, mercifully covering the pile of rubble.

The first thing to cross my line of vision, misty with tears, was a tall ghost with its arms raised to heaven. It was the unhappy rival of the mayor at the last elections. How had he been able to get here so quickly from his pharmacy in the Grand-Rue? He was shouting "Oh God!" like me, but he also added,

"I told him! I knew it! I've always said so! I've told the mayor a hundred times, a hundred times I've said to him, 'One of these days your gateway'll come crashing down! And *you*'ll have deaths on your conscience! Deaths on your conscience!'"

The crowd was growing larger. The unhappy rival took off his white coat and turned up his shirtsleeves. The others did the same. They folded their jackets on the neighbours' doorsteps and rolled up their sleeves. They made a chain and passed the Durance stones from one to the other up to the stream and threw them in. You could hear the fire engine approaching. Someone had thrown a blanket over my shoulders. They tried to pull me further away. Everyone was white with plaster, looking like worried clowns with tears running down their faces because of the pouring rain. They whispered.

"It's Pierrot ! His whole family's under that!"

The firemen arrived ready for action but not able to do anything.

"You'll have to go and get the bulldozer!"

"Right! And if anyone's still alive underneath, you'll risk crushing him!"

There were 200 now, perhaps more, making a chain to dig trenches in the ruins and look for victims.

I had a heavy, empty feeling in the pit of my stomach which made it impossible to move. My hands were no longer joined together in prayer, but were on my head. Feeling Lucinde's letter crackling in the lining, I realized just how much importance I'd placed on worthless dreams.

Suddenly I felt myself bathed in the warmth of a strange sun and it immediately freed me from that nightmare. It was my mother, my deaf mother, shouting with happiness as she shook me, enveloping me with her love. I could feel my mother's tired breasts pressed so tightly against my chest I could hardly breathe. Then they all arrived: my brother, smelling of rust, fell into my arms and kissed me awkwardly for the first time in our lives, my father whose moustache smelled of quarry stone, and my little sister held out to me by my mother. She began licking my eyebrows and lashes, trying to dry my tears. We were all on our knees, pressed close together like the members of a family carved in bas-relief on a tomb. And the rain fell on us, relentlessly, unmercifully.

At the time of the disaster, my mother had gone to fetch my sister from nursery school, my father had been doing some overtime and my brother, as I expected, had been at work with his boss. The crowd was relieved to know that all five of us were alive. They kept saying,

"My goodness! You were lucky!"

"How lucky you were!"

I started to cry again.

"What are you crying about, silly? We're all here!" my mother said.

I staggered to my feet. With the last surviving volume of Saint-Simon in the huge pocket of Uncle's coat, I began to walk towards the three-metre-high barricade that once had been our home. As well as the stones it had spewed out the cast-iron stove, which now lay with its three feet in the air on top of the debris. The organ case was also sticking out like the stem of a shipwreck with the rain drumming away on the pipes.

There was some hope! By digging a hole through the stones, I might be able to reach my mattress and the basket of Saint-Simon. I started to crawl up the heap of rubble. I'd already reached the organ case and was stretching out my arm to catch hold of it, when I heard a shrill voice. It was my mother shouting to me.

"Pierrot! What are you doing?"

"Looking for my books!"

"Have you gone crazy, or what?"

The firemen, my father, the neighbours, everybody intervened. I struggled like a maniac, wailing,

"My books!"

My mother shouted more loudly than I did.

"Idiot! It's no time to be thinking about books!"

We had nothing left: no mattresses, no sagging bed bases, no frying pans, no food or Sunday clothes. Nothing! My mother was lamenting the potato and celery stew she'd made at midday.

The rain was falling; it was six o'clock in the evening and the street lamps had just gone on. Through the neighbours' windows, we could see people getting ready for a pleasant evening with their families. But there were also perhaps a hundred worried people around us mentally making the connection between what had just happened to us and what could one day happen to them.

"The poor things! They've lost everything!"

The locksmith from Soubeyran immediately ran up and pulled my brother towards him as though he owned him.

"I'm keeping this one!" he said.

"But you have four already!"

"That doesn't matter. We'll manage. It can always be managed somehow."

My brother told me later that from that day on he never made another hollow solder and he never received another kick in the behind either. As a victim of misfortune he was now sacred.

My father, alone and dejected, went with one of the other road menders, where they drank all night and told each other tales of natural disasters.

Madame Alarthéus and Madame Bourdelle were told by neighbours that my mother was in need. They both came running in the rain; one in hair curlers and the other in slippers and padded coat. Both had been wanting my mother to work for them for some time. Madame Alarthéus won the day. It was an unequal battle between her manor house, the "Manoir des Turpins", and Madame Bourdelle's simple villa, "Lou Pantaï".

It was while all these arrangements were being finalized that I saw Madame Henry emerge from the rain with her purse on her arm. You could hear her heels on the asphalt of the boulevard. She clamped her hand on to my damp beret.

"I can take one," she said, "and no more!"

No-one said a word – not my mother, nor the authorities. Madame Henry turned me around without taking her hand from my head.

She walked along slowly. She whispered to me that life is long and although it seemed we had lost everything, I was young and I still had time to lose and regain everything ten times over.

"And what's more," she added, "without this disaster you wouldn't be here beside me and you wouldn't know how well-disposed I am towards you."

She patted my head, feeling the crackling paper of my poor banknotes and Lucinde's letter.

"I've lost my books!"

I burst into sobs. When I finished this volume, the only one to escape the disaster, I'd have no access to the rest of Saint-Simon, that is, 40 volumes. I'd never know the great saga of Versailles, in which I'd only just begun to immerse myself.

The whole time we were walking, I had Madame Henry's sympathetic hand on my shoulder as she vainly tried to console me. We had to run the last part of the way, as the rain was starting to fall heavily again on the tall cedars. We were subjected to intermittent downpours which then soaked the ground, and heavy drops splashing on the gravel and into the green chestnut trees. The horse chestnuts knocked down by the rain fell heavily, their husks exploding as they hit the ground.

Madame Henry had put up her umbrella and was sheltering me. In my confusion, it took me some minutes to realize that the soft thing pressing against my arm was her left breast.

She pushed me through the door to "Eden" in front of her. With its soft scent of lives past, the dimly lit house welcomed us as soon as we crossed the threshold. The feel of her breast against my arm was beginning to affect me and dry up that source of adult tears I'd just shed for my wretched state. It was the first time it had ever made me cry.

"You must be starving," Madame Henry said.

I gave some world-weary indication of my indifference to any such material constraints.

"Yes, yes!" she insisted. "I never eat anything in the evening, but you must."

She led me down the corridor to the kitchen, practically forcing me to sit down on a stool at a big table. She made herself busy between a cupboard and the refrigerator. She took out a ham wrapped in a tea towel and cut a big slice quickly and with an expert hand. I watched fascinated as she moved about around me. She seemed light and heavy at the same time, and very steady on her lovely legs. Watching her fly around bringing me all the treasures from her pantry, I slowly lost the desire to cry.

The kitchen was a very big square room with a very high ceiling; its scrupulous cleanliness was guaranteed by a relentless eye that picked up anything that wasn't just right. The glass door leading out to the garden had red-checked gingham curtains which touched my heart with their air of peace and tranquillity. Had Madame Henry chosen them herself?

At first I just put the food into my mouth without thinking, but slowly I began to enjoy it. She was sitting opposite me, looking at me as I tasted the good things she offered me. I'd already noticed that the way she looked at me changed progressively as she paid me more attention. It was neither harsher nor gentler. It was sharper, as though she was aware that my miserable grey coat hid the real person I was. She didn't yet know what I was hiding, but since our meetings in the bakery, she was sure I was hiding something and I was sure she knew.

"Take your hat off!" she said. "How many times do I have to tell you that men take their hats off in the presence of ladies!"

I snatched off my beret, but I couldn't eat and hold it at the same time. She seized it and hung it up on one of the pegs that looked like stag horns on the umbrella stand.

"That's right! You shouldn't be ashamed of your head. It's what's inside that counts!"

I was beginning to be completely dazed by the despair of having lost my books, of being without my family for the first time in my life, of the disaster that had just reduced us to beggary and the rain that kept pelting down.

"Wait there!" Madame Henry was giving an order.

She disappeared into a room for several minutes, leaving the door open. She came back to me with her arms full like the day she'd dressed me from head to foot for the winter. This time it was fine flannel underwear smelling of soap powder and dry lavender.

"Come!" Madame Henry said.

I had the presence of mind to hurry over to the hat rack and retrieve my beret. She gave a little kick to the door next to the potted palm. I went in behind her. It was the bedroom where suffering had been imprisoned since the death of the woman it had killed.

"The beds are always made up in my house," said Madame Henry.

She was proud of being totally organized, having tightly closing doors, watertight roofs, gleaming glasses in glass-fronted cabinets, and maintaining dignity in death.

"Don't worry," she said, "my mother died in that bed, but it's the best in the house. Get into these pyjamas. They're the last ones my husband bought before going to the war. He never wore them."

She'd turned down the plump lemon-yellow eiderdown on the counterpane and pulled back the sheet. I saw an enormous white pillow, adorned with two big initials embroidered in open-work.

"Go to sleep!" It was another order from Madame Henry. "Tomorrow is another day."

She closed the door firmly behind her. I was alone with a bed for the first time in my life. This solid, imposing piece of furniture with its well-polished walnut posts looked like a bed used by a married couple. My imagination, my intuition and the atmosphere all around where it sat imposingly in the middle of the room made me think that its occupants' nights weren't always much fun.

I slipped between the sheets in my new pyjamas, feeling somewhat overawed. I tried not to make the base creak, but to be the extra guest huddled up in the silence and unnoticed. I couldn't get rid of the idea that I was out of place in that bed and in that house. Besides, an old woman was looking at me like an interloper over on the commodious but handsome chest of drawers, beside a yellowed orange-blossom coronet under a glass dome. Her gaze was pitiless, distant, resigned and vacant, expressing a still-born life and years and years of good manners.

It was a grandmother who had gone to the hairdresser before being photographed. Beside that frame was another, which was more modern and seemed much closer to our time than the portrait of the ancestor with the soft wrinkles on her face. In that picture frame a girl was smiling shyly. She looked nothing like the other woman. There was little detail in the face to focus attention on the elegant wedding dress.

I got out of bed and tiptoed over, holding my breath at these two frozen moments of life which gave me more food for thought than I could cope with at that moment. The little portrait with the blurry face and small feet attracted me most. Behind the girl was the verandah at "Eden" just as we've always known it, without an extra flake of paint, all gilding, imitation oriental features, theatrical Arabian balconies with iron railings and trompe-l'oeil columns. In spite of appearances, that photo was much older than the portrait of the old woman with the perm, and although there was no resemblance between them, I knew it was the same person who had been changed into some-one else by 50 years of life.

I stood barefoot for quite a few minutes before this altar of an unfulfilled life: the glass dome with its coronet of orange blossom, the wedding photo, the portrait of the grandmother. Even though it looked like a room for the living, they were all imprisoned in the connecting fabric of this room dedicated to death.

"Go to sleep!" Madame Henry had told me.

There was no chance of that. The grandmother of the picture was breathing in the dark beside me, eager to let me know how she was robbed of her life. Outside in the tall trees, the rain was now easing, and falling silent, but the moisture was still lying there in the branches of the cedars.

I'd completely stopped thinking about myself and bemoaning my plight. I was totally concentrated on those three objects on the chest of drawers: the orange blossom coronet under the glass dome and the two portraits in their frames. Ridiculous though it may seem, I was longing to make up a story around those three objects.

As I was coming into the room, I'd had time to notice at the head of the bed a wooden crucifix with a carved holy water basin containing an olive twig. I turned on the bedside lamp to make sure. In the light I could see that it was a dry, old, twisted bit of olive covered in dusty cobwebs. The last hand that had put it there many years ago had trembled with the thought that for her the light of day was weighed, measured and divided up.

I had no chance of sleeping, but it was also a night when I had no thought of pleasuring myself. Life was crowding in on me with its questions, making me aware of the awful gulf between the way the world appears to an individual and the way it really is.

I could hear the grandmother's slippered feet slowly and carefully dragging over the carpet, then the desperate effort she had to make to climb into the ridiculously high bed.

The sudden realization of nothingness, of ceasing to exist, which must have struck that person, and which I would come to one day, made me feel small and insignificant. I promised myself I'd die at 40!

How could people sleep? Why weren't they continually kept awake by the unrelenting fear of the future that leads only to death? How could they not be conscious every night of how short the distance is between birth and nothingness?

All that was suddenly wiped from my mind, like chalk from a slate, as my attention was switched elsewhere. I'd just heard the loud, sharp click of a key turning in a lock and then a door shutting without any effort to do it quietly. A springy step passed by my bedroom and faded down the long corridor. A latch was lifted, quietly this time, but I heard no sound of a door being opened or shut. A honey smell filtered through into the room. It was Lucky Strike, the very soul of America.

I was as taut as a bowstring, straining my ears in the silence. It's an understatement to say that I held my breath: I drew it out so carefully and for so long that I wouldn't let it go down into my lungs.

I heard a dull sound I knew very well. I heard it from my father when he went to bed exhausted and let his belt drop on the floor. A thump followed as Victor's body hit a bed in the dark. Then nothing more except the rain on the cedars and the slow, regular thumping of my heart. I was pressed against the smooth sheets on the mattress, the first real one I'd lain on in my life, learning that poverty is not a matter of destitution but of feeling excluded from happiness. I knew where Victor's body had stretched out and what he was in the act of possessing in such a casual and familiar way.

The wall was too thick for me to make out any nuances of that act, but my inner ear made it up as it went along and that was enough to lead me to perdition.

Suddenly I was gripped by fear as a sound, different from anything I could have imagined and with the fierce intensity of a scream, shattered the silence. It was the scream of a body in free-fall being sucked into the abyss and giving a desolate farewell to life. It was the delighted cry of pain suddenly relieved; the weight of a great burden suddenly lifted and the joy of bursting into song as you stand there naked, luxuriating in the warmth of a new day. All that was contained in the one incredibly long, loud sound, like the belling of a stag. Was it a laugh or a groan? I was transfixed by that subtle blend of sounds rising and falling like a melody, now tense, now released, transmuting a joyful cry into a mad laugh.

I'd already heard that same modulation of a single note before, when it had changed me into a pillar of salt in the drawing room. It could give rise to a whole forest of appoggiaturas, but it was part of the structure of the cantata that had had such an effect on me. Here it was that something earthy, banal and beyond art suddenly burst forth. I didn't really understand it, as this was the first time in my life I'd heard a woman's orgasm.

A shiver of fear ran over my damp scalp; I was panting; my cock had shrunk to nothing between my thighs. I wouldn't have touched it for anything in the world. My mouth had fallen open hearing that new, long, complex cry, ready to simulate it and catch anything to eat or drink from it. But silence had returned, drowning the moment of that cry, already making me imagine it, reinvent it.

The rain whispering in the branches of the cedars was the only companion of that callow, idealistic country youth, destined never to understand, although the elements of the mystery had always been within his reach. Now, confronted with that litany, that manifestation of intense pleasure, he wavered between the amazement of having heard it once and the fear of never hearing it again.

With fists clenched and throat pulsating, I was torn between wonder and fear. I saw men and women as gods to whose games I would never be invited. The deep, intimate release that cry had just expressed was enough in my mind to explain the whole of life, and I'd come to the conclusion that I'd always be excluded from that fulfilment.

Some time after that cry – the clock had had enough time to strike two o'clock – I suddenly heard the most tranquil sound in the world come from the other side of the wall: Victor and Madame Henry had begun to snore in unison. A feeling of disappointed irony took over from the bitter unease that had moved me until that moment. This dual snoring cut the couple in the unknown bed down to the size of everyday married life. They snored like my father and mother, lying ordinary, innocent and relaxed in the hand of fate.

It seemed to me they should have stayed awake until death, he constantly amazed and she overcome, terrified and delighted at the gift nature had given her at birth: the ability to experience that intense joy. By snoring – and snoring so soon afterwards – they put themselves on the same level as the animal in heat – they ceased to think passion, they ceased to be amazed by it. They no longer has any distinguishing characteristic. They were part of the herd.

I was 16. I knew what a couple was, and yet I didn't really know. In my wild nights I never allowed myself to give in to pleasure, so I knew and yet I didn't really know what happens to two people after their bodies have separated and they take up their own thoughts again. The simple pulling aside of a bedspread creates a galactic space where one star travelling on its orbit and another moving away on another, without any control over their trajectories, can only say a brief goodbye.

I must have suddenly fallen asleep, with my fists still tight shut, bent over my cock in the position of the foetus who can predict what the world he must enter is like and can't foresee any good coming out of it.

A rooster was crowing loudly and, in spite of the curtains, brilliant sunlight was pouring through the slats in the shutters. It was a sparkling autumn day. Suddenly the curtains were pulled apart and the shutters banged as they were pushed open against the wall. Daylight flooded in. I closed my eyes.

"Get up!" Madame Henry said firmly. "The coffee's ready, but go to the bathroom first! I've put out a clean towel and a tooth-brush. Clean your teeth! Clean yourself all over! I don't want you to be smelling of anything but soap when I see you!"

She'd already closed the door. I hadn't had time to see anything more of her than a dark dressing gown patterned with red dragons, and her hair was loose, hiding her neck. Only the image of her lioness's stride remained in her wake.

"Go the bathroom first!" It was a big high-ceilinged room with another door leading to another bedroom. The high window looked out on the groves of trees. The bath itself was made of white marble. To me it looked like a tomb, for I'd never imagined that marble could be used for anything else than keeping the dead in the ground. It was the first time in my life I'd seen a bath. I went to the public baths every Saturday, but they had only showers. There was one here behind a curtain. It was attached to the wall above a shallow basin. I made the best use of it I could, because getting into the bath where Madame Henry's body often lay would seem like sacrilege. On the other hand, I took a good look at all the tubes and bottles lying on the shelf over the basin, as well as the bidet, which also looked as though it was made of marble. A damp towel had been casually thrown on it.

"Well!" Madame Henry called out. "Are you ready yet?"

A clock chimed dully at the end of a corridor, quite a few times, it seemed to me. I rushed back into the bedroom and grabbed my clothes. It had just struck eight and I was an hour late.

I called to her, "I'm sorry Madame, but I shan't have enough time!"

This formal language had come to me naturally, like homage I owed to this woman who was being so kind. But she stepped in front of me as I was about to rush out the door, totally preoccupied by my increasing lateness.

"You do have enough time and you'll come and drink your coffee! Everyone will understand after what happened yesterday. And if by chance they don't, you can count on me to say what's necessary!"

She was looking at me closely while I was doing my best to hide the fact that I'd heard her joyful cry the night before. But I was also drinking in her lovely unadorned face with its blue eyes. On those nights when I made use of her imaginary body, was I ever aware she also had a face? She was presenting it to me now quite naturally, either as an offering or an affront.

"Come!" she said, holding out her hand. "Come with me, you poor thing! You've lost your home."

"I've lost my books!" I moaned.

"Come! Come and drink your coffee! There are still so many things you haven't lost."

The kitchen was large and bright. It gave the impression of being organized by someone with a methodical mind. The space in the centre of the room was nearly all taken up with a heavy squat table with two solid benches which were difficult to get around. Through the window, in the distance, you could see the small building where I'd seen Madame Henry crying.

She was now sipping her coffee in gourmet fashion, her lips scarcely touching the rim of her fine china cup. Her blue eyes strayed towards that building. It was incredible how last night, which was such an unforgettable experience for me, could have left no trace on this woman's impassible features.

"Do you want any milk?"

She was buttering some bread for me with the same passive submission that women have always adopted with men since the beginning of time. I almost snatched the coffee pot from her hands.

"No! I don't want you to serve me!"

It's hard not to do or say something foolish when you feel a basic part of your character is under attack and beyond your control. That was a basic part of my character from earliest childhood. I could never bear anyone serving me, even my own mother.

"Don't you want me to serve you?"

I could see an expression of utter amazement in her wide-open eyes.

"No!" I said. "I don't!"

"You know you're not very easy to get on with, don't you?"

"No," I said. "I'm not very easy to get on with."

If ever there was the right moment to control my shifting gaze, look her full in the face for once and ask, "Why were you crying in that house the other evening?", it was now. But the moment had already passed. She pulled off my beret, which I'd taken great care to screw back on my head as soon as I'd had my shower.

"Really!" she said. "You'll never understand that you must take you hat off in the presence of a lady!"

Fortunately, barely a week ago I'd watched my mother repairing my sister's torn smock and picked up how to do it. As soon as I was alone, I'd managed with some difficulty to thread the needle, find a thimble in the workbox and firmly sew up the lining of my beret with little stitches right up to the opening on the side. I took a lot of trouble with it and it also struck me that I wouldn't be spending my 600 francs in a hurry or rereading Lucinde's letter.

"Really!" Madame Henry said again. "You don't bother whether people like you or not . . ."

She looked at me, restraining a smile so that it didn't look bitter.

"You see," she said, "you're not the only one who's late. I've missed seven o'clock mass and I haven't had time to go to the bakery. You're eating stale bread."

She gave me back my beret, scrunching it up for fun.

"You'll sleep here every night," she said, "until they find somewhere for you to live. You can come as soon as you finish work. You'll get your lunch at the school canteen."

She accompanied me to the hall while still sipping her coffee. A square pile of books took up a corner of the hall table, where she laid her hand.

"There you are!" she said. "There are fewer of them, but that's because the print is smaller and the pages are thinner, but they're all there. There's your beloved Saint-Simon! You can take them as soon as you have somewhere to put them. And don't bother about giving them back to me!"

"Oh Madame!" was all I could say.

Of all the things Madame Henry did for me, that was the most unforgettable. It still makes me weep today, with my heart so full of memories and so weighed down with the pain of being alone.

"Oh," she said, "don't imagine it's a gift! What you'll learn from that writer is to see people, everyone, as they really are. I'm not sure that will really help you to live."

She stopped speaking and very slowly sipped a little of her

coffee. Her lips moved carefully over the edge of her cup. I couldn't take my eyes off her, gazing at their shape, their colour and their fullness. There was the slightest hint of down, darker at the roots, in the shape of a circumflex accent which accentuated their sensuality. Seeing her lips, I no longer needed to look at her legs or imagine her breasts.

She put the cup down gently on the saucer sitting on the edge of the table.

"Nor that it will help you to love," she concluded.

VIII

IN THE MORNING, THE AVAILABLE FORCES IN THE TOWN
had combined their efforts to put our lives back together again as
best they could. There was a cheap, ugly, yellow-brick building
simply called the big house, which had just been repainted. It had
been built at the beginning of the century by the Compagnie
d'Alais, de Froges et de la Camargue to shelter the human wreck-
age that streamed in from all over Europe hungry and looking
for work. The toilet was at the end of the corridor, but there was
running water in the kitchen. They gave us a three-roomed flat
on the third floor, which belonged to a man who had just died of
silicosis and whose family had suddenly gone back to Piedmont.
The smell of the sulphur that had been burnt in the dead man's
room still caught in your throat.

Manosque didn't like the people who lived in the big house.
They came from outside. If they spoke French – some of them with
difficulty – they didn't understand our dialect. The Compagnie
d'Alais, de Froges et de la Camargue owned our local mine, the

Gaude mine. It had never been racist, welcoming all those poverty had driven from their homelands. Although the administrators of the company paid low wages, they salved their consciences by saying it was still ten times more than they'd have got in their own countries, in Spain, Calabria or Herzegovina. The yellow house had been built to charge them a modest rent, which was taken out of their wages. For the moment, however, they were not asking anything from us. Our misfortune earned us some respite and anyway we were the only French people in the building. They must have thought that this was certainly worth a few months' rent.

On every floor there were gorgeous teenage girls talking in foreign languages. They were reed-slim and swayed their hips as though they still had the baskets and jugs on their heads that they carried in their native lands. They smiled at me at first, then withdrew any sign of interest when they noticed I went down the corridors with my nose in a book or dreaming of 30-year-old women.

When there are not too many poor people in a community, solidarity works well. All sorts of useful things flowed into the yellow house: chairs, a table that one of Bébé Fabre's odd-job men delivered on his cart with a very bad grace. Having a roof over his head himself and a room to sleep in, he took a dim view of having to do some work for people who hadn't either, no matter for how short a time. Madame Alarthéus took three beds from her lofts, thus assuring life-long loyalty from my mother, who gave up her other three households so that she could work for her benefactress alone. My mother had long wanted to polish Madame Alarthéus' furniture. It was so beautiful!

The firm of Guigues et Chabrier delivered a coal-fired heating stove; Carnetier from the Grand Bazaar general store sent blankets; on the advice of his wife, my brother's boss opened up the wardrobe where his poor mother kept her sheets and invited mine to help herself.

At dusk Henri Gardon knocked on the door carrying a kilo of his good coffee to help revive our spirits. He slipped it into my father's hands through the half-open door, putting a finger to his lips to silence our thanks, he was so afraid of appearing ostentatious. My mother immediately got out the mill and began to grind the coffee. When we tasted the flavour in our drinking glasses, we all had Mona Lisa smiles on our faces.

However, on the fourth day, I experienced the weakness of human nature at Albert's bakery. As my father wasn't paid until Saturday, we bought our daily three kilos of bread on account. That is, we and Albert each kept a little notebook where we wrote down the price of the bread we owed each day. Every Tuesday my mother went to settle the account.

On Sunday, when the cream puffs were brought into the shop, Lucinde put a hand on my shoulder and in spite of the people waiting to be served, she drew me towards the kitchen door. Holding out the notebook, she said to me,

"There you are! Tell your mother not to bother coming on Tuesday. I've cancelled it all. And cakes for this week are a gift from me."

For the first time she gave me a kindly look. There was even the hint of a smile at the corner of her lips. But for me the real prize was something I'd lusted after for so long: that hand lingering on my shoulder, almost stroking it, but not quite daring to.

I went away with my head ringing like a bell. I raised my bag to my nose and breathed in the smell of our daily bread transformed by charity.

I imagined Albert and Lucinde, who perhaps had not talked to each other since the night of Patrocles' murder, except for the bare essentials about work. On this occasion, they must have spoken to each other.

"Have you thought about Pierrot's bread?"

"Yes. I've crossed it out of the notebook."

"That's good. And on Sunday, make them a present of the cream puffs."

That, or something like it, is what they must have said after the disaster that had taken everything we had.

At that moment I had a wild desire to quickly undo the lining in my beret and take out Lucinde's letter: "My darling . . . Albert will be in the bakehouse . . . ", tear it into four pieces and let it fall on to the swiftly flowing water filling the gutter along the footpath.

I tried to do it, but the cross stitch I'd sewed around the leather lining wouldn't give way. It resisted my efforts long enough for my conscious mind to think again, to advise me against it. It whispered that if I ever wanted to win Lucinde's heart, I'd have to offer her that letter as I reminded her of this moment when her hand on my shoulder had meant so much more than the bread she gave us.

The act of ripping out the lining, which I'd begun, thought seriously about, and then abandoned, all took place in total silence. Although it was intangible, I knew there was a power to act, but it remained uncommitted and untapped. I maintained my non-judgmental silence, like that of a judge without a case, though I was aware it was encircling and trapping me. Even today, that silence weighs on me still, condemns me and brings me down. That was the moment when my free will failed and I chose remorse for the rest of my life.

But it was also because I was so amazed. The remarkable sang-froid with which this couple accepted their crime, so naturally and consistently, just wasn't in keeping with the human kindness shown in what they had just done for us. How could charity co-exist with infamy in the souls of these simple people?

This was certainly a time for God to recognize His own and for me to reflect on my first lesson in life's mysteries.

Everyone in the town felt the solitude that descended on all the inhabitants. No more flocks passed by. Water washed out the fires under the brandy stills and, in the woods, it soaked the pine branches we used for our home fires. The distillers let it be known that they were shutting up shop.

It seemed essential to all of us to keep close together. On the fourth day after our disaster, the rain started to fall as before. Everyone at Albert's complained that the bread was soft.

"If only we still had that to rely on!" moaned Bessolote.

Auguste Faux gave us worrying details about the mayor's health. His bronchitis was turning into asthma. The bread that came from the oven to the shop under a waterproof tarpaulin no longer had its crisp crust and delicious wheaten smell. Only Jacques le Beau, who was celebrating the arrival of his third grandson, found the energy to hum "The Old Women of Our Village".

Madame Henry arrived back from church cursing creation. "*Un tron de Dieu la cure!*" she swore. "The devil take this rain!"

It was her morning greeting, but she suddenly saw me. She said nothing, watching me out of the corner of her eye. Then, for the first time, I saw her face break into a smile without any hint of sarcasm. In spite of the dull morning, which was very slow to lift, her complexion was pink and warm. Her bust emerged from a ruby satin collar like a flower petal, pinned down in the front between her breasts by a cameo brooch. It was tight-fitting and revealing. My throat went dry as I looked at her discreetly but lustfully.

She got ready to go out the side door, following close behind me. Our umbrellas were no match for the guttering in the lane, as the roof valleys overflowed with a deafening noise.

"Come this evening!" Madame Henry whispered. "I'll play you the Bach cantata."

She didn't wait for my reply. I watched her hurry off in the downpour, not very well protected by her umbrella. The water dripped from each of the spokes, splashing on to her skirt and little by little revealing the rounded contours of her lower back moving under the shiny wet material.

She cursed the overflowing gutters and the town council that should have been prepared for such an eventuality. She was exactly as we always described her, feared her, revered her. And I just followed this slow, regal, undulating movement of Aphrodite's bottom, beginning down at ankle level, then hardening the curve of her calves and finally radiating out like a rising sun in an undulation that for me was something like an earthquake. As I saw her from behind, the woman assumed the dimensions of a calm goddess.

I spent the day clearing the iron gratings over the drains with a thin broom and a rickety rake. Waves of intense anxiety made me feel sick.

When the clock struck five o'clock and the mist already prevented me from seeing the rubbish, I'd almost managed to free all the drain outlets in my area. The water rushed down the gutters. I knew it was a labour of Sisyphus and that tomorrow everything would be overflowing again.

I went home to the vast yellow building with its noise of happy children, clinging on to the bannister like an old man as I climbed the stairs. I was short of breath and I could hear my heart beating. Normally one who looked forward to that time, thinking of mashed potatoes or pasta with cheese, that evening I'd lost my appetite completely. I was churning with apprehension, as though rolling on a sickening swell at sea, more dead than alive.

When I said I wasn't hungry, there was a commotion. It had never happened before. My mother, my father, my sister (my brother was practising with the municipal band), everyone rushed with anxious cries to feel my forehead. They wanted to put me to bed and tuck me in. I shouted no, I had to go out!

I was now in a double room with a bed of my own. There was a soap box at the head of the bed, with a book always lying on it. That day, for the first time ever, I looked at Saint-Simon with a jaundiced eye.

I changed my clothes slowly, including my underpants and socks. I went to the kitchen sink to brush my teeth, which always earned me the admiration of the family, for since that first day when I'd slept at Madame Henry's house, I was the only one at home who did it. I made a careful inspection of my fingernails and toenails. My beret was new but I still felt ashamed of it, although this was hardly the moment to leave it off. When my hair flopped down on each side of my head, it made me look really stupid.

I went out dressed in my Sunday best from top to toe. Outside in the street, everything seemed to be moaning and groaning: the drainpipes, the trees, the gutters and the des Rates stream. A high, damp wind was weaving gloomily through the high foliage, shaking down showers of raindrops from the leaves. But my throat was dry as I walked underneath them. It was certainly not from any secret, erotic thought, though heaven knows, I was fond enough of them.

At the Boulevard Mirabeau, I was greeted by an oppressive silence, in spite of the usual sounds from the natural world. All that could be heard was a milkman's horn calling clients at the top of the Rue d'Aubette.

The green iron gate, which was permanently open at the main entrance to "Eden", led me on to the main path leading to the house. It had almost become a habit with me to make my way down it, pull the bell at the entrance and cry, "It's me!", then go to the grandmother's bedroom. That room was so much the embodiment of her simple life that it warned me against too much excitement. But this evening was different. Madame Henry hadn't asked me to spend another night under her roof, she'd said, "Come this evening. I'll play you the Bach cantata."

That phrase was the reason for my nervousness. I knew that something was going to happen. Something was going to upset the well-established order of my existence, shamelessly devoted to the imagination and masturbation. This time, my expectations held no prospect of happiness or hope. I was trembling as I pulled the awkward bell that always scraped the skin on my fingers. Once I'd rung, I went in. The friendly darkness softened by the light from lamps lit elsewhere in the house welcomed me into the entrance hall. There was also a subtle, indefinable smell that must have been in that house for more than a hundred years. It bespoke gentle ways, peace of mind gained through resignation to an unremarkable and uneventful life, men without passion and women without hope. All that seemed to be contained in that perfume which wasn't yet Madame Henry's, but to which hers would be added, as every thousand years or so a new layer of alluvial deposits raises up the bottom of a lake full of historical remains.

"Hurry up and come in!" an assertive voice called out to me.

I opened the door that led from the hall to the drawing room. The room was dark apart from the bright firelight. The music I heard that first day was playing softly in the background. It wove its way from my anxiety to a part of my brain where I knew it would last longer than that futile feeling of nervousness, so much longer, in fact as long as I lived. This time it wasn't coming from the gramophone with the orange horn, which had so fascinated me that first day. A strange shape on a low stool occupied a corner of the room. It was a player I'd seen in the window of Beuvin's piano shop. The cantata came from it through a loud-speaker with two wooden notes across the front of the mysterious cloth-covered hole. The movement of the flames reflected in the curves of that piece of furniture seemed to accompany the rhythm of the music.

I thought first of all that no-one was there in the darkness and that Madame Henry was somewhere else, for the sofa and the armchairs on each side facing the hearth were empty. I noticed the carpet in front of the fireplace. It was the largest object in the drawing room, and the few times I'd been in here, I'd never dared set foot on that rug. It was bright red, bordered with two large blue leaves entwined around the edge, leaving the red centre plain. A huge no-man's-land seemed to stretch between me and that carpet.

I finally noticed Madame Henry in the flickering firelight. She was sitting, almost crouching, with her arms extended over the top of the sofa cushions. She was dressed in dark red against the bright red of the carpet. The close-fitting top had a lot of small buttons, with the top ones left undone. It enclosed her breasts, but gave the impression that it would take little to free them from their constricting collar. Her feet were bare and she was wearing a pair of very finely pleated Indian-style trousers which came in at the ankle. They were also dark red.

I stood at the edge of the carpet like a swimmer who dares not take the plunge. We were both silent, with only Bach to form a link between us. I was painfully aware of everything she was and everything I wasn't. Then I did the only thing which seemed to me likely to bring Madame Henry around to recognizing what sort of thing I desired: I took off my shoes. In the shadows, where I was standing, I had the impression that it was the first time she'd turned her head towards me since I came in.

Her arm moved across the firelight and her hand was extended towards me. She didn't say a word. That gesture was enough. It invited me to lie down on the carpet. She threw me one of the sofa cushions. The only time I ever stretched out, first on my mattress and now on my bed, was when I was worn out with hard work. I'd never dreamed of women anywhere but out in the country, in a haystack or the *groussan* under the tall broom bushes on Sainte-Roustagne. Even in my wildest sexual fantasies, I'd never thought of a carpet and I had no idea how to get on to it without looking foolish. It occurred to me I should take off my jacket with the gold buttons and lay it over the arm of a chair. That done, it was easier to crawl to the cushion she'd thrown me and finally just to let myself sink down silently on my elbow, as I did when I was going to read in the sunshine beside the castle tower.

I was little more than a metre away from Madame Henry and could see her quite well in spite of the dim light. Both her presence and Bach's music drew me out of my normal state. Now I dared look at her. Time and time again I was tempted to speak, but time and time again fate, shame or something deep in my nature combined to stifle any word in my throat before it could be uttered.

Outside, the ever-present rain added its beat to the music, emphasizing the importance of that day and that moment. The extraordinary revelation of my future was about to unfold, bringing light to my darkness and filling me with wonder.

I slowly accustomed myself to the carpet; I accustomed my heartbeat to the still presence of the woman in red, the woman whose top with the little buttons imprisoned the breasts I dreamed about, as the corolla firmly holds a bud about to burst.

I also saw something standing on the parquet floor at the edge of the carpet: it was an ordinary pitcher with blackish-brown and green curves reflecting the dancing firelight; a pitcher made to be used, to be picked up at any minute, taken to the fountain and filled; a simple, unpretentious pitcher that I could easily have put down beside my birch broom.

A bouquet of asters had been placed in the pitcher, with the flowers leaning over the sides. You could see from the colours of the sparse foliage that they were the last of the season. The chrysanthemum smell they gave out clashed with Madame Henry's perfume but slowly became part of it. Everything had been planned to make the moment unique.

I understood then that Madame Henry had allowed me to get in tune with her mind, that she trusted mine, and that henceforth we both should do without the usual things that help two people to come together, the intermediaries, and above all, the words. I should be ready to breathe the more rarefied air of the level to which she invited me to rise.

I was so afraid of doing the wrong thing that I was tempted at that moment to abandon gestures as well. I would stay there all night without moving, with my head resting on my hand and my elbow on the carpet, taming my desire, making it resigned to inaction (which wouldn't be difficult as I was so afraid) and, after a long while, in the cold light of dawn, to leaving the woman who was waiting for me.

Suddenly the music stopped and was replaced by a monotonous scratching that could be heard above the crackling of the fire and the sound of the rain on the cedars in the garden. Madame Henry was suddenly standing between myself and the hearth. She had got up to raise the needle and turn the record over. Her trousers billowed out around her legs in the shape of a marvellous red tulip. The flat pleats opened out like an accordion and, just as a wave casts a silken sheen over the surface of the waters, through that ripple of red I could make out Madame Henry's legs standing still, straight and strong. I could follow their line from top to bottom right down to her bare feet, and from bottom to top right up to the solid shadow of her body hiding the place where they joined.

The tracks on those old records lasted for five minutes. The cantata was on three records with six tracks. I'd arrived in the middle of the first. When Madame Henry came back and stretched out on the carpet after the wonderful sight of those trousers billowing out around her legs, we still had five to listen to, which meant she had to get up five times to turn the record over.

I wish all men could have the almost religious experience of the expectation I lived through with my throat dry and my heart beating wildly. I half feared, half hoped that each time she whom I secretly called Hortense would notice my agitation and the effect she had on me when she bent over to stoke the fire as she passed.

I was glued to my carpet, head on hand and elbow digging into the big blue leaf. I could never hope to guess what the lady in red expected me to do to prolong the spell and make it infinitely subtle, but not so much so that it would fade away like a vision.

I noticed then that when Madame Henry had come back and stretched out at the foot of the sofa, she had lain down at an angle and her body was now parallel to mine. She had piled up three cushions under her neck so that she could see both the fire and the asters. Her hand with the fingers curved like a petal had come to rest on the carpet between the two of us.

I realized that she must also be feeling the fear sweeping through me. The proud lady with the commanding voice who thrust open the bakery door to show she'd arrived, was now quaking inside like me, a 17-year-old whose five senses were all in turmoil. Self-esteem was her only safeguard, but it was no longer strong enough to repress a shiver that had nothing to do with the autumn cold.

In the middle of the third track of the cantata, Madame Henry reduced the distance between us even further by crawling towards me, without any particular hope or intention, almost resignedly. Then, on my instep, I felt the almost timid touch of a hand that didn't dare make it a caress.

I lay there like the trunk of a felled tree, an erection being so far from my thoughts that I doubted whether I had a cock at all. I felt empty, eviscerated; I was scarcely breathing, yet unaware of it. I didn't even dare look at the hand moving gently over my ankle. I scarcely dared to imagine that this whole event was taking place for me. I'd always looked death in the face, but from that moment it was wiped from my ever-present obsessions.

The Bach cantata rose to meet that breathless pitch of emotion. The choir sang on, creating eternity for me. As it existed outside of that moment, how could Madame Henry's hand moving up and down between my ankle and calf make me understand what she wanted?

As I write this 60 years later, that hand returned to dust so long ago is more eternal to me than the stars. I look at my ankle, still alive and smooth (it's one of the parts of the human body that ages least quickly), and I evoke that hand and call to it from the depths of my sadness. Now I stretch out my own hand to meet it, but my longing finds only empty space and even Bach has faded with time.

While the fire crackled and the cedars moaned in the south wind, Madame Henry was moving her expert, delicate hand over my skin. When the record stopped in the middle of the third movement, she dared not stop and get up. You could hear the needle scratching the wax.

I suddenly wanted to say the name Victor and destroy everything, allowing me to escape. When you've dreamt of something for so long and it suddenly crystallizes, you feel a panic that totally disorientates you. Victor's name, pronounced on purpose, would have been the ultimate weapon against the spell that was being woven, but I'd have defaced a great work of art, sullied heaven, ruined fate's masterpiece carefully worked out for me. I couldn't. I hadn't the right. My sense of the comic was quite dead.

So I contented myself with half sitting up and gazing at the face in front of me, which looked like an enigmatic mask with its closed eyes. It was a beautiful face, ripe as a ripe fruit, its lips scarcely moving as if to drink in awakening desire. Her features were still, waiting for me and sure of their charm.

I murmured, "Don't you feel that everything is suddenly strange?"

It seemed as though a little sigh preceded her answer.

"Yes, isn't it?" she said.

She opened her eyes, turned towards me and her arms ended their long wait, rising towards my head then encircling my shoulders. Suddenly I felt between us the breasts held in the red tulip of her bodice by so many buttons. They were being offered to me, thrust at me. I was reaching an awkward hand towards those fascinating buttons when I heard the sound of button-holes quietly popping open one after the other, until the last one released the marvel of those soft welcoming breasts so close to my face.

She must have sensed my impatient attempt at help, which could well have broken the spell, so she had done it herself. She immediately offered her breasts to my lips with a shame-lessness long held in check.

"There!" she said. "Drink them! Love them with the rest of me! You must really love them, love them as they want to be loved!"

I reached out my hands, barely touching them, not yet daring to touch them.

"Hortense!" I said ecstatically.

The whole of her was there in her breasts: they were the outward manifestation of her inner self. They knew I'd been waiting for them for so long and that I would be the only one who had the power and patience to recall them endlessly until my dying day.

My erection, shamelessly pressed against her legs, let her know the urgency of my desire and the wildness of my heart beating against her breasts.

Then she seized my beret almost roughly and sent it flying beyond the carpet, beyond the firelight, out of reach. I was about to let out a horrified cry when Hortense stopped it before it left my lips. For the first time in my life, a woman's searching tongue was trying to enter me, filling my mouth, saying everything our silence had been trying to express from the beginning of the evening.

Now I understood why the Hindu gods I found so fascinating had so many arms and hands. I didn't have enough to touch Hortense where she wanted to be touched. I was terribly limited in my responses. Not even my night dreams had ever suggested that one day real life would demand more imagination than they could ever summon up. Nevertheless, I still had the impression of not being worthy of the delights showered upon me; life had made a mistake in offering them to me and would soon drag me from this feast in a flurry of outrage.

Hortense's body more than filled the expectations of my arms and my hands. I would never have thought that a woman could fill the hollow of a man to overflowing, press herself everywhere from head to foot, trying to become one with the other and fail to do it. If we wanted to feel the whole length of our bodies, we couldn't stay lying down without the constraint of having to rest against something. So we got up, she clutching my tangled hair with both hands and me with my fingers joined just below her waist, not daring to go lower than the two dimples in the small of her back.

And so it was standing up, clinging to each other with no support, that the storm in our minds and bodies was calmed, coordinated and subdued, so that it would last a long time, and I made love for the first time in my life.

Deep inside my ecstatic mind there still lurked a tiny worry, which gave a certain spice to my happiness: it was my beret flung in a corner somewhere out of sight and out of reach. But I was already thinking of sacrificing this mystery to Hortense.

I was ready to reveal it to her later when we were capable of thinking of anyone else again.

If I'd only known, if there was any way I could have known, I'd have burned the beret and the letter in the first heap of leaves I came across as I went out into the grey dawn. But fate had put a black blindfold over my eyes before making me spin around like a top, as in blind man's buff.

Ah, the first morning! And it was still the same one. I'd gone back to my bedroom at about four o'clock. I remember that a huge dull red shooting star with a round curving tail had made me clap my hands to my head with shock as I went out into the black night as it was rising. It also stopped me in my tracks in the middle of the roadway. I was sure that perhaps I wouldn't remember my first night of love, alas, but that I'd never forget that shooting star. I may even have been bending my knees so as to prostrate myself for the end of the world when the meteor died in the silent night.

I couldn't go to sleep. I spent the three hours left before I had to get up sniffing my skin, surprised because Hortense's smell was already evaporating. At seven I leaped out of bed, grabbed the bag as I passed and rushed to Albert's bakery. Jacques le Beau, Auguste Faux, Bessolote and Madame Donnet were already there. All these placid people, who make up the majority of people in the world, didn't even look at me when I said good morning. Lucinde, thin-lipped and frowning, was calculating the price of the bread as she did every morning. I hoped that she would be able to see I was a new person since last night, but she was in a bad mood as usual and just looked through me.

How could she get up this morning without having experienced what I'd just experienced? She knew what it was like, so why didn't she break free from the shackles of the life she was leading and run to a lover? How could she prefer this counter, this till, these endless boring calculations on scraps of paper? Tomorrow I'd return the note to Lucinde unconditionally, for I'd calmly examined all her charms and they no longer had any attraction for me. I no longer desired Lucinde. But I did indeed think of Hortense's gently curving belly and all those parts of her I'd touched. How would I dare to see her again?

Suddenly the door on the bakehouse side was pushed open by a firm hand. Madame Henry appeared at the top of the three steps, her missal held in one gloved hand and her reticule on her arm, giving that exasperated sigh, her usual morning greeting. I was right in the middle of her line of vision and even today I can't really define the look she gave me. She still embodied all the happiness on earth for me, as though I was still lusting after her with no hope of success. But my face was as expressionless as hers, as cold and indifferent as she could wish. We were both natives of the Basses-Alpes and as hard as each other. Secrets were safe with us; our emotions were kept below the surface. The triumphant look in Hortense's eyes was directed briefly not at me but at Lucinde, which is what I was watching for. I witnessed the extraordinary phenomenon of one woman sensing the privation of another.

Her free hand was clutching her first communion missal and she had just come from the silence of the church at seven in the morning, having offered up the unworthiness of her person to the Lord. Yet futile triumph emanated from her whole person. While she was wildly happy as I was, even though I had nothing to offer the Lord, the face she presented to us expressed nothing but boredom. In her eyes, the world was not a more beautiful place because she'd just made love. I contemplated this mystery with a clarity of mind that gave me no joy, but unfortunately I could find no arguments to put forward against it.

She'd said, "Tomorrow!"

I'd replied with a hint of doubt, thinking of Victor, "Tomorrow?"

She'd repeated, "Tomorrow!"

There was no arguing with that.

The wonder of it was too strong. I wasn't capable of observing her; I was hardly able to observe myself. There was that precise moment when I was finally able to crawl over the parquet floor to retrieve my beret. She watched me attentively as I did so. Before saying, "till tomorrow", she'd commented,

"Are you in such a hurry to cover your hair?"

"Well . . . No. Why?"

"You went about it so eagerly."

And so that evening, before moving on to the carpet where she was waiting for me, this time dressed in a black kimono with a pattern of entwined dragons, I took the precaution of taking off my beret and hanging it on the stand in the hall, next to the garden hats.

If Hortense wanted to inspect it, she would have to walk over there naked, offering me the sight of something she probably considered an imperfection. She had an hour-glass figure with a small waist and full, supple hips, and her flesh moved in slow waves. Although you couldn't notice it, her breasts were slightly low, like a comma on a well-written text. I'm sure she thought her body less than perfect and wouldn't make the mistake of walking in front of me without something covering her swaying hips. So there was nothing to worry about as far as Lucinde's letter was concerned.

The big Tibetan carpet had become our special place. She invited me on to it with open hands, then on her knees. She had a way of making fires which burned quietly, both enriching our shadows and, with flickering firelight, making our faces and bodies much more beautiful than they really were. These fires also gave even more life to the carpet. The designer had made a border of only two huge blue leaves in a stylized impression of an abundance of foliage.

I wasn't sure I'd remember what I felt in Hortense's arms: I've only ever cared about what the other person was feeling; as for me, orgasm has only been something superfluous, a nuisance. But I was sure I'd never forget the blue oak leaf embroidered against the weave of the carpet.

She tipped back her rosy face when she offered her breasts to me one after the other, and as I looked at her closed eyelids, I tried to work out who she really was: the much decorated heroine in the cemetery at Patrocles' funeral? The detestable middle-class woman who huffed and puffed as she pushed open the bakery door? The grande dame who had read enough of Saint-Simon to forbid me to venture into that territory and then, when my persistence forced her to admit defeat, finally gave me the books? Or could she be the one I didn't know at all: the devout parishioner who quietly entered our prim and proper church by the little door in Rue Voland to admit to heaven knows what sin? But then what could be considered a sin by this widow who always gave the appearance of an enraged Fury in pursuit of a crime? But more mysterious still, she could be the woman who cried out with joy on the night I heard her with Victor. With me she didn't cry out; there were only gentle moans and murmurs of delight.

And yet she was always the same person. I knew she had a

scattering of tiny pink warts where her armpits began and so many beauty spots I still couldn't place where they all were on her skin. When her body was above me, her slight plumpness creased softly on the side like ripples on the surface of the water. I'd longed for that body from seeing it some time ago in a painting called *The Three Graces* on a calendar. Hortense was just like one of those women.

But the magic of her breasts soon beguiled my critical faculties. Her breasts didn't match her haughty character. They were soft and defenceless, and when I filled my mouth with them, drinking them in against my tongue, I felt Hortense's vigilance melt away. It was then I knew that she was a poor soul, just as I was, and that we had only one refuge from our fears, which was to control the moment we delayed as long as possible, so that we could count all our pleasures as you count the beads on a rosary. Then she never forgot to add her breasts to my prayer. She offered them to me one after the other, teaching me to fit my hands to their curves. To please her I had to remember the way the potter, who died last year, used to stroke long-fingered hands over the sides of his pitchers. I learned from this gesture and from the outline of the bones in his fingers standing out under the tightly stretched skin, as the gentle pressure on the live clay became a virtual caress.

When the hollow of my hands knew how to cradle her offering until she was no longer aware that they were only a man's hands, an expression of exultation spread over her lips and she spoke her pleasure over and over again. Although I didn't always hear them, her tenderest whispers were really words of thanks to her breasts.

I'm sitting here with my pen in the air, for apart from the wind still blowing in other cedars, my memory is as frozen as an erotic fresco on the walls of a ruined house in Pompeii. And yet our passion was all movement, from one moment to the next, yet finding every means possible to delay the imminent approach of the orgasm we braced ourselves for and which spread through all our senses. She struggled and pulled away from me so that she wouldn't experience the whole sensation, as if she didn't want me to know everything about her, while still creating the illusion that there was nothing I didn't know. It was as though she'd entrusted a secret to someone for ever and it was none of my concern, for she never gave me that great shout of release I'd heard when she was with Victor. She pressed me to her as hard as she could and I had the impression she always expected something of me that I couldn't give her.

She'd forgotten, or never known, that on the night when Victor came to her while I was sleeping in the next bedroom, that the walls could be thin and I could still be awake. I had an advantage over her: I knew how she came with someone else. It's unusual for a lover to know that and be able to compare.

It was a comparison that made me infinitely sad. From that moment I could no longer believe in the world of pleasure. I was always sceptical and I've never found any transport of passion sincere enough to release me from that doubt. The gift of acute observation with which I've been endowed has the awful consequence of killing feeling.

Nonetheless, I received an obvious denial of this the following evening, although I've always thought it had been given to me as a precaution. At that moment I felt I'd never understand anything about women.

We were past the stage of wildly throwing ourselves at each other. We were teasing each other, panting with the urgency of it, tirelessly adding to our embraces with our lips pressed together and my hands caressing her breasts. I remember the carpet, always our arena, the shadows cast by the fire making our silhouettes seem huge on the walls and ceilings. The shadows deepened the mystery of Hortense's thick pubic hair, offered to me as she lay spread out over the cushions, for her refinement of suggestion challenged anything my most lascivious dreams were capable of inventing.

"There's something you haven't dared try yet . . . " Come here! Bring your face closer. Kneel down! Think of what you see as my mouth. Do to it what you usually do to that!"

Then she arched her back and offered that amazing forest to my lips. I couldn't take my eyes off it and put all the humble devotion I paid to my lover into my new caress. My ignorance was slowly dispelled by the slight movement of my head made by the pressure first of her two hands then of one. The words of rapturous approval she uttered became more and more difficult to understand. I'd kept my eyes open to increase my delight by the royal sight of her secret place. Then, on the crest of that dark promontory arched like the string of a bow, I saw the diamond Hortense wore on her ring finger. The finger wearing it advanced slowly between me and the gleaming pink shrine so close to my lips. The ring on that straight finger was at my eye-level, then gently and repeatedly hit me on the side of my nose. I opened my eyes wide to see everything. My lips and tongue ceased what they were doing.

"Oh! Talk to me!" she whispered. "Urge me on!"

She kept gently turning her index finger on that mysterious tip I longed to see and touch. Her fingers were parted like flower petals. They were not in contact with her body, apart from the mounds on the palm of her hand that brushed lightly over her pubic hair.

I felt like lying on the ground and weeping: I'd never reach that virtuosity, never have the gift of that delicate touch. Her hand and finger moved like a bow over a string or a swallow skimming the surface of the water.

"Talk to me! Please! Talk to me!"

I whispered words of encouragement I'd never dare say out loud. Some of these were words you always think, but don't dare say; words that timid folk who utter them use, unthinking, to exorcise their mysterious and unreasoning fear of pure pleasure; words that make us remember our beginnings in the mire; words that electrify our writhing bodies and make them finally ready to give in; words between the two of us which we'll forget, and be able to look at each other at last, completely openly and sincerely, having given everything we had to give.

My eyes and all my senses followed her efforts to reach a pitch that made her first cry out almost angrily.

"Keep talking to me!"

I had to whisper to her everything my erotic dreams had suggested to me since childhood. I was exasperated by her resistance. I was holding her tightly by the most intimate parts of her body when I felt them start to contract. The tip of my tongue went towards her but she pulled away wildly.

Suddenly I heard that wild cry. That long scream of release from pain ending in a cry of joy was terrifying. I was hearing it properly for the first time and was not about to forget it.

I understood then that Hortense couldn't get the joy she expressed at the top of her voice from another man, neither from Victor nor from me. It was herself she had to thank for that release; it was her own skill she was celebrating, her intimate knowledge of herself that neither of us could reach.

In my naïveté I thought that was all I had to learn about

this woman, and now I knew everything about her. Nevertheless, I took a while to realize it wasn't just one orgasm that made her happy, however great it might be, but that she took enormous delight in a whole series of little excitements. And there were deeper mysteries I was yet to discover.

One day when she was pleasuring herself with me, or rather on top of me, with my arms stretched out above me, pressing against her breasts firmly cupped in the palms of my hands, she suddenly burst into tears, and collapsed in a heap on top of me, sobbing, no longer thinking of me or even aware I was there. My body and my presence no longer existed for her. She wept uncontrollably, like a lost soul, with those deep sobs I'd heard one evening behind the shutters in the little house in the trees.

I was dumbfounded: it was the first time in my life someone had drenched me with tears. It was like a flood. Her tears fell from the point of her chin on to my shoulders, trickling down past my armpits to the carpet. I'd never have thought that a woman's face or eyes could fill with so many tears and overflow in such a stream.

The word grief seemed such a weak term to express what I witnessed. That day, on that carpet, I learned compassion. I suddenly realized it was quite out of place for me to confine myself to the ridiculous role of the conquering male in the face of a sorrow that cannot be assuaged. I was overcome with real pity and lay down beside her, taking her head in my hands and placing it against my shoulder. I didn't ask her what was wrong; I didn't question her; I simply stroked her cheek, her hair, her face, and gently kissed her eyelashes, moistening my lips at the source of her tears.

When she finally calmed down, without saying anything or speaking to me, I realized that if I wanted to continue living at her level, I had to remain silent and pay no attention to what I'd seen.

I don't know now, and I've never known, whether she had prepared any explanation in case I ever mentioned her tears. But the fact that I said not a word at the time helped to convince her that there was more to me than she thought, and to prepare the pit that would swallow her up.

IX

ON MONDAY SHE SAID TO ME, "DON'T COME TOMORROW. I'm not free."

I said nothing and went off. I'd taken my beret from the hat peg and it was firmly fixed on my head.

I hadn't climaxed. That's what I liked best: to leave my lover while I was still burning with desire for her. Being sated always left the worst memories.

Hortense still intrigued me with that lovely enigmatic smile, so different from the one she gave everyone else during the course of the day. I was the only one to have the privilege of the smile I now saw on her face. It was a subtle mixture of surprise and tenderness, duplicity and kindness, secretiveness and fear that I might finally find her out, finally know her.

How could she have been so naïve as not to know that her bedroom wall wasn't as discreet as she imagined? She must have taken me for someone totally insignificant if she thought I slept so soundly I didn't hear Victor come in.

She could have left it at "Don't come tomorrow", but like all liars she felt the need to add the lie, which hadn't actually been stated until then.

"Yes," she added, "my clairvoyant's coming tomorrow. She tells me the most extraordinary things about my future."

I went out into the night just before dawn and made my way back to the yellow house. That morning I didn't feel my usual eagerness to pick up Saint-Simon again. I felt for the sore spot like a sick man touching his wound. I was certainly in pain, but where, how and why? There wasn't any particular part of my body that was hurt, sensitive or painful. I simply felt as though some kind of pump had emptied me of a substance I didn't know was in me until then. My joy in life had gone with it. I wouldn't have cared if I died there and then. Even the dawn wind blowing through the tops of the plane trees no longer made me feel alive.

It was a fine day and I lived through it bent over my broom with my eyes never straying from the job in hand. I worked diligently, tirelessly, the very picture of a good hard-working lad, having no interest in any other station but his own.

I sometimes interspersed my reading of Saint-Simon with a few pages of Stendhal, whom I both disliked and admired for his relentless mathematician's logic. It seemed to me that Madame Henry had shown me this highly recommended author to counteract the effect of Saint-Simon.

That evening I took up the book with trembling hands, feverishly looking for some help from him, ready to believe his lucid aphorisms and make them my own. I didn't have far to look, as the book opened at just the right page. Someone a long time ago had shakily underlined this sentence which I found amazing: "He made the mistake of being unremitting in his attentions when, on the contrary, he should have made sure he was seen infrequently."

I decided to follow this sceptic's advice, but I did it with a very heavy heart. I kept imagining Hortense in all the ways she presented herself to me: the woman with the missal; Lucinde's disdainful customer; the heroine who wore the two discreet ribbons on the lapel of her suit on Sundays, separating her for ever from the ordinary run of women; and the person she was at night on the Tibetan carpet, the sensual lover with the purring words who held out her breasts to me before she held out her arms.

She could be two or three people effortlessly and unaffectedly. She was perfectly capable of ferreting around in her purse for the old coins she gave at mass, of worrying about 20 centimes at the bakery with Lucinde, who was practically grinding her teeth. At the same time she could show pity for my destitution by giving me her late husband's clothes and raising me up to her level through the gifts of her books, her music and finally through the gift of herself and the admission of her most intimate desires.

Similarly, she was capable of leaving my arms on Sunday to rush into Victor's on Monday, forgetting me for a week, crossing me out of her life, as she did to Victor with the same lack of concern the following week. That was an essential part of her character. You had to accept it, or go away, or die.

That's what I was thinking about on Tuesday evening, gazing at Madame Henry's shuttered windows from the end of the promenade. A soft light escaped from them, an intimate glow that seemed almost a confession of love.

"It is very difficult not to overrate joys one does not share."

I found that aphorism in Stendhal, not far from the last, but didn't think it very amusing. I remember it all. The wind was blowing a gale and creating a tumult high in the branches of the cedars. I imagined the bouquet of asters with their chrysanthemum smell, the long flames quietly darting up to the chimney,

Victor's tall body nonchalantly stretched out on the carpet with the blessing of Hortense's words of welcome. I tortured myself with these detailed mental pictures. The joys shared by Victor and Hortense seemed to me so superior to mine with Madame Henry. The carpet looked huge. There was only one thing that I couldn't place in this amorous idyll between Hortense and Victor, and that was the Bach cantata.

I was trying to convince myself not to see Hortense for as long as possible, to be seen infrequently, to literally make myself scarce. My dearest wish would be to disappear from her life without saying a word, but I knew that I was too weak for that.

I walked up the deserted boulevard in the November night. The shutters on some windows in the houses had not yet been closed. I saw people with uneventful lives sitting at the dinner table and I envied them. I felt I was in a strange, precarious state in spite of my new clothes and my new shoes (only the beret wasn't new). I'd swapped material discomfort for moral discomfort, and it was no improvement.

I nevertheless enjoyed looking through the brightly lit windows and feeling something of the blessed peace of mind enjoyed by all those people who had nothing to hide and who lived bland public lives. The dining room in the Hôtel Pascal, which I could see through the trees, was half-full of couples, families and a few lone diners fingering pieces of bread. That too was happiness I found hard not to overestimate.

How many times did I walk up and down this street, the Promenade de la Plaine? From the time the inhabitants of Manosque began strolling that boulevard, from youth to old age, like a tranquil stream moving through life, there must have been thousands of ghosts jostling each other there. This walking up and down inevitably brought me back to the bronze dog surrounded by box bushes and an iron railing, and just as inevitably to the point on the balustrade where I could overlook "Eden" and its bright light that I could have been enjoying as Victor was.

I stood there in the same place, gripping the iron railing, following Hortense and Victor's lovemaking in my imagination. I remember, eight o'clock had just struck in the Saint-Sauveur tower, as if to make me even more aware of time going by. Suddenly I saw light pour out on to the trees from the main door of "Eden". Someone had just opened it and was walking beneath the chestnut trees, still illuminated by the light from the boulevard. It was Victor, straight and tall, Victor with the Lucky Strike between his fingers strolling down the path. Victor leaving at eight in the evening! When I left Hortense, it was always at about four in the morning. This extraordinary time difference between the two of us lit up my gloomy heart like the arrival of spring.

I leaned over as far as I could to get a good look at Victor below me. A round bald spot was beginning to show on the top of his head. He seemed a little stooped and older than he really was. He walked along "Eden's" iron fence, going up the boulevard, crossing the road to stop at the urinal, then came back to the footpath on the opposite side. He walked head up, with a deliberate step, as befits someone universally feared. I followed him higher up, hidden by the trees, as though drawn by a magnet. I wanted to see his face, look at his features which should show the reason why this evening he left Hortense at eight, whereas the first time I'd heard him, it was past midnight.

I decided to go and inspect Victor at close quarters if I could. I also felt calm and at ease, now that I knew Hortense was alone behind the shutters at the villa.

Our promenade has an unusual construction: at the beginning, the two roadways, the one that goes around the town and the avenue, are on the same level. The railing separating them continues horizontally along the avenue, and it's the road under the increasingly high retaining wall that goes down the slope where the ditches were filled a long time ago. The avenue remains on the same level as the railing. The two join up in front of the La Saunerie gateway, a fortified postern erected in the 14th century.

The square in front of this gateway was unusually full of people in the evening. It was the place where all those lone souls rejected by Manosque assembled, outsiders of no fixed address with the burden of poverty and nostalgia for other places and other times. They gravitated to Inesta, a Spaniard from Asturias with a pock-marked face, who tossed chestnuts over a brazier, which he sold for 20 sous in newspaper cones.

There were cafés around the gatehouse frequented by the various social groups: ones for the working classes, one for those who worked in banks, one for the butcher-delicatessens (the grocers didn't go to bistrots); a high-class one, the Grand Café Glacier, whose windows were blanked out with whitening halfway up, to spare the clients the sight of the unattractive scene outside.

I haven't forgotten the smell of those chestnuts. I haven't forgotten the look of those Chinese shadows with their hands in their pockets, standing around the brazier roasting their chests while their backs froze. I haven't even forgotten that small things made me happy that evening: knowing that Victor was no longer with Hortense, and seeing Mireille, the newspaper seller with the smooth stockings, moving about securing the shutters of her little shop. She made a graceful sliding movement on tiptoe to engage the latches on the shutters into their fixtures. It was always useful to study those movement so that I could include them the following night in my erotic scenarios, for the incredible gift Hortense had given me on 12 November, when she revealed all her mysteries, hadn't turned me off my masturbatory fancies at night. But I couldn't include her in them any more; she was taboo. I didn't mix real sexuality with my futile dreams. The question was to find out – and I tried unsuccessfully – whether I preferred illusion or reality.

So, there I was on the footpath outside the Glacier, having forgotten I'd come to get a good look at Victor's face. I was as close as I could get to Mireille putting up her shutters and attaching them to the windows, while I tried to let my imagination go to work and to catch a whiff of her when she was standing on tiptoe, reaching up as high as she could.

Suddenly I felt myself pulled up with cyclone strength by the ear and the neck. There was a strong whiff of Lucky Strike. I was thrown into the air between a tangle of tables on the terrace. Although I was bent double, I could see Inesta's brazier coming towards me at full speed. Above me was Victor's face, teeth clenched and eyes glazed, bending my head over the glowing coals. (I was terribly afraid for my beret and Lucinde's letter.) Victor uttered the following threat:

"If you don't leave her alone, I'll blacken your face on this brazier like Yolande de Voland! You understand? Do you understand me?"

He stood me upright and with a well-placed kick sent me flying into a group of Portuguese who pretended to take no notice. Mireille didn't even turn around. I heard someone laugh, but it was at something else. Victor was so terrifying that no-one would admit to seeing him do anything.

I went off shamefaced in the direction of the big yellow house, with my heart thumping and feeling about as low as I could. My brother thought I was sick when he saw how pale I was. My mother and sister were at Madame Alarthéus' house, as November was always the time for our "wonderful dinners". I was trembling. My brother thought it was the cold. I picked up a volume of Saint-Simon, but reading was no joy at all. My mind was in turmoil and I couldn't remember anything I'd read. The sweetish smell of Lucky Strike stuck to me all night in bed. When I woke up, it was still there.

That day fate began to move more quickly, and it was my fault. I was so panic-stricken that I swore never to see Hortense again. My decision to make my visits much less frequent was far from my mind: now it was never again. I was a coward (I still am). All the "my loves" I may have uttered no longer counted when fear took over. In my memory, I confused Victor the Nazi killer with Victor the slaughterman. He'd press me against the coals in the brazier without the slightest compunction, and everyone would wait until I was dead before they did anything.

I tried to forget Hortense by masturbating, but I realized that I was just stirring a pile of ashes. There was no flesh and blood for my vice to feed on. Past memories killed all desire. Mireille seemed nothing more than a straw puppet, Lucinde perspired under her arms; their faces wore ancient tragic masks instead of the joyful smiles I imagined. Anything that wasn't Hortense was nothing. Time and time again in the evening I hurried around the corner of Gardon's grocery store; time and time again I saw Lucinde bent over the rubbish bins she was carrying out. I saw her with polite indifference, no longer even touching the note in my beret. Several times I forgot about it completely.

But as soon as I saw the tops of the chestnut trees at "Eden", now bare of leaves, fear struck and I retraced my steps. All this lasted a week. My family began to worry. I wasn't eating and what I did choke down tasted like sawdust. The world had lost its charm. The fifteenth volume of Saint-Simon lay in the corner of the box at my bed-side unopened. My mother fussed over me. I avoided her. I didn't want to be near any body that wasn't Hortense's.

One evening towards eight o'clock, violent knocking shook our door. It was more bashed in than opened. An outraged Hortense stood framed in the doorway in all her glory.

"Well?" she said.

My mother, who was serving the soup, stood there with the ladle in mid-air.

"Well?" Hortense repeated. "I'm waiting for you!" And then, "Come over here so that I can talk to you."

She pulled me out of my seat and dragged me outside, slamming the door behind her.

"Well?" she said. "What's got into you?"

I told her everything: Victor and the brazier.

"Oh, indeed!" she said. "Victor doesn't own my arse! And you'll see if I stop him from making a move all right!"

She didn't have time. Providence, or whatever you like to call it, has always got rid of my enemies all my life, to the point where the mystery of it all made my blood run cold. That providence now gave the first example of what it could do.

The butt of a Lucky Strike cigarette had been found in the hall of "the mysterious villa" where Fulgance Bécarri had been murdered. It had taken a year to establish a list of the 150 smokers in the town who used those cigarettes. One hundred and thirty-five of them were interviewed, one per day excluding holidays, and had given an unassailable account of their movements. The dossier was already enormous when the gendarmes undertook an examination of the alibis of the 15 left. Fourteen burst into tears, admitting all sorts of ordinary, stupid misdemeanours which had nothing to do with the crime in question. That left only one, Victor, whom they had ruled out straight away, given his war service and decorations.

When he saw this name in the dossier, Judge Cassarin asked for a transfer. It was refused. He walked up and down in his office for a long time before issuing a summons. He went about it as tactfully as he could, beating about the bush, before actually asking Victor the fatal question:

"Where were you and what were you doing on the night of such and such, between nine in the evening and three in the morning?"

Victor said, "Do you know what the bath torture is? I lasted for two hours in the Gestapo cellars. You don't imagine I'm going to tell you, do you?"

Madame Henry hurried over to the magistrate's office to make a declaration.

"He was with me, in my bed, on the night the murder was committed. I only let him go at five in the morning, and believe me, he was in no state to commit a murder."

"Madame," Judge Cassarin said, "it's very praiseworthy of you to want to cover . . . "

He gave a discreet laugh behind his moustache.

"Excuse me! To want to prove the innocence of this hero of the Resistance, but someone has come forward before you!"

He opened his office door and a gendarme ushered in a woman with a contrite look on her face. It was Antoinette, the faithful servant.

"Madame," the judge said, "this woman, Antoinette Tremoille,

216

got here before you. She too was in the arms of Victor Anduze that night, between eleven in the evening and five in the morning on the night of the murder!"

Madame Henry looked her servant up and down.

"You stupid fool!" she said.

But Judge Cassarin's difficulties were not over yet. The telephone never stopped ringing in his office. The clerk had to stop continually and put down his pen to answer it. The north wind was blowing in high places. No-one claimed he was guilty; everyone wanted him to be released forthwith.

A killer is always a nuisance, even if he has had to be overused, whether previously in the Resistance against the enemy or currently as he works his trade, slaughtering the ox for the family table. But there's one place where his presence is particularly alarming: in prison. A killer unjustly accused of having been overzealous in the use of his talent can decide to seek revenge and start proclaiming things that even torture wouldn't have wrested from him. In 1946, it wasn't yet the thing to forgive and forget. There were those who claimed to have a clear conscience, who began to have doubts. Some had sleepless nights. Judge Cassarin was assailed with scarcely veiled commands. But he examined his own conscience, conscientiously. He found it beyond reproach and not about to start reproaching itself now. He didn't care about promotion. The world of Manosque provided as much satisfaction as he wanted.

Victor was conveyed to Saint-Charles prison in Digne, but with great consideration and in a private car. He was given the cell of notary Loisel, a legal hack from Banon who last century had made off with the takings of a dancer from the Marseille opera. It was such a large sum – several millions of *Germinal* francs[10] – that the law couldn't help admiring such a feat and treated him well. They had built a squat toilet so that the notary did not have to go and empty his bucket with the rest of the prisoners.

Victor inherited that comfort. In 1946, the Digne prison had the smallest budget of the detention centres in France, for the good reason that there was never anyone inside except the jailers and a few poor devils who snatched a couple of candlesticks so that they'd be put in the cells for the coldest months.

The jailers never called Victor anything but *monsieur* during his brief stay among them.

However, even the squat toilet was dilapidated for lack of funds. The inhabitant of the cell frequently had to get up on a chair to make the flush work, as the original pull cord had long ago been replaced by a bicycle chain, which got stuck on the cast-iron cistern. It was also a long time since anyone had occupied the cell. The chair was worm-eaten and it needed a precise manoeuvre to balance a chair on the two foot plates of a squat toilet. They think that Victor must have been edgy, over-excited, in a rage. In short, when they found him, the chair was lying in pieces beneath him and his foot was stuck in the hole of the latrine. He'd got tangled in the bicycle chain, which had twisted around his neck before catching in its groove on the cistern. The cast-iron cistern itself had half pulled away. Victor's neck had been broken when the chair fell from under his foot. No-one tried to piece together how the accident happened. Suppositions were based on nothing more than summary observations. Who would have thought of a bicycle chain as an instrument of vengeance? It was only vaguely

10 Money decreed by Napoleon in 1803. Its value was linked to the price of gold and remained the same until 1924. [tr.]

mentioned and promptly put away in an exhibit bag, where it stayed, since any action by the law was immediately extinguished.

Judge Cassarin could do nothing but shrug his shoulders. The head jailer was transferred to Corsica for negligence; he had actually been born there and longed to go back to his native land. Everything returned to normal.

In Manosque, you could see faces that had been continually glum since Victor's incarceration suddenly brighten up, especially mine. The morning at Albert's when Bessolote and Auguste Faux told the rather dramatized story of Victor's death, I breathed easily for the first time.

"Do you think it was an accident?"

This point-blank question made people look away.

"Well! There's for and against."

"Alternatively, chance . . ."

Everyone wanted to be served more quickly than usual.

"It's going to snow!" they said. "Heavens, Lucinde, let me know what I owe you quickly. I came out in my slippers!"

Madame Henry arranged a funeral for Victor almost as impressive as Patrocles'. The mayor made a suitable and very short funeral oration, which Auguste Faux had prepared.

"But, look here!" the mayor had objected, banging the desk. "It seems to me that for Patrocles . . . "

"Let's not mix styles," the deputy said. "One was a tenor and the other, a member of the chorus!"

That year it snowed so abundantly before Christmas that we were isolated from each other. It was a week before Chrismas Eve and it was snowing extremely heavily. You could no longer make out the Gypsies' wash-house. The snow had filled the troughs and piled up on the flooring, forming an oblong mass with only the crystalline overflow showing through.

Every morning I dug out the paths leading from one shop to another with my shovel and broom. I whistled Cantata 140 as loudly as I could.

We, the municipal street sweepers, had been requisitioned to keep the town going by keeping the cleared passages on the main roads open. My hands and feet were frozen from morn till night; my teeth chattered with cold; my back was permanently sore, but I was happy thinking of Hortense. There was something I wanted more than her body, and that was to hear her voice. That was the only thing that would put my mind at ease as I worked alone in the snow-covered streets. I also wanted the tranquillity she seemed to surround herself with, and the asters in the green pitcher.

Then, something extraordinary happened: the bulldozer clearing the boulevards had raised such a hard-packed bank of snow in front of the entrance to "Eden", that Madame Henry was a prisoner behind her gate. Even the postman couldn't get in.

At the same time, the bulldozer broke down. It was pointed out to the mayor what a difficult situation Madame Henry was in. He made a gesture with his hand as if he were throwing a handful of salt over his shoulder.

"Madame Henry, Madame Henry . . . ," he said. "If I know her, she's got enough provisions for six months! And I have more than one citizen to look after."

"I pointed out to him," Auguste Faux told us at the bakery, "that Madame Henry is an important person in an election and that she must easily control a hundred votes, but you know what love is . . . "

That caused a ripple of laughter, and even Lucinde allowed herself a little ironic laugh. Everyone knew that the mayor har-boured a secret love for Madame Henry, and he suffered from never having been able to declare it to her.

One evening, despite an exhausting day, I took my pick and snow shovel to free my lover. The whole town was paralysed with cold under its white mantle. There was not a cat nor a dog to be seen. They crouched in stables, moaning, their darting eyes wide open, waiting for a cataclysm to descend on them.

The new central overhead lighting, which penetrated every shadowy corner, lit me up as though it were daylight. I worked patiently in the full light, breathing hard but spurred on by the reward awaiting me after my labours. It was ten days now since I had felt Hortense's full, soft breasts in my hands.

I cut a passage in the snow wall just big enough for me to slip through sideways. The cold crackled. The snow beneath the "Eden" chestnut trees was like a dome in front of the starry sky. It formed little hills on the ground, banking up in places. The groves of trees and the box bushes reflected the distant light of the street lamps. They were half-buried and shapeless and you couldn't tell if they were trees or ruins.

Behind the shutters was that peaceful, filtered light that disturbed me so when I thought of proud Hortense, who was so good at creating atmosphere.

I pulled the cumbersome cord that rang the door bell.

Hortense appeared.

"I knew you'd come," she said.

This time she was dressed in white, a white scarcely made more intense by a gold border on the low-cut neckline of her dress. It was a long evening dress of an opaque material that gave a slight silky swish when she moved. Although it was opaque, the dress still outlined Hortense's body perfectly.

"Do you know it's Christmas tomorrow? I dressed in your honour."

With a sudden move, she pulled off my beret and hung it on the hat peg. She turned around in front of me, holding the hem of her dress in finger and thumb as it swirled around her.

"How do I look?"

I whispered, "Disturbing."

I dared not go near her with my bleeding, chilblained hands. They'd have made her shriek with cold if I happened to touch her.

"You know the value of words, so that means you think I look beautiful."

"I've dug out the snow bank. It had shut you in. You're all right, aren't you?"

We had to start from the beginning again. Standing there in front of me she was Madame Henry and not Hortense. It occurred to me that we would always be starting all over again as long as we lived, and that Hortense would always go back to being Madame Henry and I then would always use the formal *vous* to her. Yet I always found saying *vous* to her breasts highly exciting.

"You're all right at least, aren't you?"

I was almost kneeling in front of her.

"I don't dare touch you because my hands are cold. You're all right, aren't you?"

She looked at me intently, seriously. It must have been a long time since anyone bothered to find out if she was all right. Perhaps it had never happened. I guessed that my repeating the same thing three times had awakened an automatic tendency to mock, but she restrained herself from giving me any hint of her bitter smile.

"I have enough wood," she said. "Look! There's a fire in the hearth. My cellar is bursting with provisions, and yesterday I bought a double order from Lucinde. Your hands are frozen, you said?"

She took hold of them and firmly placed them down the front of her dress. My fingers immediately spread out to cup her breasts.

"Did I bat an eyelid?" she asked. "To me your hands are never cold."

There was a Christmas tree standing in the middle of the Tibetan rug, with a mysterious little nativity scene tucked away in the shadow of its branches. The pine tree was hung with a lot of twinkling coloured decorations. Madame Henry walked around it and indicated that I should follow her.

"Come here," she said. "Come and sit in front of the fire for a while and take your clothes off!"

She crouched down between the upright of the fireplace and the armchair she'd pulled forward to make room for the Christmas tree.

"Nobody knows where we are tonight," she said. "Nobody knows we're together. Did you think of that? Do you realize what that means? Are you savouring these moments of happiness?"

Anything I could say would only have sounded foolish, so I just nodded my head.

"Sit down in front of me with your back to the fire," she said. "And look at me!"

I sat there stark naked as those watchful eyes ran over me, naked and thin. The cold hadn't left me, but it was giving me back a hundredfold the energy I'd lost to it as I dug the hole in the ice-hard snow compressed by the bulldozer at "Eden's" gate.

"Poor little thing!" Madame Henry said.

She was feeling the weight of my cock in her hand, but not as a caress to bring it back to life: it was more out of pity than desire. Her beautiful white dress with its tiny swirling pleats fell away from her body, which was as naked as mine, hardly seeming to cover it. She let down her hair around me.

"You know . . ." she said. "Just a moment, put your feet on my mother's foot warmer. Are you comfortable like that?"

We no longer needed the Bach cantata. That night, between Hortense's whispers and my unwillingness to speak, there was nothing but silence and the odd crackling of the fire flaming up in the hearth and making me come alive again.

"You know," Madame Henry repeated, "I wanted to tell you. It wasn't Providence alone that freed you from Victor."

She let go of my cock and stood up. The white dress fell in a soft heap in front of the fire. The red-gold firelight flickered on the triangle of my lover's curly black hair.

She was leaning against the mantelpiece. Her breasts were not touching the marble but were inclined towards the fire. You'd have thought that they too were pensively gazing at the fire. Any imperfections of her face lit up by the firelight were there for me to see. She had a long nose, the subtle outline of her sensual mouth had retained something of the little girl's innocent pout, and I could just see there on her cheek the next stern line that ageing would one day imprint on her flesh. I began to think of her like a fruit to be felt, but at that moment I wouldn't have put my hand on her for anything in the world. The mystery of that woman was so deep and complex that it made me feel compassion rather than love.

I'd have to work really hard to see her in the role of a bacch-ante that she'd had in so many of my erotic dreams. I didn't want to call her anything but Madame.

"It's not for nothing," she said, "that I'm standing here naked with you rather than getting ready to go and celebrate the birth of Christ."

"You couldn't have got out!" I said. "You'd never have got to church without the path I dug for you in the ice!"

"If you were a Christian, you'd know that one can reach Jesus from the deepest pit."

She came closer until she was just touching me. Don't forget that I was kneeling in front of her with my eyes and face level with her navel. And yet, at that moment it was her soul she was offering me and it was her soul I desired.

"Victor . . ." she confided in a whisper. "Don't imagine he got caught up in the bicycle chain all on his own . . . He needed help."

"You . . ."

"No! Not me! I just let it reach the ears of someone who really needed Victor to keep quiet, that he was going to talk, and talk convincingly! In large national assemblies, it's called reason of State; in small ones it's a crime."

"Is that why you can't go to meet Christ?"

She straightened up as though I'd stung her.

"Don't you talk about it," she said, "like a believer!"

"How would you know whether I believe or not? I don't know myself!"

She didn't reply, but offered her navel to my lips. It seemed to me that I was thanking the creator by letting my attentive tongue fill the hollow of the knot by which she'd been brought into the world.

"You see," she said, "I'm warming you from my centre."

From the moment I dared lay a hand on her by putting my arms around her hips, only kneeling before her to worship her sex, seeking out her secret smell, burrowing my nose into the thick hair that separated me from her heaven, she ceased to be Madame Henry and once again became Hortense. My curved fingers slid up her body, fitting the roundness of her belly, to her breasts, which she leaned towards me.

"No!" she said. "You must wait. You must let it build up for a long time. And anyway, you're not coming to me on the carpet tonight. Come with me!"

She took hold of me by the wrist. In bare feet, she was scarcely taller than me and all her arrogance, her self-satisfaction and her selfishness had disappeared. It was as though she was leading a child by the hand through the woods. I had the impression we were both humbly entering a time when all thought would cease.

"This is my bedroom!" she said proudly.

We had just gone through a double door. I saw a blue ceiling with ornamental sunken panels. I saw another fireplace in the dark with a fire quietly burning in the hearth. Its light didn't reach the walls, except for a flat, straight chest of drawers on which stood another glass dome over a wreath of orange-blossom.

I've said that she and I were humbly entering a time when all thought would cease, but the sight of that relic under glass – and now I knew to whom it belonged – awoke that gift of observation, my hell on earth, which has prevented me, which still and always will prevent me from wholeheartedly enjoying the present moment.

Neither my erect cock, my beating heart, nor my mouth already full of my lover's juices would stop me from remembering the fire in the hearth first and always. The smell of the pines that sizzled in the summer sun on the sides of La Mort-d'Imbert pass still wafted from its flames. I would always see the straight, military Empire chest of drawers, the wreath in the glass dome, the little photo of the girl on the day of her First Holy Communion (and I could see from here she was already so like Hortense today); and above all, yes, above all, that portrait in the flickering firelight of the man with the dead eyes. It was hanging above the fireplace, draped in black crepe, and portrayed a man who looked dreadfully sad, wearing the cap of an officer in the Forestry Commission. Two war medals lay on a cushion below the portrait and the frame was adorned with beaten oak leaves, but the gilding had tarnished.

I could see it all. Firstly, the old showy objects: the dome, the wreath, the First Communion photo, the portrait of a hero who died defending his country, the light wood, straight-sided chest of drawers, the drapes on the two windows opening on to the dark night, the bed with the scrolls, almost as dark as the grandmother's in the next room; then, between the bed and the fireplace, the low modern table, an anachronism, on which stood a bottle in a silver bucket, with two tall glasses on fine stems. I could already see it at some summer fair after we're dead, spread out on some second-hand dealer's cheap carpet, just a tiny part of the tragic bric-à-brac of family mementoes nobody knows or wants any more.

It was as if she could read my mind.

"Don't look at anything but me!" Hortense exclaimed. "I'm alive! Do you see me? Do you really see me!"

She seized my hands and pressed them against the roundness of her breasts.

"Ah!" she whispered. "They always feel desire! They're consumed with desire! Here, take them. Gently, my wild one! And wait!"

She slipped out of my arms and went quickly over to the little table. She didn't need to encourage me. I adored watching her move so silently yet with so much undulating pink flesh. The shadows made her body look extraordinary. It shone like solid bronze and even the flesh was more beautiful because of the darker hollows suggesting the graceful line beneath.

She took the bottle out of the bucket, and even in that position her breasts were still firm and proud. When she moved, the flames lit up the tips. She carefully filled up the two flutes. Her long hair hid the shape of her head. She was already back and pressed against me.

"Here, drink this!"

"What is it?"

"It's champagne."

"I've never tried it."

"I should think not! Drink it!"

I drank it. It was cool. It disappeared in my mouth. It was as though the liquid didn't reach my throat. I was in a hurry to put down the glass and take Hortense's breasts in my hands again. I would have tired of champagne much faster than those heavenly spheres.

"Drink some more!"

She refilled the two flutes.

"Tonight must be our night of nights. You must speak your pleasure and mine. You must . . . Wait!"

I was tipsy straight away, but in a lucid kind of way. All I could feel in my body was my erection that wanted nothing better than to prolong that wait, lingering over the slightest details of the pleasures she was anticipating.

We were standing pressed against each other, my mouth on her breasts and her belly gently fitting into mine with that subtle incandescence she knew how to ignite. I didn't enter her, just lightly brushed against it, trying to approach something tiny that kept slipping away. The only things that could tame the hidden erection that had come to meet me were my mouth and my tongue. I made her move backwards slowly towards the bed. She'd already pulled back the bedclothes well before I arrived. I had time to notice two big pillows proudly embroidered with initials; this widow had two pillows, like all the widows in the world, in the impossible hope that the head that once rested there might still be there, making a hollow in the eiderdown that would have to be plumped up again next morning.

She had crawled on her back over the vast expanse of sheet. She offered me and offered herself, inviting my mouth and my eyes to take possession of her. I began to stammer words meant only for her, daring words that were lost in her thick, curly pubic hair, with the shame and the sensual pleasure of being able to say them at last after having tried to hold them back for so long. I knew my real talent was in those lost words so quickly forgotten and so hard to remember later.

But suddenly I felt an urgent need to see her eyes. I would never have thought I'd dare to take her face in my hands. Her body, her breasts, her buttocks, everything she offered me without reserve, yes. But her face! She kept smiling and murmuring softly to me. Yes, her face was mine too. I began to chant my joy, increased tenfold by the heady effect of the champagne.

I hardly knew where to put my hands, my mouth, my cock. The sense of disappointment at not having more ways to pleasure my love made me feel almost helpless.

It was then that I noticed her eyes were open, but she closed them straight away. The strange clarity I saw in them should have warned me, but I was too busy thinking of the pleasure I was giving to pay any real attention to a sideways glance. I was too filled with wonder as I went down to look at her again and bury my face in her as though she were a bunch of flowers. I was too full of wonder at the approaching spasm gripping all her muscles and making her press my head against her so hard it would burst. I was too absorbed by the strange withdrawal, a strange instinctive flight like that of an animal feeling the approach of death. I had to hold her against my mouth with my arms around her and my hands clasped over the dimples in the small of her back, while my tongue never ceased caressing her lightly and fleetingly. I was holding a begging, insistent animal, uttering a flow of irretrievable words I couldn't make out; a being who seemed to demand and refuse at the same time, fighting against the unbearable desire of her flesh which rendered her helpless, against a release she didn't want to accept. It was against her will and in spite of her refusal, which was fervent but too late.

My face was wet from eyebrow to chin with her and myself. One of her hairs lay curled on my tongue. Happiness was that unbearable state of erection that I could still bear. Happiness, that incomprehensible state! Until then the closest I'd come to it was knowing the word. The greatest happiness was there in that woman, breathing in the atmosphere we'd just created around us with its odour of sanctity; both of us breathing it in to make it unforgettable.

Then she told me to lie down on my back. I saw her lift herself up to my level, turn and place herself exactly above my cock, but that still wasn't what she had in mind for me. It was something rarer and more precise than that.

She's naked, she's just had her hunger satisfied by my mouth, her whole body still shivering with it, making it last. Then she seizes my cock, turns around and offers me the perfect curve of her back.

"Oh, yes!"

They're not just two words, they're unforgettable desire, the flesh become word. That's what she wants. In the rush of lust spreading through me, I'm dreadfully afraid of giving way before I can satisfy her. She says, she stammers, she moans,

"That's it! You're there!"

My penis comes to life in her. I'm calm. I don't want to come yet. I'm filled with wonder at what I can see: the small of her back, her muscles, her skin with its beauty spots shimmering in the firelight, her strong neck I can't reach. I lightly touch the dimples above herbuttocks. She dare not stir. I whisper to her,

"Move! Move!"

I look at her coiling around me. She's exultant, sliding around my cock until my belly can feel her silky softness. Then a pain like a swelling wave builds in me at last. I cry out to her,

"Ah! I have to . . ."

She calls out, she encourages me, she moves furiously. I still have two minutes of absolute ecstasy before I come inside her with pure joy. You could die during or after that, and it wouldn't matter.

Orgasm stopped her words and my reason. We both howled at the same time. I sank into a semi-conscious state, sliding into sleep. I was incredibly drunk with happiness.

The last memory I have of her is of those two dimples low down on Hortense's strong back as she separated from me, left me, abandoned me.

X

I WOKE UP. THE LOUD, SHRILL CROWING OF A ROOSTER seeking an answer to his call had ended my sleep. I was filled with the presence, the body, the feel and the taste of my lover. Sensuality had resisted sleep: I had an erection like the trunk of a young tree. I put off the moment when I had to open my eyes. The pillow, the sheets, the cooled air around my head all smelled of love.

But the rooster's insistent call ordered me to come back to life. I stretched out my arm to put my arms around my lover again and hold her in the hollow of my shoulder as I'd seen my father do for my mother.

Her place in the bed was empty; her place was cold. The flat part of the pillow no longer retained the shape of the woman's head; it had already plumped up again. With my eyes still closed, I lovingly breathed in the sweet smell of her hair.

It wasn't only the rooster. The bright morning light boldly played against anything that could hold back its rays. The previous evening we'd forgotten to close the shutters on the two windows and hadn't even pulled the curtains across. The sun turned the two empty champagne flutes into a source of incandescent brilliance radiating all around them and prevented me from opening my eyes. I stood up and almost groped my way towards the crater of blinding light. A serviette lay on the low table, so I dropped it over the bucket and the glasses. Then I could open my eyes. Then I saw it.

Actually, what I saw didn't immediately impinge on my consciousness, it was so ordinary: it was my beret on the floor, two metres from the bed and one metre from the table. It was lying limply on its side. I was so used to wearing it on my head that I'd never realized how silly this little appendage perched on its top could look.

It wasn't the only thing lying there. Scattered beside it were the 100 franc notes I'd saved up and, propped up prominently against the crown, I saw a white envelope with the inscription "For Pierre".

The rooster had started to crow for the third time. The sparrows were also singing away in the trees, in spite of the snow. Water from the melted snow gurgled merrily along the guttering on the roof. I registered everything, remembered everything, including the firemen's dual-tone siren starting way in the distance and coming closer.

I fell on my knees. I thought I understood. I began to crawl towards my beret, noticing now that the lining had been ripped open. I grabbed the unsealed envelope. I took out a card written in a fine hand with all the t's crossed. It said:

Forgive me. For a long time I've had to find out what was in your beret. Now I must get started. Forgive me. I've made you my sole legatee. Go to the small house in the garden. You'll understand. One day you'll write my story, I'm sure of it. I love . . .

I closed my fingers around a key that had been slipped into the envelope beside the card. I stared dumbly at the last two words, which had been crossed out by a determined hand.

"I love . . ." I stood there stock-still, paralysed, my illusions falling away from me with the almost imperceptible movement of a receding tide.

Then, between cock crow and the gurgling of the melting snow in the guttering, I heard the slow sound of a drop spreading out in a pool of liquid. The sound came from next door, from the bathroom, where the door was open. I turned my head. In spite of the bright daylight, the light globe inside the round Japanese paper shade was still on. I got up. I knew the truth, even before I discovered it, for there was a distinct feeling of absence inside that house, and I wasn't one to miss a sensation like that. Then there were those repeated words, "forgive me", which had the ring of a farewell.

I took four stumbling steps towards the open door. I saw her from the doorway. She was half-sitting, half-lying in the bathtub. Her beautiful breasts still rose proudly level with the water, which was red because her blood was mixed with it; the hair framing her forehead still had life in it; her face was white as marble, and all at once I realized why the bath had seemed like a tomb on that first day I saw it. She'd carefully put the cut-throat razor she'd used to open her veins on the soap dish next to the taps.

I'd already faced all kinds of silences in my short life, but the silence of Hortense dead after so many happy whispers, such a short time ago, was unbearable. That time when she was so alive;

when she got off me with that graceful round movement of her back, deepening its dimples; when I gazed at her beauty spots and touched them; when she moaned with love as I did, having held her pleasure back for so long; when she lay on her side, looking so like the gentle curves of our hills, as she stared at the fire and the asters. The silence made it seem as though that time had never existed.

I began to shout to make her start. The cry slid over her still body. I was on my knees staring at her lack of response. I reached out my hands to the round globes of her breasts, caressing them as though they were still alive; they were barely cold. It took me several seconds to be convinced that they wouldn't respond to my touch. I looked deeply into her eyes, as I usually did, but they were only a surface with no life behind them. I closed them rather awkwardly, as I'd seen people do in films. I couldn't bear her blank stare.

I stood up and backed away without taking my eyes off her, never ceasing to believe, never ceasing to imagine that as soon as I went out the door, her imperious voice would call me.

"Idiot! Did you think I was dead?"

But even though I kept moving away until I could no longer see her, and even though the cock was still crowing, the birds chirping and the melting snow trickling into the gutters, there seemed a silence all around. Without thinking what I was doing, I picked up my beret again and put the bank notes back in the lining. I put it firmly on my head, stupidly even taking the trouble to tuck my hair and my ears into it.

"Go to the small house in the garden. You'll understand." I didn't know what more there was for me to understand since she was dead, but I did what she asked.

Outside, the snow was breaking up. I wasn't cold any more. The trees and box hedges were straightening up as their white mantle collapsed. A very gentle wind was reclaiming its territory.

I set out down the paths, sinking up to my ankles in the soft snow, in the direction of the small house at the bottom of the garden. I felt uneasy as I went up the ten steps of the absurdly pretentious staircase. I remembered the evening when I'd heard Hortense sobbing and when I so much wanted to comfort her. Now I was about to find out why she was crying.

I turned the key in the lock and pushed one side of the stiff double doors. I remembered seeing Hortense kick it hard. I did the same and went in. The shutters were closed. I saw an electric light switch to the left of the door and pressed it. The light revealed Hortense's secret, her poor, dead secret.

It was a bedroom with a rumpled unmade bed that had been left just as it was. It must have been like that for months. The blankets were pushed up in a ball against the walnut bedstead as though someone had hurriedly pushed them back to be more obviously naked. The sheets were crumpled here and there in little bunches, as if thoughtlessly pressed by hands and feet braced to support bodies in strange positions, like the state of sheets left by lovers.

Two immaculate pillows, each with intertwined H's embroidered on it, sat at the head of the bed, like those I'd pressed the night before in Hortense's other bedroom. To the right of the bed was a table with a large full-length portrait and three anemones in a champagne flute like those we'd drunk from yesterday evening, Hortense and I. Across this portrait of a handsome man was written in a large, confident, determined hand: "To Hortense – Philémon". That was Captain Patrocles' first name, which made us laugh so much when we were children.

A writing desk against the wall between the two windows was wide open. The flap was open and the drawers in a mess, with letters spilling out of them – blue letters like Lucinde's, letters covered with that self-important writing.

There was a fireplace with black marble sides and someone had thrown as many of those letters as possible into the hearth to burn and destroy them, but few of them had been completely destroyed. (Fine rag paper doesn't burn well.)

I had to read, had to know. All the letters began with "My only love . . ."

> I swear to you that my heart is an open book. I love you. Surely you know that? You are wrong to think that I could be attracted to anyone else. You are the only woman in my life. I can never forget your body nor your voluptuous laugh (that laugh that is so much you!) nor everything about you that gets me so excited.

The wind blowing in through the wide-open door blew the pile of letters off the desk and spread them on the floor. "My only loves . . ." were strewn over the ground like so many roses scattered over that dead passion.

Just as Hortense had set me against women by how much she must have lied to succeed in doing that one thing: getting hold of my beret to take it to pieces and remove Lucinde's letter, Patrocles' letters had set me against men. They were full of "my only love", while he died precisely because he'd had several.

I sat down on the edge of that bed, the scene of such passion, trembling with cold and loneliness. Everything had hit me all at once: the discovery of Hortense's only love; the reason why she'd gone the whole way, giving me everything she had to give, to disarm me, to exhaust me with pleasure so that she could get hold of my beret and learn the truth that would kill her.

While she was planning all that, not even one single hair of her head must have thought of me as anything but an obstacle to be overcome. There wasn't a soul in the world now to help me get through life. "I love . . .", crossed out with such force, plainly showed the awful distress that must have overcome her when she finally knew that her lover was betraying her and that was why he died.

She must have hurriedly written the note meant for me, while she was still wet from me and my arms still had the imprint of her fingers convulsively squeezed around them. At the same time as she was working out her final preparations, an idea, a conviction or a regret must have taken hold of her and life was trying one last time to dissuade her from her plan: "I love . . . " But no, it wasn't possible! Everything was pulling her backwards. The past obliterated the present. It had to be crossed out. Where she was going, everything would be crossed out. What did I have to complain about? She'd loved me as a living being. I couldn't hope to compete with a dead man.

I couldn't compete with a love that must have begun years ago and grown when death could be around the next corner; when they were hiding in that little house, listening for the sound of boots outside, the sound of a truck trying to locate the transmitter, which was the soul of the Resistance. They must have begun to love each other somewhere between patriotism and terror, between the need to act and the realization of what that action could cost them. The must have held hands in fear. It was that fear she was unable to share with me which tipped the scales towards Philémon Patrocles.

While she was in my arms, Hortense had never had occasion to feel afraid. We were at peace. Johann Sebastian Bach had taken precedence over the barbarians. The asters with their chrysanthemum perfume could spill out in profusion from the green and yellow pitcher. This bland, simple, naïve view of life could not hope to prevail against the memory of so many moments they thought would be their last. I understood – I was born to understand – the dead took precedence over the living.

I went out of that house. I took myself out of the gardens sparkling with melting snow. I went up the path towards the boulevard; I could already see the asphalt on the road. The snow was dirty here.

In the distance, between the trees, the red fire engine and Dr Martin-Charpenel's little car were parked in front of Albert's bakery. Two gendarmes on bicycles had just arrived. All those who were usually in the shop with me of a morning were standing nervously huddled in a group a little way off. Their big funereal shopping bags were sitting on the snow like so many crows. I half-knew what I was going to discover.

Bessolote was wrapped tight in a cloak, Jacques le Beau was wearing a balaclava and Auguste Faux was all black in a big baggy coat, as though he had matched his clothes to his bag. Madame Donnet and Madame Chaix had covered their heads with a *pointe*, a black lace headscarf worn by the old women in our region.

I'd unthinkingly kept Hortense's letter in my hand. I went towards the comforting group of my morning friends. Bessolote had the floor and was determined to keep it.

"*I* saw everything!" she was saying. " I arrived at seven as usual and all the lights were on in the shop. It wasn't cold any more and the snow was melting by the bucketful all around. My feet have been wet ever since. I should go and warm myself up."

"Off you go, Bessolote!" Jacques le Beau said. "I'll carry on for you."

"Heaven forbid! You arrived a good five minutes after me!"

She launched off again.

"In I go! I say, 'Good morning all' as usual. I turn around after shutting the door and that's when I see Lucinde flat on the floor with her feet sticking out from behind the counter. She was lying in a pool of blood. Her skull had been bashed in with a two-kilo weight! You have to be pretty strong to do that! And the other weight was missing from the rack!"

"What other one?"

"The other two-kilo weight! And with good reason, as you'll see! The door from the side street was wide open. I go out through it shouting, 'Help!' Then I see black smoke escaping from the bakehouse. I thought the bread must have caught fire. As I reach the oven, Jacques le Beau comes up behind me. We saw Albert's feet sticking out of the oven. We pulled him out as best we could. My dear! He'd been hit by a weight too. It was still there on the shelf! Covered in blood! But as well as that, Albert had been lifted up from the floor and put into the oven with the bread. He had a *pompe* stuck to his face. I'll never eat another one! His head was burning like a piece of coal from the Gaude mine. Jacques and I sprinkled water on him as best we could from the bucket that holds the damp cloths, but, you can imagine . . . an oven!"

"You haven't said everything, Bessolote. I . . ."

Bessolote raised her hand to interrupt Jacques.

"Wait! I haven't said everything! The second weight had been taken out of the shop, but the first, the first had been brought down on the copper tray with such force that the beam had been damaged! And under that weight was a letter . . . a blue one!" she said, finishing her story.

Her eyes were starting out of her head. She'd never felt such intense excitement in all her life.

The firemen were bringing out Lucinde's body on a stretcher

covered by a tarpaulin. Our group stood there stock-still, watching the body of the tight-lipped woman, who had managed to bear such a heavy secret for so long, being carried past us.

My remorse didn't begin at that moment. I had too many mixed emotions to deal with. I didn't have time to sort them out.

Auguste Faux leaned over towards our narrator, as he was two heads taller than she.

"And by the way, Bessolote, do you know what the letter said?"

"Well, no! How could you expect . . . "

"It's possible that in the excitement, and wanting to be helpful, you might have . . . "

"I didn't have time. I didn't think of it. I was so flabbergasted that I didn't know what I was doing! Oof! It's now I'm going all hot and cold!"

She slumped. We rushed to her aid, but valiantly leaning against the trunk of a plane tree, she refused all help.

"It's all right!" she said. "The man who did that must have been mighty angry!"

"The woman . . . " I said, my voice flat and toneless.

"What do you mean, the woman?" Bessolote asked.

With the note still in my hand, I waved my arm in the direction of "Eden" and my dead lover.

I set out, my shoulders drooping, like an exhausted old man. They followed. All these people with their black bags were like a funeral escort. The gendarmes arrived, took the note from me and read it.

"Now, just a moment! You inherit?"

"What do you mean, I inherit?"

"Sole legatee! Do you know what that means?"

I knew, but those words had not warmed my heart or lightened my loneliness.

"But you inherit! That changes everything. Always find out who stands to benefit from the crime! It's easy to cut someone's wrists!"

"And easy to say!" Auguste Faux objected.

"And as well as that, if I'm not mistaken, there's a case of corruption of a minor?"

"I'd like to point out to you worthy gentlemen," Auguste Faux objected respectfully, "that the corrupter is testator and he, the minor, is the corruptee!"

"That makes no difference. We'll get to the bottom of all that!" the gendarmes said.

They took me away and sat me down between two officers. One went to look for a typewriter and the other stoked the stove. The police station was a vast, deep, echoing building. Suddenly the voice of our mayor was heard filling the corridors, shouting,

"What does that matter? What are you thinking of? You must be out of your minds to arrest an employee of the maintenance department in weather like this! Will you be out there tomorrow breaking up the ice on the footpaths with pick axes? Do you realize, I have eight men? Eight! Three are out of action with the flu, and you want to take this one too? Will you take responsibility for my constituents who slip and break their legs tomorrow? Well, will you?"

He put a protective hand on my head, on my beret, which crackled under the pressure, but all it contained now were the banknotes.

"I'll vouch for him!" our mayor said.

The door was opened for him and, with his hand still holding my head, he went off with me like a bird of prey.

"Get to work quickly!" he said. "And begin with the town hall square. I've got a wedding at four o'clock."

* * *

As you would expect, I went through a serious religious phase that made me withdraw from the world as soon as I put away my broom, the only thing that kept my feet on the ground.

I'd found an old lady's bicycle with a green net over the spokes lying about in the store rooms under the small house in the garden. I began to do the rounds of churches, little chapels, calvary crosses in the open countryside. I fell on my knees everywhere. I wanted God to exist; I wanted eternity to be tangible. I wanted Hortense to rise from the dead, but I couldn't bear her to be pressed in between so many ordinary souls in the anonymous crowd of that universal gathering. I wanted to find her in the particular splendour of her flesh, in the tension and control of her sexual pleasure. It meant little to me that she should be an eternal spirit if she could never fill my arms again. Oh, God! Was it possible that her breasts would no longer draw my mouth to them? Was it possible that they had ceased to exist? I called to God under the heavy marble where she lay wasting away to give me back the warmth of her softly rounded belly against mine.

And so I lived through the whole of one winter and a summer. I fervently prayed, I don't really know what, in that empty world that now belonged to me: the cold hearth, the Tibetan carpet, the dead asters in the green pitcher with the slimy water. I would have nothing changed.

The world of lust and women disappeared with Hortense. Nocturnal erections no longer bothered me. As an asteroid flying too close to a planet destroys its atmosphere, Hortense's death had destroyed my joy in life. Disenchantment took hold of my imagination, giving it this melancholy cast.

Pressed on all sides, I eventually had to come back to earth. One day, I found myself standing between my mother and father before the notary, Maître Tournatoire, who wavered between polite irony and the desire to sermonize. But between us lay the large sheet of blue paper, the same blue as Lucinde's note and Patrocles' letters.

I'd insisted on appearing before him with all the attributes of my order: Uncle Désiré's long, shapeless, grey coat and my birch broom. My mother and father pleaded in vain. No, I wouldn't resign; no, I wouldn't stop being a street sweeper. The times I swept up the droppings from the *scabots* smelling of the mountains, with a wide swing like a reaper, were the only ones when I was not with Hortense.

"Of course," Maître Tournatoire said, "the taxation office will immediately take half of the pile, but rest assured, there'll be enough left for the rest of your days. The Henrys were sensible people from father to son . . ."

He sighed.

"Not like my poor father. In short, everything goes to you! There is only one condition: that you write her story! But," he added, "and Heaven knows if I understand why, she gives you your whole lifetime to do it, and she stipulates . . ."

He adjusted his glasses.

"And I quote: 'So that you can never forget me.'"

As my father was taking his leave, he turned around to the notary, adding,

"Why do you speak to him so familiarly with *tu*?"

"Why! He's 17 and I'm 60!"

"What of it?" my father said. "He's suffering. Can't you see it? You always address despair as *vous*."

One morning the Duke de Saint-Simon rose up out of my unhappiness like an island to land on. I'd always had a total lack

244

of curiosity about the rest of the world, but Saint-Simon had lived at Versailles. The lives of all those people surrounding Saint-Simon were still in my head and I wanted to hear their ghosts. I asked for a holiday, which I was certainly entitled to. The mayor granted my request on the spot. He even accompanied me to the door of his office, calling me "a good lad".

A fortnight later, my father sent me a letter, which I read as I was walking along the Grand Canal at Versailles.

> I couldn't say no. The mayor needs "Eden" to build the Hôtel des Postes. We've taken everything to the Saint-Véran property. Don't worry. You'll find everything intact. I'll tell you about the pressure I've been under.

I made a dash for the first available train, arriving in Manosque that evening. Two enormous machines were sleeping until the following day over the ruins of my dream. One of them was plunged halfway into the bowels of the house where Hortense and Patrocles had shared their love. Two cedars lay uprooted on the ground, looking awkward and pathetic in death, and I wept over them.

The other machine had already broken up the verandah, and sat on the rubble looking almost triumphant. All I could do now was remember.

Sometimes at night, when Manosque is no more than a sad little town, exuding its fear, I return quietly, and I'll return when I'm a ghost, to the bronze-coloured greyhound, still there to bear witness when everything else has disappeared around it.

I lean over the balustrade with my eyes closed. I can hear the cedars of Lebanon moaning sadly in the wind. I can see once more the small house, the groves of trees, the soft light where Hortense would wait for me behind the closed shutters.

Then I open my eyes again. Everything is neat and tidy, brilliantly lit, but for whom? No-one is there. A two-lane roadway with two wide footpaths has demolished the drawing room with the books, the Tibetan carpet and the fireplace with the asters.

If one day you should pass by this buried site, remember it was here, a long time ago, that a green and callow country lad had the misfortune to lose his innocence for ever.